A CATERED MOTHER'S DAY

Center Point
Large Print

Also by Isis Crawford and available from Center Point Large Print:

A Catered Fourth of July

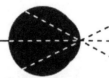

This Large Print Book carries the Seal of Approval of N.A.V.H.

A Mystery with Recipes

A CATERED MOTHER'S DAY

ISIS CRAWFORD

CENTER POINT LARGE PRINT
THORNDIKE, MAINE

Library of Congress Cataloging-in-Publication Data

Names: Crawford, Isis.
Title: A catered Mother's Day : a mystery with recipes / Isis Crawford.
Description: Center Point Large Print edition. | Thorndike, Maine :
Center Point Large Print, 2016. | ©2015
Identifiers: LCCN 2015042460 | ISBN 9781628998382
          (hardcover : alk. paper)
Subjects: LCSH: Simmons, Bernie (Fictitious character : Crawford)—
Fiction. | Simmons, Libby (Fictitious character)—Fiction. | Caterers and
catering—Fiction. | Murder—Investigation—Fiction. | New York
(State)—Fiction. | Large type books. | GSAFD: Mystery fiction.
Classification: LCC PS3603.R396 C3695 2016 | DDC 813/.6—dc23
LC record available at http://lccn.loc.gov/2015042460

For Dean Burns—thanks for your ideas

Acknowledgments

Thanks to Betsy Scheu,
for her proofreading skills

Prologue

The first call came at ten o'clock on the Thursday evening before Mother's Day.

"I thought you'd like to know that I'm doing it," Ellen Hadley said.

"Doing what?" Bernie Simmons asked as she headed over to the refrigerator.

"Doing what you suggested, of course," Ellen replied.

Bernie wrinkled her forehead. "What did I suggest?" she inquired as she lodged her cell more firmly between her shoulder and her ear, opened the refrigerator door, and took out two pounds of butter and a dozen eggs.

"You know."

"I really don't."

"Ha-ha. Funny lady."

"I'm being serious."

There was a pause and some sort of noise in the background. Maybe a door closing? Or opening? Bernie wasn't sure.

Then Ellen said, "Gotta go."

"Wait," Bernie told her. But it was too late. Ellen had hung up.

"What the hell?" Bernie muttered. She put the butter and the eggs down on the counter and tried calling her friend back, but her call went straight to voice mail. Had Ellen turned off her phone? Was there some sort of interference with the signal? Bernie tried again and got the same result.

"That's odd," Bernie reflected as she slipped her cell into her pants pocket and gathered up her supplies.

"What's odd?" Bernie's sister, Libby, asked as she studied the cupcakes on the cooling rack. They were perfect. They all had gently rounded tops. There wasn't a crack in sight.

Bernie told her, concluding with, "I don't have a clue what Ellen's talking about."

Libby shrugged. "If you can't remember, it's probably not that important anyway."

"Probably not," Bernie agreed as she got out the sugar, vanilla, and cocoa for the cupcake icing. "But why did she turn off her phone?" she asked, unwilling to let the matter go.

"Obviously Ellen's in the middle of something. She did say 'gotta go,' after all." Libby paused. "Or maybe she didn't turn her cell off," she suggested as she went over to the sink and began washing out the muffin tins. "Maybe her battery went dead."

"Possibly." *Heaven only knows,* thought Bernie, *it's happened to me often enough.* "But . . ." she began.

Libby turned her head. "You're overthinking this. Let it go."

"But it makes no—"

"Let it go," Libby repeated, a bit more emphatically this time. She placed the muffin tin on the dish rack to dry and started on the second one.

"You're right," Bernie said after a moment, and began concentrating on the task at hand.

She started separating the eggs into different bowls and after a while she forgot about Ellen's call. It was late, she was tired, and Libby was right. How important could the call be? If it was, Ellen would have called back. She was most likely dealing with some domestic drama. But then, what else was new?

It wasn't until Ellen's second call came in two days later and Bernie and Libby were staring at a man's body splayed out on a bed in room twenty-one of the Riverview Motel, while Ellen whimpered in the background, that Bernie began to understand what Ellen had been referring to.

Chapter 1

B ernie's mom had always told Bernie that she should think before she spoke, and Bernie decided her mom had been right—as per usual. It was true. Sometimes she didn't think, and what she'd said to Ellen had definitely fallen into that category. Boy, she wished she'd kept her mouth shut. That was for sure. But how could she have known their conversation would lead to such a disastrous conclusion?

She couldn't have. By any stretch of the imagination. Even her father and her sister agreed with that. But still, there was that small niggling voice in her head, the voice she kept hearing no matter what she told herself. The voice that kept telling her that if she hadn't mentioned Mother's Day, Ellen wouldn't have said what she said, Bernie wouldn't have made the suggestions she did, there wouldn't be a dead body on the motel bed, and Ellen wouldn't be in the trouble she was in.

It had all started so innocently too. When Ellen had walked into A Little Taste of Heaven, the noon rush was over, the day's baking was done, and the counter was manned. It was one of those picture perfect, Norman Rockwell kind of afternoons. The sky was a cerulean blue, the tulips and the daffodils were in bloom, the grass was a tender green, and the sun was streaming down through the leaves trembling in the breeze.

Shopkeepers had thrown their doors open and drivers were lined up at the car washes getting their rides spiffed up. Teenagers were running around in flip-flops and shorts while adults were parading around in T-shirts. When Bernie was recounting the details of the debacle to her dad, she remembered it had been a little after three in the afternoon when Ellen had come into the shop.

12

Bernie had had a smudge of flour on her cheek and some flecks of it in her hair.

"Baking?" Ellen had asked, indicating the flour.

Bernie had laughed and brushed it off. "I'm through for the day."

"Want to take a break and go to Skylar Park and watch the boats on the river?"

"By all means. I was just thinking that it's too nice to be inside."

Ten minutes later, after Bernie told Libby where they were going, she and Ellen had headed out the door. When they got to the park, it seemed to Bernie as if the whole town of Longely had had the same idea. Kids were running after other kids, moms were chasing after them, and dogs were chasing after anything that moved.

She and Ellen had sat on one of the few unoccupied benches and began drinking the freshly roasted Sumatra coffee that Bernie had brought with her from the shop, black for Ellen, and a small amount of heavy cream and one lump of demerara sugar for herself. They ate the anise-flavored biscotti that Bernie and Libby had finished baking that morning and chatted about Arf, Ellen's burgeoning dog biscuit business.

"I think we have to decide whether or not to increase production," Ellen had said.

Bernie took a sip of her coffee and watched as a pigeon waddled toward her. "Do you want to?"

"Lisa does."

"And you don't?"

Ellen sipped her coffee. "I guess I'm not as ambitious as she is. But Lisa says it's the right thing to do. She says you either grow or die."

"Sounds like something her husband would say."

Ellen nodded. "But I think Jeremy may be right."

"You don't sound very enthusiastic," Bernie observed.

"I'm not," Ellen confessed. "But I think it's the smart thing to do."

The pigeon stared at Bernie. "That means you'd have to move the business out of your house," she said.

"I know."

Bernie decided Ellen didn't look happy about the prospect.

"So where would you go?"

"There's a commercial space near Croton that we can rent." Ellen corrected herself. "Have rented."

"So it's a done deal," Bernie said.

Ellen sighed. "Yeah, it is. The place has lots of equipment. The ovens are good. Of course, it's not cheap."

"Not compared to using your basement it isn't. And then there's the fact it's a half an hour drive from your house," Bernie pointed out.

Ellen frowned. "There is that. Lisa wants to buy a new mixer, although there are a couple of twenty-gallon ones there we can use—at least for

a while. They look as if they're on their last legs."
She reached in her bag and brought out a flyer
from a restaurant supply house down on Canal
Street. "What do you think?" she asked Bernie,
pointing to a forty-gallon mixer. "This is what
Lisa wants to get."

Bernie broke off a tiny bit of her biscotti and
threw it to the pigeon. "I think I'd look on
Craigslist and get it used. It'll cost you one-third
as much, maybe even a quarter."

Ellen folded up the flyer and put it in her bag.
"That's what I said to Lisa."

Bernie threw some more biscotti crumbs out.
Two more pigeons landed and started squabbling
with the first one. "Expanding is tricky," she
noted. "You'd be working more hours."

"A lot more if you count in the commute."

"Did you point that out to Lisa?"

"She doesn't care. She has a live-in housekeeper, some Spanish lady that lives in a flat
over the garage. It's a nice flat," Ellen said in
response to Bernie's raised eyebrow. "Nicer than
my apartment after I graduated."

"That's not saying much," Bernie noted. Ellen
had lived in a stereotypical cold-water flat on
the Lower East Side. "So what does Bruce say?"
Bernie asked, changing the subject. Bruce was
Ellen's husband.

"He says it's up to me. Frankly, I don't think
he cares what I do as long as he's not incon-

15

venienced—meaning there's food on the table and the laundry is done."

Ellen took another sip of her coffee, while Bernie watched a tugboat making its way down the Hudson. Then she introduced the subject she wished she hadn't. All she said was that A Little Taste of Heaven was running a special on French macaroons for Mother's Day. Harmless, right? One would have thought, but one would have been wrong.

Ellen's expression turned grim. "I hate Mother's Day," she said, pulling at the hem of the faded brown T-shirt she was wearing.

"How come?" Bernie asked. She was curious. Mother's Day made her sad because her mom had died six years ago, but she didn't understand why Ellen felt that way. Her mom was alive and well.

Ellen laughed harshly. "Maybe because my family didn't get me anything for Mother's Day last year. Not even a card, or a bunch of flowers. Nothing. Zip. Zero."

Bernie shook her head, puzzled. "But you said they took you out to dinner at La Coquette." La Coquette was a trendy new French bistro that had opened one town over.

The corners of Ellen's mouth turned down. "Yeah. Well, I lied."

"Why?"

Ellen looked at her hands and bit her lip. "Maybe because I was embarrassed."

Bernie reached over and squeezed Ellen's shoulder. "They'll get you something this year."

"No, they won't."

"You can't be sure."

"Yes, I can." Ellen's voice started rising. "They didn't get me a Mother's Day card the year before that or the one before that either, for that matter," she continued. "So why should this year be any different? Bruce says Mother's Day is a made-up holiday and he sees no reason to make the card companies rich."

"All holidays are made-up holidays if it comes to that," Bernie observed. "It's not as if they're encoded in our DNA."

Ellen sniffed. "Try telling that to my husband."

"I will." Bernie looked down. Now she had five pigeons around her feet. She clapped her hands. They retreated.

"Do you know what he and the guys got me for my birthday last year?" Ellen asked.

"Socks?" Bernie posited. They were the worst thing she could think of—unless, of course, they were cashmere and came from Bergdorf's.

"Even worse than that. A ratchet set."

Bernie crinkled her nose. "Isn't that a tool?"

"Yes. I mean really. You know what Bruce got me for our anniversary?"

"I'm afraid to ask."

"A new iron and ironing board."

Bernie rolled her eyes. "That's bad. You should

17

stop ironing. That's what Chinese laundries are for."

"I don't iron. This was his way of telling me I should. We didn't even go out," Ellen continued. "Bruce went off and played golf with his buddies instead."

"Nothing like being ignored," Bernie observed.

Ellen sniffed. "I'll say." Her eyes misted over and she turned her head away for a moment to get control of herself. "It's like I'm a piece of furniture."

"Well, maybe expanding your business will be good."

Ellen turned toward her. "How do you mean?"

"You'll be away more, so you won't have time to do all the stuff you do at home now."

Ellen made a dismissive noise. "I'm still going to do everything around there."

Bernie fed another crumb of biscotti to a second pigeon. "Why? How old are your boys now?" she asked. It was a rhetorical question. She knew the answer, but Ellen told her anyway.

"Ethan is twelve, Ryan is fifteen, and Matt is seventeen."

"So they're old enough to help. They're more than old enough. You do everything around there. You clean, you cook, you food shop, you walk the dog."

Ellen's shoulders slumped. "I know."

"You should stop."

"I don't mind doing it all," Ellen protested.

Bernie snorted. "Yeah. I can see that."

"It's true. I'd just like everyone to pick up after themselves and put their laundry in the basket instead of leaving it on the floor." Ellen worried her cuticle. "And a thank-you once in a while wouldn't hurt either."

"Well, I still don't see why they can't do their own laundry and take out the trash," Bernie persisted. This was not the first time that she and Ellen had had this discussion. It annoyed her that her friend allowed herself to be treated like a dishrag. "After all, you *are* working full time now."

"I've tried giving them chores," Ellen replied. "But they don't do them."

"So make them."

"They don't listen to me."

"My dad would have kicked our butts if we didn't do our jobs," Bernie observed. "Maybe you should talk to Bruce."

Ellen frowned. "Bruce is part of the problem. In fact, Bruce *is* the problem. His dad never lifted a finger because his mom did everything, and Bruce thinks I should do the same for him."

Bernie sighed and stretched out her legs. By now she had a flock of pigeons milling around her. She should never have fed them the biscotti crumbs. She leaned over and waved her arms. "Shoo." The pigeons retreated a couple of inches.

"So what would happen if you didn't do every-one's laundry or take the garbage out or cook dinner?" she asked.

Ellen answered promptly. "The dishes would pile up and no one would have any clothes to wear and everyone would yell at me."

"Eventually they'd get the idea."

"No, they wouldn't."

"How do you know if you don't try?" Bernie asked.

"I have tried."

"Yeah, but for how long? One day? Two days?"

Ellen crossed her arms over her chest. "I don't want to talk about it anymore," she declared. Which was the way most of the discussions she and Bernie had on this topic ended.

"Fine," Bernie replied. "Your choice." She would have killed Bruce by now, but then she never would have married a man like that in the first place.

"I like the biscotti," Ellen said, changing the subject. "I like the texture."

"They are good, aren't they," Bernie replied, happy that her and her sister's hard work had paid off.

It had turned out that making the biscotti was trickier than Bernie and Libby had anticipated. They needed to be crisp enough to hold their shape when you dunked them in coffee, but not so hard that they hurt your teeth. Plus, there was the fact that they had to be baked twice. Then there were the flavors. She and Libby had been fiddling around with the biscotti for over a month, but in the end, aside from the ones they'd made with chocolate and a dash of chili, they'd settled on anise and almond, the old tried and true. Sometimes you couldn't beat the classics.

"So when are you going to move?" Bernie asked Ellen.

"We're in. We signed the lease two weeks ago. We just have to bring in our supplies." Ellen lapsed into silence as she watched a sailboat out on the Hudson. "Bruce and I used to have one of those, a twenty-four footer. Then the kids came along and we sold it. You're lucky you're not married," she said suddenly.

Bernie dusted the crumbs off her pink silk blouse, which caused the pigeons to surge forward. "You just need to find a way to make everyone pay attention."

"I've tried," Ellen wailed. "You know I have, but nothing I say seems to penetrate."

Bernie stamped her feet and the pigeons retreated for the third time. "That's the problem. You have to stop talking and start acting."

"And do what?" Ellen put both of her hands out palms up in a gesture of defeat. "Tell me. I've tried not doing the dishes or doing the laundry, but it didn't faze them in the least. Clearly my family has a higher capacity for dirt and disorder than I do."

Bernie finished off her biscotti. "I might have a solution for you."

Ellen leaned forward. "Tell me."

"You could always fake your own kidnapping. That would certainly get everyone's attention."

Ellen's eyes widened. "Seriously?"

Bernie snorted. "Of course not seriously. I was kidding. But you could go off to a spa for a couple of days."

Ellen leaned back. "I like it," she said.

"Then you should do it," Bernie replied, thinking that Ellen was referring to her second idea instead of her first.

Chapter 2

Up until Ellen's call on Saturday evening, Bernie and Libby had had a pretty uneventful day. Business at the shop had been slow but steady. They had sold out of their chocolate salted caramel cupcakes and lavender and honey crème brûlées as well as their basil chicken salad, pasta primavera, and Moroccan lamb stew. At a little after seven Bernie and Libby ushered their last customer out, locked the front door, cashed out, wiped down the counters, and swept up.

Afterward, they retired to the kitchen, where

they began boxing up the French macaroons they were featuring for Mother's Day. After that was done they planned on meeting Marvin and Brandon at RJ's for a drink, then getting a good night's sleep because Mother's Day morning was always a busy one, what with frantic dads and unruly kids hurrying in to buy last minute treats.

"I wonder what Mom would have thought of the macaroons," Libby said as she carefully slid six of them into a clear plastic box and put the top on.

Bernie looked up from cutting lengths of deep blue velvet ribbon. "I'm sure she would have approved. She always liked new things."

"Mrs. Salazar was asking about the little cupcakes with the candied violets on top that Mom always did for Mother's Day."

Libby reached for a ribbon. "We can do those next year."

"Dad would like that."

"He liked anything Mom made."

"This is true."

The sisters worked in silence for the next twenty minutes. At seven forty-five Bernie's cell rang. She wiped her hands on her apron, picked it up, and looked at the screen.

"It's Ellen," she informed Libby as she answered.

First Bernie heard, "I'm in so much trouble." Then Ellen began to laugh hysterically. "What's the matter?" Bernie asked.

Libby moved closer so she could hear.

"I don't know. I don't know anything anymore." There was another cackle of hysterical laughter from Ellen.

"Ellen, tell me what's going on."

"I should never have listened to you, Bernie."

"I don't know what you're talking about," Bernie told her. She'd been up since five in the morning and was not in the mood for drama.

"You know, Bernie. Your suggestion. Your brilliant plan."

"What suggestion, Ellen?"

Ellen's answer was another burst of maniacal laughter.

Libby raised an eyebrow, demanding clarification. Bernie shook her head in response. She had no idea what Ellen was talking about. She decided to try a different tack. "Okay," she said. "At least, tell me where you are."

"I'm at the Riverview Motel. Room twenty-one."

"Jeez, that's an oldie but goodie. What are you doing there?"

"Now, that's a good question. An excellent question. Of course the better—"

Bernie interrupted. "Ellen, stop. Just tell me what's going on."

This time Ellen let out something between a laugh and a sob. "How can I tell you when I don't know? I thought I did, but now . . ." Her voice trailed off.

Bernie looked around the kitchen and saw her evening plans disappearing. "Are you on something?" she asked, although she couldn't see Ellen ingesting anything that didn't come from Whole Foods. Was acid organic? Probably not.

"Like what?"

"I don't know. Pills. Acid. Bath salts."

"Are you nuts?" Ellen's voice rose in indignation. "I have three kids, for God's sake."

"Right. Moving on. Are you hurt?" Bernie asked. "Should I call nine-one-one?"

"No," Ellen cried. "Absolutely not. Whatever you do, for God's sake don't do that."

"Are you sure?" Bernie asked.

"I'm positive," Ellen said. "I couldn't explain. I don't know who it is."

"Who who is, Ellen? You're not making any sense at all."

"I did a bad thing, Bernie. A really bad thing. You'll come, won't you? Please."

Bernie grimaced. She'd really been looking forward to a shot of Scotch and a visit with Brandon. "Do I have a choice?" Ellen started sobbing on the other end of the line and Bernie immediately regretted her comment. "Of course I'll come. I'll be there as soon as I can," she promised.

"Thank you. Thank you so much." Ellen hung up, leaving Bernie looking at her phone.

"What was that all about?" Libby asked.

Bernie shook her head as she put her cell back on the kitchen counter. "Your guess is as good as mine."

"Why doesn't she call Bruce?" Libby asked as she quickly finished tying the bow on top of a box holding the six chocolate macaroons with a hazelnut praline filling. She fluffed out the loops on the ribbon and added, "Isn't that what husbands are for?"

"Theoretically." Bernie picked up a broken macaroon that was lying on the prep table and ate it. It melted in her mouth, leaving behind the taste of chocolate and hazelnuts. "Maybe she didn't call him because this has to do with him."

"What did he do? Kill someone?"

"Bruce?" Bernie laughed at the idea. "Not hardly. He'd outsource it. He's not a get-your-hands-dirty kind of guy."

Libby sighed as she looked at the unboxed macaroons.

"You don't have to come," Bernie told Libby, correctly interpreting her sigh. "It's okay. I know you don't like Ellen very much."

"I never said that," Libby protested.

"You don't have to."

"It's not that I don't like Ellen, it's just that she complains all the time. She whines more than I do."

Bernie laughed.

"But I'll come," Libby told her sister. "Of course, I'll come. You're going to need my help."

Bernie smiled. "Like that's going to happen."

Libby smiled back. "Funny, how it always seems to. I wonder what Ellen's doing at the Riverview Motel anyway."

"I guess we're going to find out," Bernie said. Then she ran upstairs to tell her dad where they were going. A minute later she was down with the keys to the van. Her dad's routine injunction of "be safe out there" floated down the stairs after her. Libby was waiting outside.

"I'm surprised Dad didn't want to ride along," Libby observed.

"He said to call him if it's anything interesting and he'll get Marvin to drive him down. He thinks Ellen is probably being hysterical."

Libby made a *pffft* noise with her lips. "Well, she does tend to get a tad overwrought."

"There is that," Bernie allowed.

"More than a tad," Libby added.

Bernie didn't say anything because it was true.

Chapter 3

The Riverview Motel on Route 72 had been built over seventy years ago at a time when people went out for leisurely Sunday afternoon drives. Once the motel had been an elegant stopping place for tourists bent on enjoying the scenic pleasures of the Hudson Valley. Now Route 72 was a forgotten road and the Riverview Motel was strictly for the locals. It was *the* place to go if you were a teenager and wanted to have a party, or you were older and wanted to have an assignation.

The sign signaling the turnoff to the motel was sited ten feet off the road and had never been replaced. Over the years, it had come to tilt sharply to the left, giving the picture of the Hudson River a tipsy feel. The weather had done its work as well, and by now the blues had faded to grays, while the boats on the river and the people on the shore had been reduced to white and black smears.

A few of the letters on the sign had vanished as well, so now the sign read, THE IVERVIEW OTEL. It had been that way for as long as Bernie and Libby remembered, the owners, Isaac and Mina, having no desire to invest money in fixing it. As Bernie pulled into the parking lot she noted that the grass and the ivy seemed to be winning the battle in their fight with the macadam.

Libby pointed as three wild turkeys looked at them, gave a couple of squawks, and hurried off into a cluster of weeds that were invading the parking lot perimeter. "Isaac should sell this place before it falls down."

"I don't think he really wants to," Bernie replied as she maneuvered around a piece of cement.

"Then he should fix the place up," Libby stated.

"He could," Bernie said. "But he obviously likes things just the way they are. I'm guessing that he prefers to spend his money on his fishing trips."

"That salmon was really good," Libby allowed, remembering the four pounds of king salmon Isaac had given them from his last trip as a thank-you for storing the catch from his freezer in theirs when his power had gone out last winter during the ice storm.

"Good!" Bernie exclaimed. "It was great. I hope he goes on another trip soon."

"Me too," Libby replied. It really was the best piece of fish she'd ever tasted. "Dad is talking about going down to the Carolinas with Clyde. They have mahimahi down there."

"Not as good as salmon, but good enough," Bernie said. Then she changed the subject. "Boy, I had some great times here," she reminisced while Mathilda let out an ominous creak as she jounced into and out of a deep rut.

"That doesn't sound good," Libby noted.

"That's because it's not," Bernie said. "We need to get a new van." She said this at least once a week.

Libby patted Mathilda's dashboard. "Don't listen to her. We won't abandon you."

"You really think talking to her helps?" Bernie asked her sister.

"Yes, I do." Libby gave Mathilda a final pat. "Just because she's a machine doesn't mean she doesn't have feelings."

"I'm not even going to comment on that," Bernie said, concentrating on keeping Mathilda out of the largest of the potholes dotting the parking lot. "This is even worse than when I was here, and that's saying a lot."

Libby pointed to the Subaru parked in front of room twenty-one. It was the only vehicle in the lot. "There's Ellen's car."

"No parties tonight," Bernie observed as she parked next to it. "In my day, the place would have been full."

"I wouldn't know," Libby said. Unlike her sister, she had never been into that scene.

Libby got out first and Bernie joined her. Except for the rustle of leaves in the breeze and the occasional barking dog, it was quiet out. Libby was just thinking about what it would take to bring the Riverview back to life when she thought she saw something moving across the way. She nudged Bernie.

"What was that?" Libby pointed to the grove of trees the turkeys had vanished into.

"What was what?" Bernie asked, looking in the direction her sister was pointing.

"I'm not sure. I thought I saw something moving out there."

Bernie squinted. She didn't see anything, but

then it was hard to see at dusk. "Sorry, but I don't see anything."

"There was something there," Libby insisted.

"Well, there isn't now. It was probably a turkey."

"It wasn't a turkey," Libby said. "It was bigger."

"Then a deer."

"It was smaller than that."

"Well, whatever it is, it's gone now," Bernie said impatiently.

Libby shook her head.

"Why are you shaking your head?" Bernie demanded.

"What if it was a person?"

"Or a vampire," Bernie suggested.

"You should stop binge watching *True Blood*." Then she changed the subject. "Where is Ellen anyway? She had to have heard us pull up. I mean it's not as if Mathilda is quiet. Given what you said, I would have thought she'd have opened the door, if not been waiting outside for us."

"I guess we'll find out," Bernie said. She turned and knocked on the door. "Ellen."

Ellen didn't answer.

Bernie knocked again.

No response. The wind picked up, rustling the leaves of the sycamore trees. A frog croaked somewhere.

"So where is she?" Libby asked after a minute had gone by. "I mean her car is here."

Bernie licked her lips. "I don't know."

Libby sucked her breath in. "I have a bad feeling about this, Bernie."

"So do I," her sister admitted.

"Maybe we should call the police."

"Ellen specifically asked me not to do that," Bernie reminded her sister, putting her hand on the doorknob and pushing.

The door creaked as it swung open. She and Libby walked in.

The room looked exactly like all the other rooms in the motel Bernie had been in over the years. It was small and dingy with white walls, a badly painted seascape hanging over the bed, a beat-up-looking TV, and a small refrigerator.

"This place needs to be aired out," Libby observed. "I think someone was wearing too much cologne or something." She sniffed. "What is it? It smells so familiar."

But Bernie didn't answer. She was too busy looking at the bed.

Someone was in it. And it wasn't Goldilocks.

Chapter 4

For some reason, the first thing that both Libby and Bernie noticed were the man's hands. They were down at his sides. Then they noticed that his legs were straight out, and he was looking up at the ceiling. Clearly he was dead. The staring eyes and the mark around his throat left no doubt about that.

They stopped in their tracks. Libby put her hand to her mouth.

"Oh my God," she whispered.

"Who is he?" Bernie asked reflexively, not expecting an answer.

Libby shook her head. "I don't know." There was something about him that looked familiar, but she couldn't figure out what it was.

"He looks like he's laid out for a wake," Bernie observed.

"I don't know. I've never been to one," Libby replied, her eyes glued to the dead man on the bed.

One thing was undeniable. The guy lying on top of the thin, white, chenille bedspread was big. Libby figured him for six foot three and almost three hundred pounds at least, although it was a little hard to estimate with him being horizontal and all. His feet hanging over the bed looked like gunboats, and Libby guessed that the white sneakers he was wearing were probably a size thirteen. He had a full beard, a gold earring in his left ear, and was dressed in cargo pants and a short-sleeved shirt. He looked ready to go out for a walk in the park, except that is, for the ligature mark around his throat.

Bernie was about to take a step toward him when she heard a low moan and turned. It took her a moment to spot Ellen crouched down on the floor in the space between the bed and the wall with her back toward the nightstand. The nightstand lamp was off, which was why Bernie and Libby hadn't seen her in the shadows when they'd come in.

"Oh my God. What happened? Are you all right?" Bernie cried, the words tumbling out as she rushed toward her friend.

"I'm good," Ellen said, and giggled. "I'm ducky. Just fine. Peachy-keen in fact."

"Are you hurt?"

Ellen shook her head. "No, I'm not hurt, Bernie. I told you I'm okay." Although the dazed look in her eyes clearly said otherwise. "Why wouldn't I be?"

"Let's guess," Libby said.

Bernie took a couple more steps and crouched down in front of Ellen. The two women were so close that their knees were touching. Even though the light was dim, Bernie could see there wasn't any blood on Ellen's white T-shirt or her pink shorts, and there didn't seem to be any bruises on her face, arms, or legs.

"Are you sure you're not hurt?" Bernie asked again.

"I'm sure," Ellen answered. "One hundred percent. Absolutely." She giggled.

Libby leaned over Bernie. "What happened?" she asked.

Ellen shook her head and whimpered.

Libby persisted. "Who is the guy on the bed?"

Ellen started to cry. "I don't know," she managed to get out between sobs.

"How can you not know?" Libby demanded.

"Because I don't," Ellen replied, crying harder.

Bernie reached out and stroked Ellen's hair. "Are you sure?"

"Yes," Ellen whispered.

"Please, you have to tell us what happened," Bernie begged.

Instead of answering, Ellen wrapped her arms around her knees, hugged herself, and started rocking back and forth.

Bernie and Libby exchanged looks. This wasn't going well. *She's in shock,* Libby thought as she caught sight of a bottle of Canadian Club sitting on the other nightstand. Maybe the Canadian Club would help.

Libby nodded in the bottle's direction. "Why don't I pour some of that into a glass?" she suggested to Bernie.

"Good idea," her sister told Libby as she took Ellen's hands in her own and began rubbing them.

Libby looked around for a glass and when she didn't see one she went into the bathroom to find one. It wasn't that Ellen couldn't drink straight from the bottle; it was that Libby thought that amenities should be observed if possible. As she stepped inside, she noted that the bathroom tiles were cracked and there was a yellow stain around the bathtub drain. Two threadbare towels hung over the towel rack next to a large white T-shirt that said Arf. A pair of well-worn pink and white slippers sat below the shirt.

A pink cosmetic case sat on top of the toilet. *Probably not the dead guy's,* Libby reasoned. He didn't seem like the pink type, she thought as she opened the case up and went through it. It contained a woman's deodorant, a travel-sized toothbrush, a new-looking tube of toothpaste, and small jars of moisturizer, cleanser, and foundation. Evidently, Ellen had been planning on staying overnight. At least.

Interesting, Libby thought as she grabbed the glass that was sitting on the sink, gave it a quick rinse because it didn't look too clean, went outside, and poured Ellen a good-sized shot of Canadian Club, after which she put the bottle back on the dresser. As she did, she could hear her father yelling that this was a crime scene and she was mucking everything up, but at the moment she didn't really care.

"Here," she said, coming around the bed and holding the glass out to Ellen.

Ellen shook her head.

Bernie reached out her hand. "Give it to me." Libby handed her sister the glass. Bernie took it and held it out to Ellen's lips. "Have a sip," she ordered. "It'll make you feel better. Really."

A few seconds went by, then Ellen said, "Okay," in a little girl voice and took a swallow.

"Better?" Bernie asked as Ellen grimaced and wiped her mouth with the back of her hand.

Ellen nodded and took another sip.

"So when did you get here?" Libby asked.

Ellen looked up. "I . . . don't . . ."

"I saw your things in the bathroom," Libby explained. "It looks as if you were planning on staying the night."

Ellen didn't say anything.

"Were you?" Libby persisted.

A tear dripped down Ellen's cheek.

"Talk to us," Bernie pleaded. "We can't help you if we don't know what happened."

"I know," Ellen said. She handed the glass back to Bernie, put out her hand to steady herself, and stood up. Then she turned her face to the wall so she wouldn't have to look at the man in the bed, and slowly sidestepped her way out, halting when she reached the dresser.

"Can you tell me what happened here?" Bernie asked.

Ellen licked her lips. "Here?"

Libby nodded to the man on the bed. "Who is he?"

"How many times do I have to say I don't know?" Ellen replied, her voice shot through with a thread of anger.

"Was he here when you arrived?"

"No . . . Yes . . . I mean." Ellen clenched her fists.

"Don't tell me you don't know again," Libby told her.

Ellen bit her lip and stared straight ahead.

"Why did you call us, if you won't talk to us?" Bernie asked.

"I was hoping—" Ellen stopped.

"Hoping what?" Bernie asked.

"That you could . . . you know . . . help. Like make him go away."

"You mean like get rid of the body?" Bernie cried incredulously. "Are you nuts? Is that what you think we do?"

Ellen put her hands to her mouth. "I'm so . . . so . . . sorry. I don't know what I was thinking." Tears were rolling down her cheeks. "It's just that I'm so scared. I don't think I can deal with this."

Bernie gave her another pat on the shoulder. "We'll be here for you every step of the way."

"But you have to tell us what happened," Libby repeated for the third time. "We can't help you if we don't know."

"Do you want another sip of the Canadian Club?" Bernie asked Ellen.

Ellen shook her head.

"Okay then," Bernie said. "I want you to take a deep breath, start at the beginning, and don't leave anything out."

Another minute passed, then Ellen blurted out, "He was here when I came back."

"Back from where?" Bernie wanted to know.

Ellen answered promptly. "Ted's." Ted's was a local discount liquor store, one of those places where all the stock is in cartons. "I decided I needed something to drink."

"So you *were* sleeping here?" Bernie asked.

Ellen nodded. Two quick movements of her head. *Like a bird pecking at food,* Libby thought.

"That was the plan. I figured no one would look for me here."

"Oh God," Bernie said. Suddenly she remembered the conversation she and Ellen had had in the park. "What did you do?"

Ellen raised her hands, then let them flutter down to her sides. "I just wanted my family to notice me," she said in a plaintive tone, skirting Bernie's question. "Is that such a terrible thing to ask?"

"Not normally," Libby replied before Bernie could. "I guess it depends on what you do to achieve those ends. For example, burning the house down would certainly get your family's attention, but not in the way you would want." Libby was going to say more, but Bernie shot her a look and she shut up.

"Please tell me you didn't kidnap yourself," Bernie said.

"You were the one who suggested it," Ellen told her.

"I was kidding," Bernie yelled. "Kidding. I told you to go to a spa."

"This seemed better," Ellen whispered.

"Oh my God," Bernie said, not for the first time. "I can't believe you did this."

"Did you leave a ransom note?" Libby asked.

Ellen nodded. "In an envelope on the dining room table. I cut out the letters for Bruce's name from a magazine and pasted them on the envelope."

"What did the note say?" Bernie asked.

"I told him to come alone and that I'd kill myself if he didn't come up with the money and have it here by two in the morning at the latest."

"So how much were you asking for yourself?" Libby couldn't resist inquiring. "A lot?"

Ellen opened and closed her mouth. Nothing came out.

Libby nodded to the dead guy on the bed. "Was he in on this?"

"No," Ellen cried. "No. I already told you I don't know who he is. I'm so ashamed." She put her hand over her mouth. "I'm going to be sick," she announced, and ran to the bathroom, leaving Bernie and Libby standing there.

"What a god-awful mess," Libby said to Bernie as Ellen slammed the bathroom door shut behind her.

"That," Bernie replied, "is a massive under-statement."

40

"I'm surprised the cops aren't here already," Libby observed.

Bernie bit at a cuticle. "They will be soon. That's for sure."

Chapter 5

Libby reached in her pants pocket for a square of chocolate, then remembered she'd left the candy back at the shop. Drats. Just when she needed it too. "Bernie, we have to call the police."

Bernie grimaced. "Tell me something I don't know." She nodded her head toward the bathroom. "She's going to freak when they show up," she said, lowering her voice to a whisper. "She's going to come apart."

"She is already."

"Yeah, but she's going to go even further down that path."

Libby swatted at a fly buzzing around her head. "I would file this under really, really bad concepts."

"I can't believe she did this." Bernie pressed the palms of her hands against her eyes. "I can't believe she took me seriously."

"I know," Libby assured her. "Really I do."

"I just . . ." Bernie stopped talking and shook her head.

Libby went over and put her hands on her

sister's shoulders. "Bernie," she told her, "you have to keep it together."

Bernie took a deep breath and let it out. "Better." Then she pointed to the man on the bed. "We need to find out who this guy is. Hopefully he has some ID on him."

"The police aren't going to like our doing that," Libby observed.

"They're not going to know," Bernie said.

"H-E-L-L-O. Fingerprints. DNA," Libby said.

"Watch and learn," Bernie said as she pulled a Ziplock bag full of walnuts and almonds out of her tote, shook the nuts into a side pocket, slipped her hand into the bag, and wiggled her fingers. "Tada! No fingerprints on the body. Am I brilliant or am I brilliant?"

"You're brilliant."

Bernie curtsied, choosing to overlook the sarcasm. "Thank you. Thank you. Thank you." She moved a strand of hair off her forehead with the back of her hand.

Libby sighed. "We're still going to have a lot of explaining to do when the police get here." She could picture the upcoming scene and it wasn't a pleasant vision.

"Not as much as Ellen," Bernie observed.

"True." Then Libby leaned over to her sister and asked her the question that had been bothering her ever since they'd walked into the place. "You don't think Ellen had anything to do

42

with this, do you?" she asked, keeping her voice low. *This* referring to the body on the bed.

"No, I don't," Bernie responded, "and I'll tell you why." She pointed to the mark on the man's throat. "Ellen is five foot two and one hundred and forty pounds at the most. I don't see how she could have strangled him, do you? Especially with what looks like some sort of rope, some sort of thin rope."

"Or a garrote," Libby suggested.

Bernie thought about the Spanish weapon. "You don't see a lot of those floating around Westchester."

"You also don't see a lot of corpses in motel rooms," Libby pointed out. "Especially motel rooms around here."

Bernie nodded. "True. But even if it was a garrote, Ellen still wouldn't have the strength to kill this guy with something like that. Shooting, yes. This, no."

"I guess she wouldn't," Libby allowed. "But somebody did."

Bernie straightened up. "Someone large, someone almost as tall as the guy on the bed, someone with strong hands."

Libby sighed. "If Ellen is telling the truth, it also means that that someone had to have known that she had left her room so they could place the body in here."

"Which also means whoever it was had to have

been following her," Bernie said. "Ellen told us she went to Ted's"

Libby nodded. "That's right." She thought for a moment. "Twenty minutes is about the time it would take to get to Ted's, buy a bottle, and come back."

"You can kill a man in a lot less time than that," Bernie noted.

"Yeah. Like two seconds." Libby chewed her cheek as she looked around the room. Everything seemed in order. "There are no signs of a struggle," she observed. "If the killing had taken place here, there would have been. Of course, Ellen could have cleaned them up."

"Which seems unlikely," Bernie replied. "First she kills this guy, then she cleans up, then she calls us for help?"

"To get rid of the body."

"She said she was sorry about that."

"I hope so. Why not just leave? Why call us?"

"I'm guessing because she was so panicked she couldn't move."

Bernie brushed a speck of lint off her black T-shirt. "So given that we're agreed with the fact that Ellen didn't kill this guy—we are, aren't we?"

Libby nodded.

"We're left with the question of how this guy got here. I think there are three possibilities." And Bernie ticked them off on her fingers through the plastic bag. "Either this guy was killed in this

44

room, he was killed in the parking lot, or he was dead already, and whoever the killer was saw Ellen leaving and decided to take advantage of the opportunity and put the body on the bed, after which, he drove off."

"Highly unlikely," Libby said. "Most people don't drive around with dead bodies."

"Except for Marvin."

"Ha-ha. It's his job. He owns a funeral home."

"I know. I just couldn't resist the opening. Anyway," Bernie said, getting back to business, "we're agreed our dead guy was probably not killed in the motel room, right?"

"Right," Libby said. "There's the parking lot. Maybe the person I saw—"

Bernie interrupted. "You never said it was a person," she countered. "You said it was a deer."

"No. You said it was a deer. I said I wasn't sure. Anyway, maybe he had something to do with this."

"Well, if he did, he's long gone by now." Bernie tapped her fingers on her thigh. "But for the sake of argument, let's say you're right. Let's say this hypothetical person did kill him. It still doesn't answer the question of why the dead guy is on the bed. Why not leave his body in the woods?"

"Maybe the dead guy was intended as a message to Ellen," Libby suggested.

"Doubtful. To what end?" Bernie extended her hands, palms outward. "She's a housewife, for heaven's sake, not a Mafia member. She runs a dog biscuit company; the only places she goes are the grocery store and the soccer field to watch her kids play ball."

"All I know," Libby said, pointing to the dead guy, "is that he didn't get here in some space-time continuum accident."

"No kidding." Bernie flexed her fingers in the bag. "You know how they always say on crime shows how dead bodies speak to them? Well, this one's not saying anything to me."

"And a good thing too," Libby responded. "Bad enough to deal with a dead body, let alone one who talks."

"That would make him a zombie, in which case I'd be out of here." Bernie slipped the Ziplock bag off her hand and held it out to Libby. "Hold this for a moment, would you?"

"Why?"

"I want to document everything."

Bernie reached into her tote and took out her phone. When she was done, she put her phone back in her tote, took the Ziplock bag from Libby, put it back over her hand, and started going through the dead man's pants pockets.

As Libby watched, she couldn't help thinking of her mom emptying her dad's pants pockets before she did the laundry. "Mom would not have approved of what you're doing," Libby found herself blurting out.

Bernie straightened up. "She'd have a fit. But then if Mom was alive we wouldn't be doing this."

"That's for sure," Libby said, remembering how their mom had acted when their dad had discussed his cases around the dinner table. She'd always say, "Can't we talk about something more pleasant? Any luck?"

"Not even lint." There were six pockets, three to a side, and all of them were empty. No wallet. No cell phone. No keys. No nothing. Bernie clasped her palms together and brought her fingers up to her lips. " 'Curiouser and curiouser,' as the White Rabbit would say."

"Either this guy left his stuff behind because he didn't want to be ID'd or someone took it because they didn't want him to be identified."

"Either way the result is the same," Bernie noted, taking the Ziplock bag off her hand and stuffing it back in her tote.

She and Libby were about to check out the parking lot when they heard a *clunk* coming from the bathroom.

"Ellen," Bernie called. "You okay?"

"I'm fine," Ellen replied. She gave a strangled laugh. "Part of the towel rack fell off the wall. I'm putting it back on."

"Do you need any help?" Bernie asked.

"No. No. It's all good."

"Call if you need us."

"Don't worry, I will," Ellen replied.

Bernie and Libby heard the sound of water running.

Ellen's voice floated through the noise. "I'm washing up. I'll be done in a minute."

"Take your time," Bernie responded. "But when you come out we have to talk, okay?"

Ellen didn't answer.

"Ellen, we really do," Bernie said. "This is serious. You could go to jail for this."

There was still no response.

"Maybe she can't hear you over the water," Libby suggested.

"It's not that loud. Anyway, she could hear me fine before." Bernie started tapping the fingers of her left hand against her thigh. The bad feeling she'd had ever since she'd knocked on the motel room door kicked itself up a notch. "I'm not liking this. I'm not liking this at all."

Which was when Libby remembered the bathroom window. She put her hand to her mouth and groaned. "Oh crap."

"Oh crap, what?" Bernie asked.

"The bathroom window. I bet she climbed out it."

"Don't be absurd." Bernie took a deep breath and let it out. "She wouldn't. She couldn't."

"She might have."

Bernie shook her head. "Those windows are small. I don't think she could squeeze through one of them. Anyway, they were always painted shut."

"Maybe not this time," Libby said as she headed toward the bathroom with Bernie following.

Libby banged on the door. "Ellen," she cried. "Open up. Come out this second."

There was no response.

Libby tried the door handle. It didn't budge. The door was locked.

"Let me try," Bernie said, moving in front of Libby.

"Be my guest," Libby told her.

"Ellen, don't be stupid." Bernie jiggled the door handle. "Damn," she said when it didn't move. She cursed under her breath and put her ear against the wood. All she could hear was running water. "I think you're right. I don't think she's in there."

"We should have called the police," Libby said.

"They'll be here soon enough," Bernie conceded as she studied the door. It was old and flimsy-looking and the upper hinge didn't look too sturdy.

An idea occurred to Libby. She put her hand to her mouth.

"What?" Bernie asked, even though Libby hadn't said anything.

"Do you think Ellen's trying to kill herself?"

"She wouldn't do that," Bernie replied. But then she hadn't thought Ellen would do something like this either. Bernie's heart started racing. "Ellen," she yelled, pounding on the door with her fists.

When there was no answer, Bernie rammed into it with her shoulder. The door shuddered, but stayed intact. She tried again. She thought she felt the door move slightly but she couldn't be sure.

She was rubbing her shoulder when Libby said, "Here, let me help."

Bernie nodded her appreciation. "All right then. On the count of three."

"Three it is," Libby said as she got into position.

At three both sisters hit the door full-on. There was a splintering noise and one of the hinges gave way.

"We probably could have picked the lock," Libby noted as she pushed the door open. "Isaac will not be happy."

"No, he won't," Bernie noted as both sisters charged into the bathroom.

The room was empty.

The window was open, just as Libby had predicted.

Bernie stared at it. "I don't believe it," she said. She felt angry and hurt and betrayed and relieved that Ellen wasn't dead all at the same time.

"Come on," Libby cried, pulling her sister out of the bathroom. "We're wasting time."

"I'm going to kill her," Bernie growled as she followed her sister out of the motel room.

"First we have to get her," Libby observed.

Libby and Bernie jumped as the motel door slammed shut behind them. From where they were, they had a clear view of Ellen standing on the driver's side of her Subaru, frantically trying to open the car door.

Chapter 6

Ellen," Bernie yelled. "Wait. Don't go. Please. We have to talk."

Ellen paused for a nanosecond and tugged at the car door one last time. The door didn't budge. Bernie watched a look of horror cross Ellen's face as she realized the door was locked. She patted her pants pocket for her keys. They weren't there. *I bet she left them in the motel room,* Bernie thought as she watched Ellen start to walk to the rear of the car. Then Ellen changed her mind, pivoted, and headed for the trees that ringed the parking lot. She was running, but not very fast. Being thirty pounds overweight was slowing her down.

Bernie cursed under her breath while she reached down and took off her Manolos being that it was hard to run in stilettos. She couldn't believe she was going to have to chase Ellen down.

"Come on," Bernie cried, grabbing Libby's arm. "She's getting away."

Libby didn't move. "Good. Let her." She'd had enough drama for the moment.

"We have to catch her."

"No. We really don't. We can wait till she comes back for her car keys." And she walked over and went to open the motel room door. It was locked. Great! A self-locking lock. Just what they needed. "Or maybe not."

"Well, I'm not waiting for her to come back," Bernie announced.

"And why is that?"

Bernie stuck out her chin. "Number one, we don't know if she's coming back here or not, and number two, I'm damned if I'm going to be made a fool."

"So because you're pissed, I have to chase someone through the woods wearing flip-flops?"

Bernie raised her hand. "Hey, come with me or not. It's up to you. But I am going to catch Ellen and find out what's going on if it's the last thing I do. Ellen," she yelled as her friend disappeared into the trees.

Then Bernie took off.

"Oh, for Pete's sake," Libby muttered as she watched Bernie go. She could stay, but she knew she wouldn't. Her sister was her sister even if she was an idiot. However, this was a bad idea. She didn't like running under the best of circumstances and these were not the best of circumstances. At least, if she were wearing sneakers . . . but she wasn't. She was wearing shoes that had been developed for walking on the sand, and she didn't see any sand here.

She could hear her sandals making a slapping noise on the tarmac as she ran. On top of everything else, it was hard to see. Her night vision had never been great and the sun had set since she and Bernie had gone into the motel room and there was no moon out. All Libby could see of Bernie was a gray shape moving in front of her. Then her sister entered the woods and Libby lost sight of her altogether.

When Libby got to the forest, she paused to get her bearings. She was trying to decide which way to go when she heard twigs cracking in front of her. Then she heard Bernie shouting Ellen's name.

"Okay, then," Libby said to herself as she headed toward the sound.

As Libby ran, she wondered what her sister was going to do if and when she caught Ellen. Was she going to tackle her? Hold her down? What?

Meanwhile, Bernie was a hundred yards or so upfront. "Please, stop," she called out to Ellen, but Ellen kept going.

By now she and Ellen were running through the trees that had overgrown the parking lot and taken possession of the cornfield that had been there when the land was a farm. Bernie cursed the low-hanging pine branches that kept hitting her in the face as she raced through the woods.

Libby was right. I shouldn't be doing this, Bernie thought as she stopped for a moment to catch her breath and pluck a thorn out of her heel. *But I especially shouldn't be doing this without shoes.* But pride made her keep going. She stopped again a few yards later, bent down, and rubbed her right foot. She could feel welts and cuts. She didn't even want to think about what she was stepping on, let alone the condition of her pedicure. When had she gotten her last tetanus shot anyway? She put her right foot down, picked up her left foot, and flicked off a pebble that had lodged itself in her arch. In the future, it might be a good idea to keep an extra pair of running shoes in the van.

"It's going to look really bad if you run away," Bernie yelled at Ellen after she'd straightened up.

Ellen didn't reply. All Bernie heard was the sound of twigs snapping and brush being pushed aside, a good indication that Ellen was still moving.

Bernie tried again. "Please, Ellen," she begged. "Don't do this."

Ellen's voice floated back to her. "I'm sorry," she said. "I made a mistake. I should never have gotten you involved. Go home."

"I can't do that," Bernie called back. "I am involved."

"Just pretend you were never here," Ellen said.

Bernie could hear Ellen gasping for breath

somewhere in front of her. *She can't be that far,* thought Bernie. *If I keep her talking, maybe I can sneak up on her and tackle her.*

"That's not possible," Bernie said as she very carefully lifted her right foot up and put it down. There was no sound. This was good.

"Sure, it is," Ellen replied.

Bernie lifted her left foot up and slowly brought that one down. "What about the dead body?" she asked. "How do I explain him?"

Ellen's breath sounded a little more regular. "You don't have to."

"Really?"

"Yes. Really. No one is here. No one knows you saw anything. Just don't tell anyone and you'll be fine."

"Is that your plan?"

Ellen didn't answer.

"What if I'm not fine with it?" Bernie asked. *Just keep talking,* she silently ordered Ellen as she lifted up her right foot and brought it down. There was a crackling noise as she stepped on a twig. "Damn," Bernie said out loud.

Suddenly, she heard rustling up ahead. "Wait, Ellen," she called after her. "Please stay where you are. The two of us can talk this out."

"I don't think so," Ellen said. "I don't think so at all." And she was off again.

Bernie closed her eyes. The noise Ellen was making was coming from the right, which meant that Ellen had turned and was heading in a slightly different direction. She concentrated on picturing the lay of the land.

If her memory served, there was an open field after the trees and then a road and a housing development. The road—she thought it was Danbury Circle West—circled back and around to the motel. Ellen was going to follow it to get her car. She didn't know that the door to the motel room had slammed shut. Or did she? Maybe she was planning to wiggle her way back through the bathroom window.

Or maybe Ellen wasn't going back to the motel. No. She had to. She needed to get her car. She couldn't just leave it there. And then all of a sudden Bernie knew. When Ellen had been going to the rear of the car she must have had a key hidden underneath the fender in one of those little metallic boxes. Ellen just hadn't had time to get it. Bernie groaned. She had to beat Ellen back to her Subaru and get that key.

Chapter 7

B ernie started running again. After a couple of minutes though, she felt shooting pains going up the front of her calves and she remembered why she'd given it up. Shin splints. She kept on going anyway, brushing the ever-present low-hanging branches away from her face as she ran. She'd gone a couple of hundred feet when she stepped on something that stabbed her in her instep. She cursed and kept on going, but then she stumbled on a rock and twisted her ankle. This time she fell to the ground. She was just getting up when Libby bumped into her.

Libby screamed. They both went down.

"Sorry," Libby said, hoisting herself up. She rubbed her side where Bernie's elbow had jammed into her.

"Jeez," Bernie said after she'd gotten her wind back. "Watch where you're going, why don't you?"

"I didn't see you."

"Obviously," Bernie replied. She dusted herself off. Maybe if they hurried they could still beat Ellen back to the Subaru. But when Bernie tried to get up, a searing pain shot through her ankle. "I think I sprained something."

"Fantastic." Libby couldn't help herself. Her thoughts immediately went to all the work she was going to have to do by herself. She knew she should be more charitable. She was trying, but she wasn't succeeding.

Bernie used a rock outcropping next to her to pull herself up. She took a step and groaned. Her ankle was throbbing. "I think I'm going to need your help getting back."

"What about Ellen?" Libby asked.

"I blew it," Bernie admitted.

They both fell silent.

"I don't hear her. You think she stopped?" Libby asked.

"Maybe. Or maybe she made it to Danbury West."

"Where?"

"That's the road that goes to Clearview Gardens. It circles back to the motel."

"You think that's what she's going to do?" Libby asked.

"That's what I would do," Bernie said. "I was hoping I could beat her back to the Subaru and get her car keys."

"Not at the pace you're going now, you're not," Libby observed.

"Maybe, but she's got longer to go and she's not exactly fleet of foot."

"She's faster than you are at the moment," Libby retorted.

Bernie didn't say anything because it was true. Instead, she reached up and repinned her hair.

"Plus," Libby added, "she did climb out the window and you never thought she could do that."

"True," Bernie conceded. She thought about the route Ellen was going to have to take. "But if she cuts through the trees, she still has to walk over the field, and back up the road."

"If she doesn't retrace her steps like we are."

"She can't. We'd hear her if she did."

"It doesn't matter. We still can't catch her, especially since you can't walk."

"I can too," Bernie protested.

"You can hobble."

"Limp."

"Same thing."

"No it's not. Limping is faster." Bernie took a step to prove her point. She groaned as the pain shot up her leg again. "This might be a little trickier than I thought," she conceded, stopping and leaning against a tree for support.

"How bad is it?" Libby asked her sister. "Do you think you broke something?"

"No. I think I just need to ice it," Bernie said. "I think it's a bad sprain."

Libby took Bernie's arm and put it across her shoulder to help take some of the weight off her sister's foot. They'd walked a few more steps when Bernie held out her hand. "Wait. I have to stop again." She felt around, found a rock, and leaned against it.

"Has it ever occurred to you that it's time to stop being so stubborn, call the police, and tell them what happened?" Libby asked her sister.

"Yeah, it's occurred to me," Bernie said. "Maybe they're already there with Bruce."

"If he called them," Libby said.

"He'll call them," Bernie prophesized.

"Why do you say that?"

"Because he's that kind of guy."

"And if the police aren't there?" Libby asked.

Bernie turned to face her sister. "Listen, I just want to hear her story first before we throw her to the lions. After all, Ellen came to us for help."

"And then she ran away."

"Because she was terrified."

"Or because she killed the guy," Libby said.

"I thought we agreed that she didn't," Bernie replied.

"Maybe I'm changing my mind," Libby said.

"She's my friend, Libby. I've known her for over twenty years."

"And she's always been a pain in the ass."

"This is true."

"Sometimes there's such a thing as being too loyal." Libby scratched her arm. It felt as if something had just bitten her. "She doesn't have to know it's us. We could always call the police from the pay phone on Oakwood Drive, the one near the strip mall that sells Maltese puppies, and tell them there's a dead body in the Riverview Motel. Then we'll get you home and ice that ankle."

"As simple as that?" Bernie said.

"Yes. As simple as that," Libby replied.

"But I'll know. Also there are probably video cameras at that strip mall and they'll see us making the call."

Libby brushed a moth away from her face. "As

long as we're on that subject, have you thought about what we're going to say to the cops about the body in the bed?"

"That we found it."

"And then they'll say, 'why didn't you call it in immediately?' and we'll say . . . ?"

"We'll explain," Bernie said.

"Too bad the person who summoned us to the Riverview Motel won't be able to vouch for us."

"She will," Bernie replied.

"If we find her."

"When we find her." Bernie took a deep breath. "She needs us."

"She certainly isn't acting that way," Libby observed.

Bernie sighed and rubbed her ankle. The throbbing was getting worse. She could feel the pulsing in it. "On one hand, I'd like to wring her throat. On the other hand, I feel bad for her."

"Bad? Are you nuts?" Libby squawked.

"No. I think that she must be terrified given the way she's acting."

"So you've said." Libby snorted. "I have to say, I think that's a charitable interpretation of her actions."

Bernie crossed her arms over her chest. "I don't think she killed him and you don't think so either."

"Then why is she lying, Bernie?" Libby demanded. "Why did she run away?"

"I told you. She panicked. Remember she was the one who called us here."

"I'm not forgetting. I'm also not forgetting that she faked her own kidnapping," Libby replied. "Talk about boneheaded moves. Maybe from a teenage girl, but from a mother of three boys? Seriously."

"Stupid? Absolutely. Childish? Without a doubt," Bernie replied. "But that doesn't make her a murderer."

Libby scratched a bite on her calf. Mosquitoes loved her. "All I know is that if it weren't for Ellen all the macaroons would be packed up and we would be done."

"I can't argue with that," Bernie told her.

She slowly began putting weight on her ankle and winced as the pain shot up her leg again. God, what she wouldn't give to be home right now with a couple of packages of frozen peas on her ankle and a glass of Scotch in her hand.

She didn't say anything else for a minute, just sat there listening to the night sounds and letting the breeze wash over her. She thought she heard an owl in the distance, but she wasn't sure. Suddenly she was very tired. She knew she should get moving but she really didn't want to. Then she had an idea.

"Libby," she began.

"No. Absolutely not," said Libby, cutting her sister off. She was way ahead of her.

"You don't know what I'm about to say," Bernie protested.

"I've got a pretty good idea. You want me to go after Ellen by myself and I'm not going to," Libby told her.

"I'm not asking you to go after her, Libby," Bernie said. "I'm just asking you to beat her back to her Subaru and get the key from under the fender."

"And then what?"

"Wait for me."

"What if she wants her key back?"

"Don't give it to her."

"What if she attacks me?"

Bernie snorted. "Ellen? Don't be ridiculous. She's not going to attack you."

"What if she does? After all, you didn't think she'd climb out the window either. Or what if she decides to run away?"

"Libby, please," Bernie answered. "I would do this if I could, but I can't. I realize there's no good solution here, but finding Ellen and talking to her is the least bad one. All I'm asking is for you to stall her until I get there."

"How are you going to get there? You can hardly walk."

"I'll manage. I'll just rest a lot." Bernie took Libby's hands in hers. "Please, I'm begging you."

"I'm not sure that leaving you is such a good idea."

"I'll be fine. I swear I will," Bernie promised when Libby hesitated. "I'll call if I have a problem."

"Promise?"

Bernie raised her right hand. "Sister swear."

"You'd better."

"I will." Bernie gave Libby a gentle shove. "Now go."

As Bernie watched her sister leave she thought about the disaster this evening had turned into and about how it was all her fault. She probably shouldn't have come—Libby was right about that—but how could she not have? And now she was stuck with a sore ankle and a bunch of unanswered questions—questions she couldn't let go of. Why had Ellen run? Who was the guy in the bed? What had happened to him? Bernie was still thinking about that as Libby trudged off to the Riverview Motel. Hopefully, she would arrive in time.

On the other hand, Libby wasn't thinking about how she'd keep Ellen from getting the key if she got there first, or about the body in the bed, or even about her sister hobbling alone in the dark. She was thinking about how relieved she was to be getting out of the woods. She didn't like places like this in the daytime, and in the nighttime she liked them even less. You couldn't see where you were going, things kept hitting you in the face, you could hear strange rustles and creaks, and even though Libby knew there were no bears or wolves in Westchester, she couldn't help thinking that there were.

And then there were the vampires—she could kill Bernie for bringing them up. She didn't even want to think about them, but once she'd summoned them up she couldn't get them out of her mind, which was why she picked up her pace as much as she could, not that that was saying a lot.

It had been a long day and she was exhausted. In addition, even though Libby's eyes had become accustomed to the dark, she still had to feel her way along as tree trunks and rocks jumped out at her and vines and twigs tried to ensnare her feet. She paused every tenth step or so to untangle one of her flip-flops from a small branch or low-lying bush or take out a small rock or pebble that had gotten lodged in there, because the last thing she needed was to get injured the way Bernie had.

Ten minutes later, even though it felt like at least an hour to Libby, she could see the outline of the motel haloed in the dim light of the streetlights through the trees. When she squinted, she could see that the Subaru was still sitting next to their van in the parking lot. She had beaten Ellen after all. She didn't know whether she was relieved or not.

"I'm right behind you," Bernie said when Libby phoned to tell her the news.

"How far behind me?" Libby asked, but it was too late. Bernie had already hung up.

It took Libby another couple of minutes before she reached the edge of the woods. If she had been looking up she might have seen the three men silently crouched behind Mathilda, or the two police cars parked a little way off in the distance, or Ellen standing next to the squad cars. But Libby wasn't looking up. She was looking at the ground because she was afraid she was going to trip and fall. Out of the corner of her eye, off to the left, she saw a flicker of light. When she turned her head and focused on it she saw what had made the flicker—a small, round metallic object at the base of a pine tree, about ten feet away.

As she got closer, she realized that what she'd spotted was a watch lying facedown on the ground. *Maybe it belonged to the dead guy,* she thought. Maybe their luck was about to change. Maybe the watch had an inscription on the back. She was reaching down to get it when she heard someone yell, "There she is."

Libby froze and looked up. Then someone was shining a light in her eyes. It was so bright it blinded her and she put up her hands to shield her eyes from it.

"Got her," Ellen's husband yelled as he dug his fingers into Libby's shoulders.

Then Libby heard Ellen yelling, "Leave her alone, Bruce. I told you she doesn't have anything to do with this."

Libby didn't say anything. She was too dazed.

Chapter 8

Bernie called her dad at eleven-thirty that evening. Sean, in turn, called Marvin and told him they had a situation and he needed him pronto. Then he hung up before Marvin could ask him what was going on. It took Marvin twenty minutes to throw some clothes on and get down to the Simmons's place. When he arrived, he could see Sean sitting on the bench in front of the shop, impatiently jiggling his leg up and down. He was wearing a slightly wrinkled short-sleeved plaid shirt and a pair of frayed khakis and looked as if he'd dressed in a hurry.

"What happened?" Marvin called out to Sean as Sean levered himself up with the aid of his cane and started walking toward the Kia. "Are Libby and Bernie all right?"

"They're fine," Sean snapped. "Just dandy."

Oh, oh. What have they gotten themselves into now? Marvin thought.

Sean pointed his cane at Marvin's passenger. "What's she doing here?"

"She wanted to go for a ride."

"Hilda is a pig. Pigs don't ride in cars. They don't have 'wants.'"

Marvin took his hands off the wheel and

crossed them over his chest. "That's what my dad keeps saying."

"For once he and I are in agreement."

Marvin sighed. "I already told you, Mr. Simmons, she's used to people and Juno's husband wouldn't take her."

"That doesn't mean you had to," Sean pointed out.

"Libby wanted me to, and really, I kinda like her. It's like having a dog, only better, because she's smarter. So what's going on? Why did you call me?" Marvin asked, getting back to the important stuff.

Sean stopped in the middle of the sidewalk. "I'll tell you what's going on," he sputtered. "Your girlfriend and her sister have about as much sense as a turnip. I should have gone with them. If I had, none of this would have happened."

"None of what would have happened?" Marvin said, trying not to yell.

"In a moment," Sean told him.

Marvin clenched his teeth and reminded himself there was no point in arguing. He got out to help Sean into the car, but before he got to him Sean waved him off.

"I can manage by myself, thank you very much," Sean snarled.

Marvin took a step back. "Sorry," he said, putting his hands up in a gesture of surrender.

Sean got in the Kia and slammed the door shut.

Hilda oinked a hello, which Sean ignored. "At least she doesn't have to sit in the front seat," Sean complained when Marvin got in.

"She thinks she does," Marvin replied, closing his door.

"Ridiculous," Sean muttered. "She's a pig."

"She thinks she's a person."

"You're crazy too."

Marvin ignored the comment and asked where they were going instead. He'd learned that, in general, a good rule of thumb was not to pick a fight with your future father-in-law if possible, especially when said father-in-law was furious.

"The Riverview Motel," Sean snapped.

Marvin put the Kia in drive and they took off. Sean nodded, lit a cigarette, opened his window, threw the match out of it, and stared at the passing scenery as he smoked his cigarette. Smoking calmed him down. That's one of the things he liked about it.

"Is Libby okay?" Marvin asked after a moment of silence.

"Depends on how you define *okay*."

"Is she hurt?"

"No."

"Is Bernie hurt?"

"No."

"Then what's going on?"

"They're being held for obstruction of justice," Sean said.

"You're kidding."

Sean glared at him. "Do I look like I'm kidding, Marvin?"

Marvin shrunk back in his seat. "No."

Sean took another drag of his cigarette and thought about how he was going to handle the situation and what a pain in the ass his daughters were.

"So what happened?" Marvin finally worked up the courage to ask.

Sean took another puff of his cigarette and turned to him. "You want to know what happened? I'll tell you what happened. Evidently, Bernie's friend Ellen concocted a phony ransom note ordering her husband to go to the Riverview with money or his wife would die. Naturally, Bruce called the cops and when they got there they found an unidentified white male Caucasian on the bed in the motel room and Ellen outside the motel getting ready to drive away.

"The police were questioning her, when a short while later Libby and Bernie arrived on the scene, and the police took them into custody as well. Any other questions?"

Marvin shook his head.

"Good," Sean said. "Drive."

So Marvin concentrated on the road and on keeping Hilda from sitting on his lap. She'd grown quite a bit bigger in the time since he'd gotten her and he was a little bit nervous about how large she was going to get, even though she was a mini Vietnamese potbellied pig and those weren't supposed to get very big.

Traffic was light to nonexistent and it took Marvin a little less than fifteen minutes to drive down to the Riverview Motel. This time Sean didn't correct Marvin's sliding through stop signs. In fact, he didn't say anything to Marvin and Marvin didn't say anything else to him. There was no point. One thing was for sure though. Sean was really, really pissed.

Once he and Marvin arrived at the motel, it took Sean another twenty minutes to persuade the powers-that-be to release his daughters into his custody. He was only glad that his archenemy Lucas Broadbent, aka Lucy, chief of the Longely police, wasn't there to gloat.

"Dad," Bernie began when she and Libby got out of the squad car, but Sean put up his hand.

"Don't say anything," he instructed his daughters as they followed him and Marvin back to their van. "Not a word. I am not a happy man at this moment," he added unnecessarily, that being fairly self-evident. He started walking toward the Kia as fast as he could manage while Marvin hung back.

"Are you okay?" he asked Libby.

Sean stopped and turned around. "She's fine, Marvin. You two can talk later," he rapped out. "Right now you need to get me home."

Libby almost said, "I'm not fifteen, Dad," but she had the good sense not to. Instead she motioned for Marvin to go with her dad. "I'll call you," she mouthed.

"Make it soon," Marvin mouthed back. "I miss you and so does Hilda."

"And I miss you guys," Libby said.

Sean turned to Marvin. "Enough of that nonsense. Come on. I'm tired and I want to get to bed."

Marvin blew Libby a kiss and hurried after Sean.

"Boy, Dad's not happy," Bernie observed when she and Libby got into the van. "I haven't seen him this pissed in a long time."

"Not since you totaled the Blazer, to be exact. I told you," Libby said to Bernie once she had started Mathilda up. "I told you nothing good could come of this."

Bernie rubbed her ankle. It was even more swollen than it had been. Walking on it probably hadn't helped. "And you were right. Does that make you feel better?"

Libby shook her head. "Not even remotely."

Bernie rested her ankle on the dashboard. At least that would help ease some of the pressure. "Too bad Bruce called the cops."

"Can you blame him? What would you have done?" Libby asked her sister.

"I don't know. Maybe call us," Bernie answered.

"Have you thought that Bruce knew the note was fake? Has that occurred to you? Maybe he called the cops because he wanted to teach Ellen a lesson."

Bernie sighed. "Well, she certainly got one, that's for sure." Then she changed the subject. "How mad do you think Dad is?"

"On a scale of one to ten, one being the lowest and ten the highest, I'd give him between an eight and a nine," Libby answered. "He's still talking to us."

"Kinda."

"It's better than the 'silence of death.'" That was when Sean didn't speak to anyone for days.

The only good thing, as Bernie remarked, was that Sean got over things pretty quickly. Most of the time. The sisters just hoped that this was one of those times.

Chapter 9

Sean didn't say anything when he and his daughters went upstairs. He didn't say anything when Libby went to get Bernie an ice pack and she and Bernie something to eat. He didn't say anything until after his daughters sat down on the sofa and Bernie put her foot up on the coffee table and draped the package of frozen peas over it.

"Feel better?" he asked Bernie.

"Yes, thank you."

Sean gave a curt nod. "Good."

"Can I get you anything?" Libby asked her dad. "A brownie? There are a couple of pieces of rhubarb pie left."

Sean shook his head. "No. Nothing."

"Coffee?"

Sean glared. "I said nothing."

Libby shrugged. "I was just asking."

She and Bernie exchanged a glance. Their dad was talking a little, but he wasn't eating. What did that mean? This was a new one on Bernie and Libby. He'd never, ever said no to something they'd made.

The atmosphere in the room was glacial. No one said anything. Five minutes went by. Libby watched the second hand of the clock on the wall going round. She listened to its ticking and the occasional car going by outside. She could hear Bernie shifting around, trying to get comfortable, and her father tapping his fingers on the arm of his easy chair. Finally, she couldn't stand it anymore. She leaned forward.

"Dad," she began. "We're sorry—"

Which was as far as she got before Sean cut her off.

"You're sorry?" he asked, each word encased in a block of ice. "You're sorry?"

Libby and Bernie looked down at the floor. They felt as if they were ten again.

"You could be sitting in jail right now. You could still be sitting in jail. That's a real possibility because you're not out of the woods on this yet. Not by a long shot."

Bernie looked up. "It's my fault."

Sean shook his finger at Bernie and then at Libby. "No. It's both of your faults. I expected better from both of you. Neither one of you should have touched anything. You know not to. You should have called the police as soon as you walked into the room and saw that man lying on the bed. Then you should have gone outside and waited for them to arrive."

"What about Ellen?" Bernie asked.

"What about her?" Sean threw back. "You should have dragged her out with you."

"Hey, you haven't always followed the straight and narrow," Bernie pointed out indignantly.

Sean glared at her. It was a glare that in Sean's day had reduced the men under his command to quivering lumps of Jell-O.

"Okay," Sean said slowly. "If that's the tack you're taking, we don't have to talk about this at all. Good luck. Let me know how it all turns out. I'm going to bed." And he started to get up.

"No, no," Bernie said quickly. "I'm sorry. I shouldn't have said that."

"We're sorry," Libby amended. "For everything."

Sean's expression softened. "As well you should be." He lowered himself back down.

Bernie bit her lip. "We were wrong. We shouldn't have done what we did."

"So why did you?"

"I just . . ." Bernie waved her hand around while she thought about how she was going to frame her next sentence. "I guess . . . things got away from me."

Sean raised an eyebrow. "Really?" His tone was not congenial.

"We were surprised," Bernie explained.

"Stunned really," amplified Libby.

"Everything happened so fast. We got Ellen's phone call and ran over there. . . ."

"And then we saw the body on the bed," Libby added. "It was the first thing we saw and then Ellen was crouched down by the bed, half hidden. We didn't see her immediately, and when we did, we thought she'd been hurt."

Bernie shifted the package of frozen peas on her ankle. "We didn't know what to think."

"I see," Sean said. But he didn't. Not really. By the time he'd gotten to the Riverview, the man's body had been bagged and tagged and in the ambulance and the CID squad was working the room. "You're talking about the body Ellen claims to know nothing about, correct?"

Bernie nodded. "Correct. And Ellen was hysterical."

"She really was, Dad," Libby reaffirmed. "We couldn't get anything out of her."

"She's always hysterical."

Bernie left off with the peas. "That's exaggerating a little, don't you think?"

"Really?"

Bernie leaned over and rubbed her ankle. "Okay. It's not." If Ellen wasn't a total Drama Queen she was pretty close to it. "But not like this."

"So her plan didn't exactly work out, did it?" Sean continued.

Bernie licked her lips. "No, it didn't," she allowed.

"Well, she did want attention," Libby observed.

"Yeah, but she didn't get the kind she was aiming for," Bernie replied.

"Amazing," Sean said. "Truly amazing." He tut-tutted. What people came up with never failed to amaze him.

"Ellen probably thought Bruce was going to break down in tears or something when he got to the motel room and found out she was okay," Libby observed.

Sean thought of his response if his wife had pulled a stunt like that. Breaking down in tears would most emphatically not have been what he would have done. Wringing her neck would have been more like it. "She's definitely living in a fantasy land, I'll say that for her." Sean leaned back in his chair. "Why would Ellen do something like that?"

Bernie repositioned the frozen peas. "Because she felt neglected. She felt that no one in the family paid any attention to her."

"Couldn't she find something a little less dramatic to make her point?" Sean asked. "Your mom used to order pizza from Domino's when she felt like that."

"Oh," Bernie said. "I thought that was a treat."

Sean laughed. "I know Ellen gets worked up over things, but talk about exercising bad judgment. I gotta say this is really high up on the list of the stupidest things I've heard of, and I've heard of a lot of them."

"Ellen told me she'd tried everything else, but nothing worked." Bernie thought of her and Ellen's conversation in the park. "I should never have said what I did."

"Someone who wasn't off somewhere in la-la land wouldn't have taken your suggestion and run with it."

"And then when we were looking at the body she told us she had to go to the bathroom and she took off," Libby said. "We tried to catch her, which was another mistake."

"I think she overheard us talking about calling the police and got spooked," Bernie added. "We probably should have talked outside."

Sean massaged his temples. "Leaving Ellen's craziness aside, the thing that interests me is the body on the bed. Who is he?"

"We don't know," Bernie replied. "He didn't have any ID on him. We checked."

"And Ellen said she didn't know who he was or how he got there?" Sean continued.

"That's what she said," Libby responded.

"And you believe her?" Sean inquired.

"I want to," Bernie said.

"That's different," Sean pointed out.

"I know," Bernie said.

Sean turned to Libby. "And where do you stand on this?"

"With Bernie," Libby said.

"This makes no sense at all," Sean observed. Then he reached for the remote and turned on the TV. The sound of *Law and Order* filled the room. "I'll tell you one thing though," he said. "I'm going to enjoy being on that fishing boat. At least it'll be peaceful there."

Chapter 10

I t was a little after six-thirty the next morning when the doorbell of the Simmons's flat started ringing.

"You've got to be kidding me," Libby said, stifling a yawn as she looked out the living room window and saw Ellen Hadley's sons standing outside. She automatically pulled down the hem of the oversized T-shirt she had been sleeping in, the one that was from the gristmill down the road, and sighed.

She was exhausted, as was her sister and her dad. They'd all fallen asleep late. It had been a little after three in the morning when Sean had finally calmed down enough to be able to drift off, while Libby and Bernie had come up from downstairs after two-thirty, which was when they had finished boxing up the macaroons. Even though they'd both had trouble keeping their eyes open, they couldn't fall asleep and, once they finally did, they had both tossed and turned in their beds for the rest of the night. Neither one could get the picture of the dead man lying on the bed out of their minds. There was something about him, both sisters agreed, something nibbling at the corners of their minds. But what it was neither Libby nor Bernie knew.

RING. The doorbell went off again. Libby could see Ethan, Ellen's youngest son, pushing on it.

"What is going on?" Sean barked as he stalked out of his bedroom.

Libby explained.

"What the hell do they want?"

"I'm guessing to talk to us about their mom," Libby replied.

"Well, I don't want to talk to them," Sean declared. "Tell them to go away or I'll come down and shoot them."

"I don't want to talk to them either, Dad, but I think we have to."

"I'm serious," her father said.

"So am I. I'll ask them to come back later."

"You do that."

"I will." Libby had too much to do to deal with Ellen Hadley's children right now, especially with Bernie semi-out of commission. She had to start prepping for Mother's Day. She had to slice up the bread, start it soaking, sauté the spinach, and cube the Gruyère for the strata. Then she had to make the filling for the chocolate babka: roll out the babka dough, put the filling in it, roll it back up, braid it, and allow it to rise for another hour before she put it in the oven.

Lastly, she had to make the Grand Marnier syrup and slice the navel oranges that would be served with it. Libby loved the dish. It was truly beautiful. The oranges looked like cut glass, but she wished she wasn't making it today because julienning the rind was extremely time consuming. This, of course, was in addition to all the rest of her prep. In fact, just thinking about everything she had to do before they opened the shop made her feel like going back to bed and putting her head under her pillow.

Well, she couldn't do that, but she could wake Bernie up and have her peel the potatoes for the Spanish sausage and potato omelet they were serving. Libby was just about to knock on Bernie's door when her sister came out of her room.

"Who is making all that racket?" Bernie demanded.

"Ethan," said Libby.

Bernie flipped her hair out of her eyes. "Ethan?"

"Ellen Hadley's son," Libby explained. "The youngest one."

"God, I hope everything is all right." Bernie tied her bathrobe sash. Her bathrobe was a peach-colored silk and matched her nightgown. She'd gotten it on sale from one of the fancy lingerie stores on Madison Avenue and it was still one of her favorites.

Libby snorted. "Not in this case. They probably dragged Ellen off to jail. Or maybe she's found another body somewhere and she wants us to come over and dispose of it."

"That's rather harsh, Libby."

"Given last night, I don't think so, Bernie."

Sean smoothed his hair down with the flat of his hand. "Well, all I can say is one of you better go down and tell Ethan to stop making so much noise before he wakes up the neighborhood."

Ethan leaned on the bell again.

Bernie pointed to her ankle. "I'd go but . . ."

Libby held up her hand. "I know. I get it."

"It's not my fault," Bernie protested.

"Actually, this *is* your fault," Libby countered.

"I don't care whose fault it is," Sean snapped. "One of you needs to get down there pronto."

"I'm going," Libby said, never mind that she was so tired that her bones were aching. She went into her bedroom and put on her bathrobe.

"Libby, be nice," Bernie said to her sister as she went by her.

"Nice? At this time of the morning? I wouldn't count on it if I were you," Libby replied as she opened the door to the flat and headed down the stairs.

How did people exist on three or four hours of sleep a night anyway? she wondered. She certainly wasn't able to. In addition to her back bothering her, her head was hurting and each ring of the doorbell was like a sharp knife through her eyes. Boy, she wished they were closed on Sundays like they usually were, but they made too much money on Mother's Day not to stay open.

"I'm coming," she cried as she descended the stairs.

The ringing continued. She got to the door and jerked it open. "What is wrong with you?" she demanded. "Don't you know what time it is?"

Ethan jumped back, looking, Libby decided, like a surprised deer.

"Ah," he stammered. "Sorry." He swallowed and looked down at the floor. Skinny, all hands and feet, and the youngest of the three, he was still in his pajama bottoms and a Batman T-shirt and looked as if he'd just rolled out of bed. Which he probably had.

His two older brothers standing a little ways behind him didn't look much more put together. Matt, the seventeen-year-old, had on a pair of stained khaki cargo shorts and an old stretched-out T-shirt that read *Mets Forever*, while fifteen-year-old Ryan, the blond wannabe gangsta of the group, was wearing baggy pants and an over-sized white T-shirt. They both looked as if they'd been up all night.

"Sorry about my little brother," Matt said, reaching out and lightly cuffing Ethan on the top of his head. "I told him to ring once, but he never listens."

Libby highly doubted that, but she wasn't about to get into a debate. "I don't care. You guys have to go home."

"Please," Ryan said, stepping forward. Libby thought he looked as if he'd been crying. In fact, all three of them looked as if they had been. Ryan held out a heavy plastic bag. "You have to help my mom." He nodded toward the bag. "There's three hundred and seventy-five dollars in there, in quarters. That's all we could come up with on short notice."

"But we'll mow lawns," Matt said.

"And I can walk dogs," Ethan added.

"So we'll get more." Matt nodded toward the bag. "We know this isn't enough, but we'll come up with more. We promise."

Ethan raised his right hand. "I swear."

"We all do," Matt said, looking like twelve instead of seventeen.

"Take it," Ryan told Libby, placing the bag in her hands. It was so heavy she nearly dropped it.

Ethan's voice cracked. "Mom said we should talk to you. She said you'd know what to do."

"Did she? Well, she was wrong." Libby held the bag out to Ryan. "Take it."

Ryan backed away. "No. No. It's for you and your sister."

"I don't want it," Libby said.

"You have to take it," Ryan insisted. "My mom said you and your sister would know what to do, and my dad said it too."

"Your dad?" *That's not what he said last night,* Libby recalled.

"Definitely," Ryan said.

"No, he didn't," Matt said.

"Yeah he did, dodo," Ryan answered. "He was yelling that she should go ask her friend Bernie to figure it out since she was so smart."

Matt looked disgusted. "He was being sarcastic, moron."

"Shows you how much you know," Ryan told him.

Libby interrupted. "So if your mother wants to talk to us how come she's not here?" she asked, figuring the boys would say "because she's in jail," but they didn't.

"Because when my dad wouldn't let her drive

his car, she locked herself in the bathroom and wouldn't come out," Ryan explained.

"Seems to be a pattern," Libby cracked.

The boys looked at her.

"Forget it," Libby said, regretting her comment. "Go on."

"The money's our idea," Matt continued. "We know you and your sister do this kind of stuff and that you do it for money, so we got all our spare change together."

"We don't know what's going on," Ethan said. He screwed up his face. Two tears trickled down his cheeks. "Except it's really, really bad."

"Don't be such a wuss," Ryan said, cuffing Ethan on the head again. "She'll be fine." But to Libby's ears he didn't sound convinced.

Ethan reached up and rubbed the spot Ryan had hit. "Stop it. That hurts. I'm gonna get brain damaged from you."

"You can't," Matt responded, "because you already are."

"Ha-ha, Matt. Very funny."

"No, Ethan. True." He turned to Libby. "Please," he said. "We have no one else to go to."

Libby sighed. Before she knew what she was saying, the word *yes* had fallen from her lips. Looking at the pleading expressions on their faces had done her in. "All right," she conceded. "Come on up."

Chapter 11

Half an hour later, everyone was settled upstairs in the Simmons's flat drinking iced Mexican hot chocolate and eating day old cinnamon rolls, strawberry muffins with peach butter, and peanut butter and chocolate chip scones.

Ethan nodded toward the plastic bag in the middle of the table. "You can count the money if you want to."

"No need. It'll be fine," Sean assured him, now that he'd calmed down and gotten over his initial annoyance. After all, he reasoned, he and his daughters had intended to look into what had happened at the motel anyway—if only to satisfy their own curiosity.

"It's all there," Ryan said. "I swear."

Sean raised his hand. "I believe you."

Matt resettled his baseball hat on his head. "So you'll help our mom?"

"If we can," Bernie interjected.

Ryan ran his hand through his hair. "She's in deep doo-doo."

"Tell me something I don't know," Sean said.

Ryan spread his hands apart palms up "So what do we do now?" he asked.

Sean leaned back in his armchair. "I always find it helps to start at the beginning."

The three boys nodded and sat up straighter, waiting for Sean's next question.

"Now, you said your mother is home. Is that correct?" Sean asked.

Ryan nodded. "Yeah. She and my dad walked in together. He looked really, really pissed and she was crying."

As Sean took a sip of his iced chocolate, he reflected that he loved the cinnamon in it and the slight taste of almond. "What time was this?"

"Around ten. Maybe ten-thirty," Matt said. "I'm not sure."

Sean made a mental note to call Clyde later and ask him what the police were thinking of this whole fiasco.

Matt continued. "I'd just gotten back home from picking up my two idiot brothers at the movies when my dad walked in the door with my mom. They were both acting weird."

"Did either of your parents say anything to you about what had happened or about where they'd been?" Sean asked the boys.

"Kinda," Ethan responded. "Mom told us she'd made a mistake."

"Now there's an understatement if ever I heard one," Libby said, the words tumbling out before she could stop them. "Sorry," she amended, catching sight of Ethan's quivering lips. "That came out wrong." She handed Ethan another muffin to atone for her faux pas.

"Did your dad say anything at that time?" Sean asked.

Matt answered. "Yeah. He told us to go to our rooms and not come out until he said to."

"And did you?" Libby asked as she held out the plate of cinnamon rolls. Ryan and Matt each took one. Libby couldn't imagine what it would take to feed these guys everyday as she watched the rolls disappearing into the boys' mouths.

"Well, yeah," Ryan said.

"Could you hear what they were saying?" Sean asked.

The three boys looked at each other and shook their heads.

"I was listening to my music," Ryan explained.

"Me too," Matt agreed.

Sean looked at Ethan.

"The same. I was playing Halo."

Sean frowned. "Halo?" he asked. "What's that?" The kid certainly didn't look angelic.

"It's a video game," Ethan explained, surprised. Even his mom and dad knew what Halo was.

"Weren't you curious about what happened?" Bernie asked. She knew that in a similar situation she and Libby would have had their ears pressed up against the door.

Ethan shrugged. "I figured it was just the usual."

Bernie wrinkled up her forehead. "The usual?"

"Fighting," Ryan said. "We always put our headphones on when they fight," he added by way of explanation.

"They do that a lot?" Sean asked.

"Yes," the three boys said together.

"Definitely," Matt amplified. "Especially since Mom started her dog biscuit business. They're always fighting about that."

Bernie leaned forward. "What are the fights about?"

Matt looked glum. "About the way the house looks and how the laundry's not done. You know, stuff like that."

"And then we heard them later too," Ryan added.

"Later?" Sean asked.

"Like three in the morning," Ryan explained. "Or two. Something like that." He looked at his brothers for confirmation and they nodded. "They were yelling at one another. I mean really loudly."

"They woke me up," Ethan said.

"Which is saying a lot," Ryan said, "because Ethan can sleep through anything. He once slept through the firemen putting a fire out in our garage."

"Did not."

"You so did."

As Sean finished off the last of his muffin, he reflected that if he stopped eating his daughter's baking he'd probably lose twenty pounds. "What were they saying, Ryan?"

"Dad was screaming that this was the stupidest stunt my mom had pulled in a long line of stupid stunts, and that it was time she faced the music, and they didn't have money to mount a reasonable defense, and that if she ended up in court she'd have to go with a court-appointed one, and whatever happened to her was fine with him because he was tired of her nonsense, and Mom was crying and saying she knew she shouldn't have done what she did, but she was desperate. Then she said that she didn't have anything to do with what happened in the motel and Dad said he didn't believe her. It was really, really bad." Ryan looked down at his hands and stopped talking.

Matt took up the tale. "So I went into the living room and asked what was going on, and Dad screamed at me to go to sleep and Mom told me again to talk to you guys like soon, and then she ran into the bathroom and slammed the door."

"So what happened at the Riverview?" Ryan asked. He reached up and began to twirl a strand of blond hair around one of his fingers.

"You don't know?" Sean said.

"Not really," Matt answered. "Was there like a dead body? There was, wasn't there?" he said, looking at Sean's, Bernie's, and Libby's faces.

"Yeah, there was," Bernie replied.

Ethan leaned forward. "Did you see it?" he asked eagerly.

"I did," Bernie said.

The three boys leaned forward expectantly. They reminded Sean of baby birds waiting to be fed.

"You might as well tell them," he said to Bernie. "They're going to find out anyway."

So Bernie did. She took a deep breath and filled Ellen's sons in on the previous evening's events. She'd expected shock. She'd expected horror. That's not what she got.

"Wow. A body," Matt cried as he grabbed another muffin and devoured it. "That's illin'."

Sean looked at him.

"Rad," Matt translated.

Sean gave up.

"I wonder how he got there."

"So does everyone," Sean said dryly.

"Maybe he was a bum or something," Matt suggested. "And the door was like opened and he just wandered in."

"Yeah," Ryan said, enthusiastically taking up the tale. "Exactly. Like he was almost dead and looking for a place to lie down and die."

"Kinda like Goldilocks, only worse," Bernie suggested.

Ryan pointed his finger at her. "Good one."

Ethan frowned as he realized something. "Do the police think my mom had something to do with it?"

"That seems to be the general consensus," Sean remarked.

Matt wiped his hands on his T-shirt. "That's totally lame. Anyone who knows my mom knows that. She captures mice in these live animal traps and takes them outside. It drives my dad crazy. She's never even spanked us."

Ryan nodded. "And believe me, I deserve to get my butt kicked."

"She spanked me once," Ethan piped up.

"That was because you almost set the house on fire," Ryan said. "He's a real pyro."

"Am not," Ethan cried.

"Are too," Ryan said. "You keep on stealing matches."

"That's because I don't want you to smoke."

"Your brother is right," Sean said. "It's a bad habit."

Bernie raised an eyebrow. "Really, Dad?"

"Yes, really," Sean said, not even looking a tiny bit abashed. "When Ryan gets to my age he can do what he wants."

Libby clapped her hands. She glanced at the clock. Her prep time was slipping away. "Can we get back to business, please?"

Ryan slid down in his seat and looked contrite. Sean did not.

He took another sip of his iced chocolate. "Is your mother still home?" he asked.

"Why wouldn't she be, Mr. Simmons?" Ryan demanded.

"They're not going to arrest her or anything, are

they?" Ethan asked, alarm in his voice. "You can make sure that doesn't happen, right?"

"We'll try," Sean said, torn between the desire to reassure and the need to be truthful.

"She was home when we left," Matt said. "She hadn't come out of the bathroom yet."

"And your dad?"

"He's gone," Matt said. "He told Mom he couldn't stand living in a lunatic asylum anymore and took off."

"Do you know where he went?" Libby asked.

"He usually goes down to the park by the river," Ethan volunteered. "He says looking at the water calms him down."

"We should talk to him," Bernie said. "We should talk to them both."

"We should," Libby agreed.

Ethan finished off his iced chocolate. "You're going to take our case, right?" he asked Sean, Bernie, and Libby, searching their faces. His eyes began misting over. "Please," he begged. "You gotta."

"We will," Sean said, answering for his daughters.

Ryan laced his fingers together and cracked his knuckles. "So what happens now?"

"Now we talk to people and see what we can find out," Bernie said.

"Like who?" Ethan inquired.

"What do you mean?" Bernie asked.

"I mean who are you going to talk to?" Ethan replied.

"Your mom's friends, your dad, your mom's business partners."

"Can we help?" Ryan said eagerly. "I mean, we know everyone."

Bernie rubbed her ankle and smiled. "If we need you, we'll let you know."

Ryan nodded. "Because that would be pretty cool, being involved in a murder investigation."

"What about the dead guy?" Ethan asked.

"What about him?" Sean said.

"How are you going to find out who he is, Mr. Simmons?"

"The police will probably know, Ethan."

"And if they don't?" asked Matt.

Bernie answered. "I'm sure they will, and if they don't, I guess we'll show his picture around."

Ethan leaned forward. His eyes were wide. "You have his picture?"

"On my phone," Bernie said.

"That is so cool. Can I see it?" Matt said.

"Bernie, you didn't tell me you have a picture," Sean said.

"I forgot, Dad."

Sean raised his voice. One didn't forget things like that. He would have dismissed one of his men if they had done something like that. "Forgot?"

Bernie bit her lower lip. She was sorry she'd said anything. "There was just too much going on."

"Let us see," Ryan begged.

"I don't think that's appropriate," Bernie said.

"Let them have a look," Sean said. He didn't add, "and me too." "Maybe they know who it is."

Bernie made a face. "I don't know what Ellen would say."

"She asked for our help, didn't she?"

"I guess you've got a point there, Dad." And Bernie asked Libby to hand her her phone. She clicked it on and went to the photos. She'd taken four snaps from different angles. The three boys gathered around her to take a look.

"Wow," Ryan said. "I can't believe it. That's Manny."

"Manny?" Libby asked.

Sean looked at the photo. He didn't recognize him. "So who is this Manny?" he asked Ellen Hadley's sons.

"I don't know. I've seen him in my mom's business partner's vehicle a couple of times," Matt said.

"Lisa?" Libby asked.

The three boys nodded.

"Dad doesn't like her very much," Ethan volunteered. "He says Mrs. Stone's a home wrecker."

"No, he didn't," Ryan said.

"Yeah, he did," Ethan retorted. "I heard him saying that to Mom."

"When?" Ryan demanded.

Bernie interrupted before Ethan could answer.

"Does the guy in the photo have a last name?" she asked.

"I guess," Ryan replied. "I mean everyone does, right? Except for maybe Prince. And Cher."

"So do you know it?" Libby asked.

Ryan shook his head. "Not really."

"Me either," Matt said.

"Me three," Ethan said. "I think maybe it starts with an *R*. Or a *B*. Something like that. Actually, I'm not really sure."

Libby looked at Bernie's and her dad's expressions. She could tell they were thinking the same thing she was. Did Ellen know who the dead guy was after all? Had she been lying about that as well? And if she was, why was she?

Chapter 12

T he rest of the morning went pretty much as Libby thought it would. Once they'd shooed the Hadley boys out the door, she, Bernie, and her dad went downstairs to finish prepping for the day. Bernie sat on a stool with her leg propped up and rolled out the croissants and iced sugar cookies, while Sean restocked the cooler, reconciled the register, tied up the cartons for recycling, and did the dishes in the sink. For her part, Libby dealt with the oranges, the strata, and the rest of the food they were serving.

By nine-thirty a scrum of men and children waiting for A Little Taste of Heaven to open had formed. Libby took one look and sent Amber out with coffee for the men and milk and chocolate chip cookies for the kids. At the dot of ten, Amber opened the doors and everyone rushed in. It was mayhem for the next two hours, Libby pressing her dad into service at the register. By twelve-thirty they'd pretty much sold out of everything they had in the shop and the next half hour after that was dead except for a few stragglers. At one o'clock, Bernie sent Googie and Amber home and locked the door.

After finishing cleaning up, Libby and Bernie closed A Little Taste of Heaven for the rest of the day and they and their father drove over to the cemetery to visit their mom, Rose, a ritual they'd been observing on Mother's Day since she'd died. It was a perfect day for a visit and, although the weather announcer was predicting rain in the afternoon and clouds were massing in the East, at the moment it was bright and sunny. The temperature was in the high sixties, with just enough of a breeze to move the branches of the willow trees back and forth.

Libby had bought a bunch of anemones, Rose's favorite flower, the day before, and Libby took those along in addition to a picnic lunch, a lunch they traditionally ate on the stone bench in front of Rose's grave. Bernie and Libby always filled their picnic basket with Rose's favorite foods and this year was no exception. Their lunch consisted of bacon, lettuce, tomato, watercress, and avocado sandwiches on store-made ciabatta rolls slathered with homemade mayo, a shaved fennel, raw artichoke, and clementine salad, an assortment of French macaroons, bunches of green grapes, and a thermos full of sweet tea to drink.

Sean sat on the bench and thought about Rose. He started to smile.

"What are you thinking about, Dad?" Bernie asked as she took a red and white checked table-cloth out of the picnic basket and began spreading it on the bench.

"I was just thinking about the time Rose got me Canoe for Father's Day and I didn't wear it, and she couldn't bear to waste it, so she took to wearing it even though it was a men's cologne.

"I remember," Libby said. "We used to buy it for her for Mother's Day."

Bernie smoothed the cloth out with the palm of her hand and began taking out lunch. "Until I introduced her to Chanel Number Five."

"Your mom always made the best out of everything," Sean observed.

"She did, didn't she?" Libby said as she studied the anemones she'd arranged in a tall glass beaker she'd brought from home.

"I love these flowers," Bernie said, looking at

the red and purple blooms. "I wonder if they'd be hard to grow."

Libby snorted. "For you? Yes."

Bernie stopped smoothing down the small red and white checked tablecloth she'd draped over the bench. "What's that supposed to mean?"

"That you have a black thumb, just like Mom and I do."

"Look at the black raspberries," Bernie said.

"Those were volunteers."

"But I didn't kill them."

Libby straightened up and went over to help Bernie. "I suppose we could scatter some seeds and see what happens," she conceded. "It couldn't hurt."

Sean didn't say anything. He'd watched his wife kill every plant she'd ever tried to grow and as far as he could tell his daughters were tending in the same direction. "She would have liked this meal," Sean said instead, after he'd taken a bite of his sandwich.

"I still think we should have done Mom's meat loaf," Libby observed. "She liked that even better than the BLTAWs."

"I think she liked both the same," Bernie replied. "Anyway, we did meat loaf last year and we're going to do it again next year. A little variety is never a bad thing."

Libby stifled a yawn. The sun was making her sleepy. She felt like lying down in the grass and taking a nap. "With vanilla frosted cupcakes."

Bernie fished a piece of artichoke out of the salad and ate it. "Definitely," she said as she wondered why more people didn't eat artichokes raw. When handled correctly they had a delightfully nutty taste. "We already discussed that."

"I wonder if Mom knows we're here," Libby mused.

"On some level I think she does," Bernie said. She had combed her hair out of her face and secured it in a ponytail the way her mom had always liked it, just in case she was around and watching.

Sean looked up from his sandwich. "Doubtful," he said after he'd taken another bite. It was late and he was hungry.

"Why do you say that?" Libby demanded of him. She was too tired to be hungry and the bug bites she'd gotten chasing Ellen through the woods still itched.

Sean swallowed. "Because I think dead is dead."

"Then why are we doing this?" Bernie asked.

Sean spooned some salad onto his plate. "As a way of keeping Rose's memory alive. They're two different things."

"And what better way to keep her memory alive than with food," Libby observed.

"I can't argue with that." Bernie took a bite of her sandwich. Even if she did say so herself, the bacon was perfectly done and the avocado and watercress were spot on foils for it. "Mom was all about meals, that's for sure. Too bad she didn't feel that way about detecting."

Sean poured himself a glass of sweet tea. "I think she would have made an exception in this case. She always liked Ellen."

Libby corrected him. "She didn't like her, she felt sorry for her. Remember, she was always saying 'oh, the poor dear' and telling her how great she looked? She never told her she needed to lose five pounds or that she shouldn't wear that skirt."

"Well, Ellen needed the encouragement, you didn't," Bernie told her.

"I did too," Libby answered hotly.

"I'm sorry, but you can't possibly compare your situations. Ellen's mom was downright mean," Bernie noted.

Libby made a face.

"You weren't at Ellen's house, but I was." Bernie pointed to herself. "Her mom was always telling her she was fat, that she should do something with her hair, that she looked awful, that she was ugly and no one would ever marry her because she looked so bad. It just went on and on and on."

Libby looked shocked. "And I thought I had it bad because Mom was always telling me to get my hair off my face."

"If I had a daughter, I'd never say stuff like that," Bernie remarked. "Not ever."

Sean took a sip of his tea. "That is abusive. But what if your daughter was wearing something that was totally wrong for her? Would you say something?"

"I'd find a nice way to say it," Bernie replied.

"So you believe in constructive criticism?"

"Yes, I do," Bernie replied. "Ask nothing, get nothing."

"That's what Mom thought," Libby said.

"If she didn't," Sean said, smiling, "she wouldn't have married me. She said I was her fixer-upper project."

Libby and Bernie both laughed. For a moment everyone was silent as they contemplated the day. In the spring and the summer the cemetery was usually filled with dog walkers and runners, but today it was empty. The only sounds were the chirping of the birds, the chiding of the squirrels, and the occasional barking of a dog.

Bernie took another bite of her sandwich and wiped her hands on her napkin. "I think Mom would be upset if we didn't help Ellen."

Sean finished the last of his sandwich and checked to see if there was another one in the basket. He was happy to see there was. "I'm not disagreeing." Sean began taking the wax paper off the sandwich. As he did, it occurred to him that Libby and Bernie wrapped sandwiches the same way that Rose had. "I think she would have too."

"Would she?" Libby demanded. "I'm not so sure. After all, Ellen got us into trouble. I think Mom would have been pissed at her for that."

Bernie frowned. "Ellen did what she did because she was terrified."

"So you keep saying."

"Because it's true."

"You have no evidence to support that assumption."

"And you don't have any for the opposite point of view."

Libby turned to Sean. "Dad, what do you think?"

Sean bit into his second sandwich before replying. "What I think is that Ellen didn't get you into trouble; you got yourselves into trouble."

"Okay. I got you in trouble," Bernie said before Libby could say anything. "Satisfied?"

Libby stretched and stood up. "Minimally."

Bernie broke off a piece of her roll, tore it into little pieces, and threw it out for the birds. "Even if what you say is true, and I'm not saying it is, I still think Mom would have wanted us to help Ellen. She always had a soft spot for her."

"I suppose." Libby grumped. She knew what Bernie and Sean were saying was true. She just didn't want to admit it. Instead she went over to Rose's grave and pulled out a handful of dandelions that were getting ready to bud.

She started walking to the trash can with them when Bernie said, "Libby, don't. We can make a salad out of those. Or put them in one."

Libby looked down at the handful of greens she was holding. "We can, can't we?"

Bernie nodded.

Libby ran possibilities in her head. "Actually that would be kinda nice, especially if we combined the greens with some arugula and butter lettuce. Then we'd have bitter, spicy, and smooth. With the addition of a little olive oil, a little lemon juice, and some pecorino cheese and a few walnuts, it might be quite delicious." She brightened. "We can try the combo out tonight."

"Exactly. Or," Bernie suggested, "if you get more we could make a wilted salad. We still have bacon we can fry up."

Sean chimed in with, "Anything with bacon is good for me."

"I wonder if dandelion greens would sell," Bernie mused.

"We could put them on the menu and see," Libby said. "After all," she observed, "they are a spring vegetable and I'm pretty sure Morgan Farms grows them, so we can source it locally. We could do something with them and shad roe." She drew an imaginary sign with her hand. " 'Try the ultimate spring meal.' I don't know why we always forget about field greens," she added. She pointed to a clump of dandelions twenty feet away that were growing near a large headstone. "I think I'll do a little gathering."

"Those are flowering," Bernie pointed out. "You're supposed to gather dandelions before they bloom if you want to eat the leaves. Otherwise they're tough and bitter."

"But those aren't," Libby said, nodding to a group of younger dandelions Bernie hadn't seen.

"You're right. They're not." Bernie reached for a macaroon. "My mistake."

She bit into it as she watched Libby wander over to a group of headstones that were located next to a weeping willow. The headstones looked as if they hadn't been cared for in a while and Bernie wondered to whom they belonged, but she didn't care enough to ask Libby. Instead she was thinking about all the different kinds of field greens there were and about who grew them and about making salads out of them decorated with violet and nasturtium blossoms when she saw Libby waving to her.

"Bernie," she called.

"What?" Bernie asked.

"I think I know who the dead guy in the bed is," Libby cried. "I think I know which Manny Ellen Hadley's sons were talking about. They were talking about Manny Roget."

Sean did a double take. "You're kidding me, right?"

Libby shook her head. "I am most definitely not."

Sean stood up and walked over to where Libby was standing. "I thought he was dead. I thought I heard he'd been killed in an accident in North Dakota or something like that."

"Maybe not," Libby said.

Bernie hobbled over to join them. "That would certainly make things interesting," she opined.

"I'd say it would make things very interesting indeed," Sean said, looking at the headstone that had sparked Libby's memory.

Chapter 13

Really," Clyde said when Sean called his friend to tell him the news.

"Yes, really," Sean replied.

"I'll be over in a half hour."

"Clyde, there's no rush," Sean protested.

"Yeah, there is. Otherwise I'm going to have to go to my mother-in-law's, and since she doesn't like me and I don't like her," Clyde told Sean, "this is perfect. The wife can't argue with my fighting crime and making Longely a safer place. Now everyone is happy, especially me."

Twenty minutes later Clyde was at the door.

"Nice tie," Sean said, managing not to laugh when Clyde came in.

Clyde looked down. The tie was bright blue

with pink and yellow poppies splashed across it. "Jeez." He took it off and jammed it in his jacket pocket. "I forgot I was wearing it. My mother-in-law's pick."

"I guess she *really* doesn't like you," Bernie observed.

"Hasn't for the last twenty years," Clyde said, sitting down in his accustomed chair. He reached for one of the brownies Libby had put out on the table and poured himself a cup of sweet tea. "Your call came in the nick of time," he said to Sean before biting into a brownie. He sighed with contentment. "Perfect," he said, chewing slowly. "Not only does my mother-in-law have lousy taste in clothes, she can't cook worth a damn." He looked at Libby. "I don't suppose you have any actual food around?"

She smiled and got up. "I think I can rustle something up."

"Much obliged," Clyde told her. "Tell me again what you told me on the phone," he said to Sean as Libby went downstairs.

So Sean did.

Clyde's eyes widened as he listened. "I thought maybe you were kidding me," he said, leaning forward.

"Nope. Libby's pretty sure," Sean said.

Clyde leaned back in his chair and took a sip of his sweet tea. "Have you told anyone else?"

"Like Lucy?" Sean shook his head. "Considering

that Libby and Bernie were there at the scene—no. I think I'd like to leave their names out of it if it's all the same to you."

"Thanks a lot for leaving it to me."

Sean grinned. "One of the many benefits of being off the force."

"I'll figure something out," Clyde said.

"I know you will," Sean told his friend. "That's why I called you."

Both men fell silent for a moment.

"Is Libby one hundred percent sure?" Clyde asked Sean, breaking the silence.

"No," Sean said. "Not one hundred percent, but probably"—he paused for a moment—"eighty-five percent."

Clyde ate another brownie. "So why didn't she recognize him at the motel?"

"I guess he's gained a lot of weight, right?" Sean said to Bernie.

"That's what Libby said," Bernie told Clyde. "And boy was she right."

"What did I say?" asked Libby. She'd just come upstairs with food for Clyde.

"That Manny had gained a lot of weight, which was why you didn't recognize him at first," Sean repeated.

"He sure had." Libby put the tray down and offered Clyde a platter consisting of kalamata olives, salami, roasted red peppers, cherry tomatoes, and homemade roasted artichoke hearts finished off with a sprinkle of Asiago cheese, plus a few slices of Italian bread.

"Perfect," Clyde said as he dug in. "Raymond Manford Roget." He shook his head as he ate a couple of olives. "I heard he was dead."

Sean nodded. "That's what I said too."

"Well, he is now. No doubt about that." Bernie reached over and broke off a small bunch of green grapes. She put a couple in her mouth, then readjusted the pack of frozen peas on her ankle and sat back.

Libby sat down on the sofa. "The beard and the weight threw me off, but his eyes are the same and so is that little crease in his nose. I thought I recognized the face when I saw him on the bed, but I couldn't put a name to it. Then I saw the family headstone and it all came together."

"Manny Roget." Clyde repeated the name. His eyes got that faraway look they always got when he was remembering the past. "He certainly got himself in trouble. For years he was Mr. Upstanding Citizen, not even a parking ticket, and then boom!"

"If he did what they say he did," Sean reached over and snagged a brownie. Sweets were definitely his downfall.

"Which was?" Bernie asked.

"Melinda Banks and Kitty Price accused him of imprisoning and raping them."

Bernie wrinkled her nose. "Those names don't sound familiar."

"They weren't here for that long. Thank heavens," Sean said. "Something bad always seemed to happen when they were around. Anyway, the DA bought their story and Judge Munoz signed a warrant for Manny's arrest, at which point he got the hell out of Dodge. Basically, he disappeared off the grid."

Clyde nodded. "The interesting thing, though, was that rumor had it the whole thing was a setup and that the girls had gotten paid to testify because Manny was fooling around with this girl and the family didn't like it and this was the way they took care of the problem."

"I never heard that," Sean said.

"I did," Clyde replied. "From a lot of different people. They said Manny had been warned off, but he didn't listen."

"That's pretty extreme," Libby said.

"If it's true," Clyde replied. "I never pursued it."

"Do you think it was true?" Bernie asked.

Clyde thought for a minute. "Knowing the two girls, I wouldn't be surprised if it was."

"This is news to me," Libby declared.

"You were at Buffalo State," Sean answered.

"And where was I?" Bernie demanded.

"In Oakland."

"I guess Mom didn't keep us up on *all* the local news," Libby said as she leaned over and snagged herself a hazelnut macaroon. It was one of the last ones left. *They really were a lot of trouble to make, but boy were they worth it,* Libby thought. And no matter what anyone said about chocolate and raspberry being the best combination, in her mind you couldn't beat hazelnut and chocolate or chocolate and coffee. She could live on these forever.

Sean laughed. "Not on the news she didn't deem fit to pass on."

"When I knew Manny he was such a . . . ."

"Dork," Bernie said, finishing Libby's sentence for her.

"I can't picture him doing something like that. I mean the Manny I knew was afraid to keep a library book out late, afraid he would get into trouble." Libby separated both sides of the macaroon and licked the filling, after which she ate the meringues. It was like eating an Oreo, only better. "What?" she said to Bernie, who was staring at her.

"Nothing," Bernie said. "I've just never seen anyone do that, is all."

"Makes it last longer," Libby explained as she wiped her fingers on a napkin.

"I wonder what made him come back here," Bernie mused. "I sure as hell wouldn't."

"This place didn't hold good memories for him for certain," Sean agreed.

Clyde ate a piece of salami. "I wonder where he was staying."

"Most of his family is gone," Sean noted. "They've either moved away or are in the ground."

"There's old Miss Randall," Libby said. "Wasn't she his second or third cousin? Something like that."

"You should go talk to her," Clyde said to Libby. "See if she knows anything."

"Thanks a lot," Bernie said. "Why don't you?" To say Old Lady Randall wasn't grouchy was a little like saying cows don't moo.

Clyde finished off his sweet tea and poured himself another glass. "Because I don't have to." He raised a hand to keep Bernie from interrupting. "This isn't my case. She wouldn't talk to me anyway. She's never forgiven me for giving her a parking ticket in front of Elwood's General Store."

Sean raised an eyebrow. "Why'd you give her a ticket?"

"Because she was parked smack dab in the middle of the street. Her driving skills have always left a lot to be desired," Clyde explained in a massive understatement.

"Makes sense," Libby said. "So what are you going to do while we talk to her?"

Clyde smiled. "Stay here and eat lunch. Talk with your dad about our fishing trip. Show him the fishing pole and tackle box I'm lending him."

"I didn't know you fished," Libby said.

Clyde smiled. "It's been a while, but I figured it's time to get back to the ocean before I get too old to hook a big one," he replied absentmindedly as he contemplated making himself a sandwich.

Chapter 14

Despite Clyde's suggestion, Libby and Bernie didn't go visit Old Lady Randall immediately. Instead, they decided to go back to the motel first and look for the watch Libby had seen before Bruce Hadley had grabbed her and scared her half to death.

"We should have done this earlier," Bernie noted as they pulled into the Riverview Motel parking lot. In the daylight, the place looked even shabbier than it did at night, the tattered yellow crime scene tape adding another depressing note to the cracked asphalt, peeling paint, and sagging roof.

"With what time?" Libby demanded. She parked next to the woods. With Bernie's ankle still in rough shape, Libby was the one who was doing most of the driving. "I think I know where I saw it," she added, turning off Mathilda and getting out of the van.

"I hope it's still there," Bernie said.

"It will be," Libby said with more confidence than she felt.

She walked to the place she thought she'd seen the watch and looked around. All she saw was scrub grass, weeds, cigarette butts, a used condom, and a couple of empty cans of Bud. She squatted down and looked more carefully. If the watch was there, she wasn't seeing it. It should be though. Libby was pretty sure this was the spot. She was almost positive she'd been facing the fourth motel room down from the end when Bruce had grabbed her. Which meant either she was mistaken or someone had taken it. Maybe she was wrong about where she'd been standing. In fact, the more she thought about it, the more unsure she became. She felt as if everything from that night was in little fragments and she couldn't put the pieces together.

"The police could have taken it," Bernie suggested when she limped up to her.

"Possibly," Libby said. That was the obvious explanation.

"Probably," Bernie said.

Libby closed her eyes and tried to run the events of that evening through her head again, and again she failed. Everything had been so confusing. She'd seen the watch; she'd been going toward it when all hell had broken loose. There had been the lights, and people yelling, and Bruce grabbing her, and Ellen yelling at him to leave her alone.

Now that she thought about it, she didn't think that anyone else had noticed the watch. They'd been too busy screaming at her. In fact, she was pretty positive they hadn't. So if they hadn't picked it up, that meant the watch should still be here. Unless Bernie was right and the forensics guys had swept the place for evidence, which they clearly hadn't done, because if they had there wouldn't be trash lying around. Of course, she *could* be in the wrong spot.

Libby had just opened her eyes and was doing one last visual sweep of the ground in front of her before she moved on to another area when she sensed someone behind her. So did Bernie. The sisters whirled around at the same time.

A man was standing in back of them. "Do you mind if I ask what you ladies are doing here?" he said.

"Not at all," Bernie answered.

She put the guy at somewhere between twenty-six and thirty. He was definitely good looking, Bernie would give him that, even if he was a little too preppy for her taste. He looked to be average weight and height. He had regular features, short dark brown hair and hazel eyes, and was neatly dressed in a white polo shirt, a pair of khakis, and a pair of Docksiders sans socks.

Libby was a little less polite. "I'm looking for something, if you must know."

"Indeed, I must." The man waggled his eyebrow and crossed his arms over his chest.

Libby couldn't help it. She burst out laughing.

"And what would that be?" the man continued.

"A watch. I'm looking for a watch," Libby answered. "Now it's your turn."

"To what?" the man asked.

"To introduce yourself."

He made a deep bow. "I am the Joker."

Bernie couldn't help smiling. "Funny you don't look like him." She took a step forward. "Seriously, who are you?"

The man grinned. "Who are you?"

"Do you always answer a question with a question?" Bernie asked.

The man's grin grew wider. "Do you?"

Bernie laughed. "Okay. You win. I'm Bernie Simmons." She gestured to Libby. "And this is my sister, Libby. Now it's your turn."

"Not a problem." He gave a small bow. "My name is Cole Webster and I'm in charge of this place. At least for the moment."

"Where's Isaac?" Libby asked.

Cole smiled. "Where do you think?"

"Fishing," Bernie promptly answered.

Cole grinned. "The lady wins the prize."

"How long is he gone for?" Bernie asked.

"A while. He and Mina are somewhere out in Alaska. Some small town, somewhere. Mina had a heart attack recently."

Bernie put her hand to her mouth. "Oh no."

"It's nothing serious. Just a minor one. But they decided to take a break. They're even talking about catching a cruise from Anchorage down the inland passage."

Bernie raised an eyebrow. "A cruise? I can't picture either of them doing that. They never sit still."

"I know." Cole suppressed a yawn. "Sorry about that, but I haven't gotten much sleep recently. I guess it's a case of 'gather ye rosebuds while ye may,' and all that stuff. I'm Mina's cousin," Cole said by way of explanation.

"You don't look like her," Bernie observed.

"Distant cousin," Cole explained. "My parents moved to Seattle years ago and I'm back East trying to reconnect with everyone. I was visiting Mina and Isaac when Mina had her attack, and it just so happened that an opportunity for a good trip came up and I convinced them to take it."

"That was nice of you," Libby said.

Cole swatted at a bee buzzing by. "No. It's nice *for* me. This is total self-interest. Isaac and Mina are the ones doing me the favor. I'm between jobs and this is perfect."

Now the bee was buzzing around Libby's face. "What do you do?" she asked, taking a step back.

Cole grinned. Bernie noticed that his teeth were perfect. "I'm embarrassed to say."

"Try me," Bernie said.

Cole kicked at a pebble and sent it flying into the woods. "It's just such a cliché."

Bernie and Libby waited.

"Okay. Fine," Cole said, looking them in the eye. "I used to be a bond trader, but I got laid off, so now I'm trying to write a novel about my experiences on the floor."

"How's it coming?" Bernie asked.

"Slowly. Very slowly." Cole waved his arm around in a gesture that encompassed the Riverview and the nearby woods. "This is ideal for me. Lots of free time. Nowhere to go. No more excuses. But I'm really glad about one thing. I'm glad I was here for that . . . thing . . . that happened. I would hate for Isaac to have to deal with that."

"Have you told him?" Libby asked.

Cole shook his head. "Communication is hard where he is, and I figured if I told him he'd insist on coming back, and there's really no need to do that. Do you think I'm wrong?"

Bernie shook her head. "No. I don't."

"Good." Cole rubbed his hands together. "So what can I do for you two ladies?"

"We're looking for a watch," Libby said, and she explained why they were.

He pointed to his wrist. "Is this it?"

Libby studied it. "Maybe. I can't be sure."

"Because I dropped it the other day when I was picking up the trash." Cole gestured toward the woods with his hand. "But look if you want."

Libby demurred. She felt slightly foolish. "That was probably it."

Cole scratched his chin. "That was really quite something."

"It was awful," Bernie said.

"So you saw him?" Cole asked.

"Unfortunately. Ellen called me when she found him."

Cole took a deep breath and let it out. "She seemed like such a nice lady too. I never would have thought she would have done something like that."

Bernie corrected him. "She is a nice lady and she didn't do that."

Bernie decided that her tone must have been fiercer than she thought, because Cole took a step back, put up his hands, and said, "Whoa. I hope if I get into trouble one day I have a friend like you."

"You registered her that night?" Libby asked.

"Well, yeah." Cole gave her an are-you-kidding-me? look. "Of course I did. I'm the only one around at night. I do registrations, maintenance, the whole deal. The only thing I don't do is clean the rooms—not that there are that many to clean these days. Lucky that I pay Maria on a per room basis." He shook his head. "She already told me she's not cleaning up the dead guy's room when they release it—not that I blame her."

Bernie leaned against a birch tree to take the weight off her foot. "So what did Ellen say when she registered?"

Cole shook his head. "Nothing really. She said

she wanted a cabin on the end. She said she was doing something to surprise her husband."

"That's one way of putting it," Libby said dryly.

"If you say so," Cole replied.

Obviously Cole hadn't heard about the ransom note yet, Libby thought.

"She paid in cash," Cole continued. "I gave her the key, then I went in the back to take a nap. I was up late the night before writing," Cole explained. "Next thing I know, the cops are knocking on my door, telling me to stay put and not go out. That they have a possible kidnap situation going on. I don't mind telling you they practically scared the bejesus out of me."

"I can imagine," Libby said.

"Then, when I found out that there was a dead guy and the dead guy was Mano . . ." Cole bit his lip and looked down at the ground for a moment. "Boy, talk about truth being stranger than fiction. I couldn't have written that. No one would believe it. They'd say it was too much of a coincidence."

"Mano?" Libby said.

"Yeah. The dead guy. That's what he told me his name was. I figured it was short for Manolo, even though he didn't look Spanish. But these days you never know."

"You met him?" Bernie asked, confused.

"Yeah. He used to come by sometimes, maybe once or twice a week. We'd sit, have a couple of beers, play some chess." Cole looked at the girls.

"You two look odd. Did I say something wrong?"

"This guy was big, had a full beard, an earring?" Bernie asked.

"That's him. Why? What's going on?"

"I'm just surprised is all," Libby said, a puzzled expression on her face. "The dead guy's name was Manny, Manny Roget."

"Maybe," Cole said, "but that's not how he introduced himself to me when he came by to see Isaac."

"Did he give you his last name?" Bernie asked.

Cole shrugged. "Nope. Of course, I didn't ask either. Maybe I should have, but I didn't. It didn't occur to me to."

"What did he want to see Isaac for?" Libby asked.

"Well, Mano told me he wanted to apologize to Isaac for all the trouble he caused back in the day. Said he'd finally worked up the courage to talk to him, but when he came by, Isaac was at the ER with Mina and I was holding down the fort. I told him I'd relay the message, which I did."

"What did Isaac say?" Bernie asked.

Cole ran his hand through his hair. "Not much really. I think he was too worried about Mina to process what I was telling him. Mano came back a couple of days later, but Isaac was taking Mina to the hospital for some tests so he missed him again. Anyway, he and I got to talking and it turned out that we both liked to play chess, so we got in the habit of playing once or twice a week." Cole paused for a moment before continuing. "I mean, he seemed like a nice guy. In a way I had to admire him."

"How so?" Bernie asked.

"He bottomed out, and then he pulled himself together."

"Bottomed out?" Libby asked.

"He told me he had some drug problems and then he was on some heavy head medicine. It was something I could relate to. The drug part, that is. After I lost my job, I kinda went off the deep end for a while. Course not as bad as Mano. I never tried meth, thank heavens. But the point is he straightened himself out. Next thing on his agenda was losing all the weight he had gained. He was embarrassed by that. He told me he used to be really skinny."

"He was," Libby said.

"But," Cole continued, "I guess if you're addicted to something it's better to be addicted to junk food than some of the other stuff that's out there." Cole patted his belly. "Fortunately, I've never had a problem in that direction. Live healthy, live long, I say."

"Do you know how long Manny has been back in Longely?" Bernie asked.

Cole scratched his ear. "Not really. Maybe nine months. Maybe a year. Maybe less. Obviously, I'm not really sure." He glanced down at his watch. "Oops. How time flies when you're having fun. Gotta go, ladies, the plumber is going to be here any minute and I have to talk to him about the leaky toilet in unit seventeen, but come back and visit whenever you want to." He grinned. "I can always use the company."

"He seems like a nice guy," Libby noted as she and Bernie walked back to the van. "Good looking too."

"Too clean cut for my taste," Bernie commented, painfully climbing back into the van. She wished her ankle would heal already. "I'm not a big fan of preppy."

"No kidding," Libby rejoined.

The two sisters spent the rest of the drive over to Miss Randall's house dissecting what Cole had told them. When they arrived, they weren't any closer to knowing anything relevant than they had been before they spoke to him.

Chapter 15

Old Lady Randall lived in a classic old Victorian painted lady. The house, Bernie thought, belonged in San Francisco with the other ladies of a certain age. It was in great shape. Every ten years or so, Old Lady Randall gave it the equivalent of a face-lift and repainted it. Bernie particularly liked its latest incarnation featuring shades of green, dark green, and coral. Even though it had been nine years since the last paint job and the paint was alligatoring a little on the dormers and the weather side of the house, it still looked good.

The deep-set front porch had rocking chairs that were made to while away a summer afternoon and the flower boxes on the windows were overflowing with pink geraniums. The three large ferns hanging from the porch ceiling swung slowly in the breeze. It was the kind of house that had been built in the days when one had a staff. To say it required an enormous amount of upkeep would be a massive understatement, but the house was Old Lady Randall's baby and she found a way to do what needed to be done. Bernie and Libby used to catch glimpses of her in her housedress mowing the lawn with her push mower or clipping the hedges with a pair of large metal pruning shears.

"She's got to be eighty," Bernie said to Libby as she turned into Seymour Street.

"At the very least," Libby said, slowing down to avoid hitting a squirrel.

"Maybe she's gotten better with age," Bernie posited hopefully.

"Doubtful," Libby said as she turned into Old Lady Randall's driveway. "In my experience, people never get better with age, they just get more of whatever they are."

Bernie sighed. It was not an encouraging thought. "Well, it would be hard for her to get any grumpier."

"We'll see," Libby said. She was not optimistic.

The last time she and Bernie had been at the house they'd been selling Girl Scout cookies and Old Lady Randall had threatened to call the police on them if they didn't get off her porch. When they'd told their mother, Rose had sighed and said she was a lady with problems and they'd do best to steer clear of her. Which they had.

Libby was remembering that as she parked Mathilda next to the garage. She and Bernie got out of the van and walked up the path to the porch. As she did, she noticed that the grass needed cutting and the laurel hedges needed pruning.

"This house is huge," Bernie commented, slowly mounting the four steps to the porch. She'd forgotten how big it was. A family of ten could probably live in there comfortably. She looked around. The grass might be a little too long, but the porch was pristine. There wasn't a speck of dust on the floor, all the chairs were neatly aligned, and none of the plants had a leaf out of place. *They probably wouldn't dare,* Bernie thought.

The sisters stopped at the door.

"Go on," Libby said to Bernie. "Ring the bell."

"No. You."

"Flip you for it."

"Are you sure?"

"I'm positive."

"Well, don't sulk when you lose."

"I'm not going to sulk and I'm not going to lose."

"Works for me," Bernie said. She reached into her pocket and brought out a nickel. Then she flipped the coin up in the air and caught it. "Call it."

"Heads."

Bernie placed the coin on the top of her hand and uncovered it. "Tails. You lose."

"But it's your case," Libby protested.

"It's our case and you're sulking."

Libby sniffed. "I wouldn't go that far."

"I would," Bernie told her.

"I can't believe you're scared of a little old lady."

"And you're not?"

"No," Libby lied.

"Then ring the bell."

"I will." *This is ridiculous,* Libby thought, walking up to the door. It was ornately carved oak, with a mail slot in the middle. Two etched glass windows took up the upper half. After a thirty-second pause, she lifted her finger and rang the bell. As she did, a fat, ginger kitten scampered up the porch, ran between Libby's feet, and started meowing. Libby bent down and petted it while she waited for Old Lady Randall to come to the door.

"Ring it again," Bernie instructed after a minute had gone by without any results.

"Why don't you?" Libby retorted, still petting the cat.

"Because I didn't lose the bet."

"Jeez," Libby muttered. She rang the bell again. She could hear it echoing inside the house. Another minute went by. The cat started meowing again. An uneasy feeling began to settle in Libby's stomach. She turned to Bernie. "I think something's wrong."

"She's old. It might take her a while to come to the door," Bernie said.

"It shouldn't take this long," Libby observed.

"You don't know," Bernie answered. "Maybe she broke her leg and she's in a cast, or maybe she's gone deaf, or maybe she's not home."

"No, she's home," Libby replied. "She's definitely home. I saw her car in the garage."

Bernie shrugged. "That doesn't mean anything. She could still be out. Maybe someone came and picked her up and took her to the grocery store or she had a doctor's appointment."

"Maybe," Libby said, unconvinced. The cat was still meowing. "Boy, she really wants to go in," Libby noted as she bent over to pet her some more. Her fur was glossy and she looked well taken care of.

"She?" Bernie said.

Libby picked the cat up and took a look. "She. I

guess you'll just have to wait," she said to the cat, putting her down. The cat's tail twitched, she meowed and rubbed against Libby's ankles. "We should probably talk to the neighbors and see if they know where Old Lady Randall is."

"Hold up a sec." Bernie walked over and peered in through the window. Even though it was covered with a crocheted curtain, she could still see inside. "There's a pile of mail on the floor," she told Libby. Then she moved aside so Libby could have a look.

"Maybe Old Lady Randall has gone away on vacation," Libby suggested.

"Or she could have fallen," Bernie said.

Libby looked at the neighbors' houses again. "Hopefully one of them has a key for the house. I think I'll go ask."

But before she could do that, Bernie reached over and turned the doorknob. It was heavy brass, the kind they don't make anymore, and felt warm in Bernie's hand. The door swung open, hitting the wall with a smack. The noise broke the quiet and Libby jumped. Bernie watched the cat run into the house and down the hallway. Bernie frowned.

"I'll tell you one thing," she said. "Old Lady Randall wouldn't have gone away and left her place open."

"No, she wouldn't," Libby agreed. "Unless, of course, she forgot. Maybe she forgot," she said, trying to be positive. "After all, she is eighty."

"Maybe," Bernie said, but she didn't believe it and she could tell from Libby's expression that Libby really didn't believe what she was saying either. After all, not six months ago Alice Finkelstein had complained that Miss Randall was after her for the twenty-five cents she owed her from last year.

Bernie and Libby stepped into the entryway. The house was cool and dark, stranded in a perpetual autumn. A large, ornate, gilded mirror sat on the wall opposite the door. Underneath it was what looked to Bernie's eyes like a marble-topped seventeenth-century chest of drawers. There was an expensive oriental on the tile floor.

"Miss Randall," Bernie called out.

Miss Randall didn't answer. Bernie felt as if the house had swallowed up her voice. The only sound she could hear was the cat meowing and the ticking of a clock somewhere inside. She and her sister exchanged glances.

"Are you thinking what I'm thinking?" Libby asked Bernie.

"Unfortunately, I think I am," Bernie replied. She bent down, scooped up the mail, and went through it. It was all flyers. No letters.

She carefully put the mail back where she'd found it. Then she and Libby walked into the kitchen. The cat was sitting in front of a cabinet, meowing.

"I bet that's where her food is," Libby said, opening the door. There was a big bag of dry cat food inside. Libby got a bowl out of another cabinet and put a little food in. "Don't worry," she said to Bernie as the cat ran over. "I'll put everything back."

"You'd better," Bernie said absentmindedly as she surveyed the kitchen. She loved it. She could cook here. The kitchen was old, but in impeccable condition. The light blue stove, fridge, and dishwasher all looked as if they'd come straight out of the fifties, as did the white cabinets.

Bernie went over and touched the fridge. "I bet this is the real deal."

"I bet you're right," Libby replied.

"Boy, I'd love to have one of these, but with all the mod cons."

"When we win the lottery," Libby replied, putting the cat food back where it belonged.

Retro was in again and fridges with retro styling on the outside and modern conveniences on the inside were going for four to six thousand dollars a pop.

Bernie began opening and closing drawers. They were all neatly lined with lavender-scented paper.

"That's a bit much," Libby said, taking a step back.

"What?" Bernie asked.

"The lavender."

"I don't smell it," Bernie said.

"Well, I do," Libby replied. The fact that Libby's sense of smell was keener than Bernie's had always been a point of contention between the sisters.

"If you say so," Bernie said, opening and closing another drawer.

The silverware drawer, the drawer with the kitchen utensils, the drawer that held pot holders and kitchen towels, and the drawer that contained coupons, all of which were clipped and filed, were immaculate.

"Just like ours," Bernie said.

"Heh-heh," Libby commented. "I wish."

"I bet she doesn't cook much," Bernie observed as she opened the last drawer. There was neat and there was crazy OCD neat. This drawer was filled with twine and scissors and a bunch of loose keys in a plastic container. All of the keys were neatly tagged. "Look at this," Bernie said, holding up a small key in a plastic bag. Inside was a note that read, *In case you need salmon, Isaac.* "I guess Old Lady Randall knows Isaac."

"That's nice of him," Libby observed.

"He's a nice guy," Bernie said.

"Yes he is. So are we done here?" Libby asked. She was feeling increasingly uneasy about being in the house.

Bernie dropped the plastic bag with the key back in the drawer and closed it. "Yes. We are."

The *crunch* of the cat eating followed Libby and Bernie as they left the kitchen. Walking through the dining and living rooms, Libby couldn't help but think of her mom's dictum of "a place for everything and everything in its place." If ever a place exemplified it, this one did. It was even neater than their flat when Mom was alive. But, whereas Rose had always liked light, Old Lady Randall had a different sensibility. The windows in the living and dining rooms were covered with a heavy damask that muted the light and absorbed noise.

The floors were polished, the furniture gleamed, the orientals looked like the real deal, and Bernie was almost positive the lamp on the dining room sideboard was a Tiffany, and the pictures in the dining room were Edward Hopper drawings. The only signs of disarray she could spot were a couple of crumpled up tissues and an ashtray full of pistachio shells on the coffee table in the den.

The cat joined them as Libby was commenting on the fifty-two-inch HD TV on the opposite wall. "It looks brand new."

"Newer than ours," Bernie replied.

She was beginning to think that Old Lady Randall had gone to visit a neighbor after all. There was certainly nothing except the mail to indicate that anything had happened to her. Bernie almost suggested that she and Libby leave—she didn't even want to think about what would happen if Old Lady Randall came in and found them standing in her house—but by that time Libby was heading toward the stairs and Bernie figured what the hell, they might as well take a quick look-see as long as they were already inside. At least this way, they'd know whether or not Manny had been living here. If he was, they'd tell Clyde and one of his minions could deal with Old Lady Randall.

The cat bounded up after them. The ginger tabby kept twining herself around Bernie's and Libby's ankles until midway up the stairs Libby scooped her up, carried her the rest of the way, and put her down on the top step. The cat looked at her for a moment, then dashed off into the first room on the left. Unlike the others on the second floor, this door was open.

Chapter 16

The tabby started meowing loudly.

"God she's noisy," Libby said as she followed the cat into the room.

Bernie corrected her. "Verbal. She's verbal."

"Whatever." Then Libby gasped.

"What's the matter?" Bernie asked, alarmed at Libby's expression.

Libby pointed. One more step and she would have planted her foot squarely on Old Lady

Randall's stomach. She was splayed out on an oriental rug in the middle of her bedroom, wearing a housedress. One slipper was on and the other one was lying a short distance away. Her eyes were wide open, as was her mouth; she was staring at the ceiling, a circle of blood pooled around her head. Libby put her hand to her mouth.

"Oh no," Bernie said, stepping inside.

Both sisters looked down at Old Lady Randall. She was smaller than either Libby or Bernie remembered her. She looked fragile, but most of all, with her white hair and wrinkled, age-spotted skin, she looked old. Libby couldn't believe she'd been terrified of her all this time. She felt ashamed of herself.

"Do you know what her first name was?" Libby asked.

Bernie thought for a moment. "I think I remember Mom calling her Clara."

"Did she ever get married?"

Bernie thought for another moment. "I'd have to ask Dad, but no, I don't think so. Why are you asking?"

Libby shrugged. "No reason. No reason at all, really. I think we should start calling her by her name. Clara, Clara Randall. Somehow given the circumstances, Old Lady Randall seems disrespectful."

Bernie wrinkled her nose. The room smelled of

old age, lavender, and death. "I don't think she's going to care."

"Maybe not," Libby said. "But I do."

Bernie shrugged. "Sure, why not. If it'll make you happy it's fine with me." She pointed to the towel lying next to Clara Randall's outstretched hand. "She must have been getting ready to take a bath."

"Maybe this was an accident," Libby suggested as she watched the tabby butt her head against Clara Randall's outstretched hand. "She could have fallen and hit her head. It's possible."

Bernie gestured around the room. "Hit her head on what?"

Libby nibbled on her lip again. "The bed post? The dresser?"

"They're too far away."

"She could have hit her head on one of them and staggered over here and collapsed," Libby answered. She went over and examined the four carved cherrywood bedposts and the matching dresser. She pointed to the right-hand post at the end of the bed. "There's blood on this. So it was an accident."

"Maybe," Bernie said. "But I can't see Clara Randall leaving the front door open."

Libby contemplated the implications of Bernie's statement. "So," she said after a moment, "what you're saying is that someone came up here and killed her. Someone with a key to the house."

"I suppose I am." Bernie automatically readjusted the belt on her dress. It kept sliding off to the side. She could hear rain starting to fall outside. "Especially if Manny was staying here. That's certainly a link."

The cat gave up on Clara Randall and began rubbing her head on Bernie's ankles.

"That's certainly a big red flag," Libby agreed. "On the other hand, she could have been expecting a neighbor or a delivery. She could have left the door open for them."

Bernie looked down at the cat. "What do you think?" she asked her.

The cat looked up at her and meowed.

"I think that's unlikely too," Bernie told her. Given what she knew of Old Lady—sorry, Clara Randall's personality—she seemed like the kind of person who would have kept her door locked at all times.

Libby sighed. "I know."

Bernie shifted her weight onto her good foot. "Everything up here and downstairs looks in order, so I think we can rule out a burglary gone wrong."

Libby closed her eyes for a minute and pictured the possible train of events. "Unless whoever was responsible came upstairs and Clara Randall surprised them so they killed her and fled without taking what they were looking for."

"Possible," Bernie conceded. She thought of

the Hoppers downstairs and the Tiffany lamp and the oriental rugs, all of which were worth a sizable amount of money. Most people, though, wouldn't take those; they'd take cash, jewelry, and electronics. "Let's take another look," she suggested.

Which they did, but there was no evidence of a TV in the bedroom, and as for jewelry, the only thing the sisters found was a jewelry box full of fake pearls and Timex watches.

"Maybe there's a safe here somewhere," Bernie said.

But if there had been, it wasn't there now. At least, it wasn't anyplace in the bedroom that Bernie or Libby could see.

Libby thought about the small safe her mom had kept to store her marriage certificate in. It was still in her dad's bedroom. It was so light she or Bernie could pick it up and carry it down the stairs. "The attacker could have taken it."

"I don't know," Bernie said. "Clara Randall strikes me as more of a safety deposit box person."

Libby nibbled on her cuticle, realized what she was doing, and stopped. "It looks as if Clara Randall died after Manny. I don't think she's been dead that long." She rubbed her temples. She could feel a headache coming on. One murder was bad, two was worse. "But I guess we'll have to wait for the autopsies to find out for sure."

Bernie bent down and scratched the ginger

tabby underneath her chin. She began to purr. The sound filled the room.

"Do you want to call the cops or should I?" Libby asked.

"You can after we finish looking around."

"I think we should call them now."

"And not finish what we started?"

Libby shook her head. "I don't know, Bernie . . . given last time."

"This is different. We're not going to run into the police this time."

"I think Dad would disown us if he had to bail us out again."

"He didn't bail us out. We didn't get ourselves arrested."

"Don't be so literal. I was talking figuratively."

"He's not going to have to. No one is coming through the door."

"And you're sure of that?"

"Reasonably."

Libby glanced down at Clara Randall. She fought an impulse to close her eyes and cross her arms over her chest.

"Listen," Bernie said, "we need to know if Manny lived here or if he didn't, and the sooner we find out, the better. If he did live here maybe there's something in his room that will shed light on what's going on." Bernie picked the cat up. The tabby leaned her head on Bernie's shoulder. "Besides, we owe it to Ellen to follow through on this. Mom would have wanted us to."

Libby frowned. She swatted at a fly that was hovering around her face. "Raising the ugly specter of guilt, are we?"

Bernie grinned. "Absolutely."

"Well, just because you feel guilty doesn't mean that I have to."

"Sisters share. Remember?"

"Ha-ha-ha. Funny lady," Libby retorted.

"That's what Mom always said. Anyway, Mom liked Ellen. You know she did. We also owe it to Ellen's kids," Bernie continued. "They paid us. We agreed to take the case. We're morally obligated to follow through."

"That's true," Libby reluctantly agreed. She couldn't argue with that. A vision of Ethan, tears trickling down his cheeks, floated through her mind, and she caved. "Okay," she said, "but let's get in and out of here fast."

Bernie curtsied. "Your wish is my command."

"Yeah, right," Libby muttered.

"We will," Bernie promised as she and Libby stepped out into the hallway.

Chapter 17

The cat meowed and Bernie resumed scratching behind her ears.

"She certainly seems starved for attention," Libby noted as she looked around.

The upstairs hallway was spacious and well lit. An oriental style runner ran down the center of the floor while a matched pair of antique Chinese Fu Dogs sat on mother-of-pearl inlaid tables across from one another and staring at each other. If the dogs had been meant to protect Clara Randall, they had failed miserably. The walls were dotted with photos and the sisters stopped to take a look at them. They were all family photos, most of them of Clara Randall when she was younger.

"She was attractive," Bernie noted over the cat's purring.

"Very," Libby answered, looking at a picture of Clara Randall. She and a girlfriend were hugging. Both of them were wearing white skirts and striped, long sleeve, boat-neck T-shirts and had their faces turned to the camera. They were both sticking out their tongues.

"I bet she was twelve or thirteen when this was taken," Bernie said.

"I wonder what happened to her," Libby mused. "She looks so happy there."

"Whatever it was, I hope it doesn't happen to us," Bernie said as she walked down the hall scanning the other photos.

They were all family photos of one kind or another. Some were in black and white, others were faded Polaroids. Most had been taken by amateurs, although a few on the wall had been taken by professionals. All of the pictures had been expensively framed and hung with great care.

There were pictures of Clara Randall with her dad and mom, at her high school and college graduations, and away on holidays at the beach and lake. The thing that struck Bernie the most as she looked at them was Clara's progression from happy to unhappy, which the photos showed. Clara Randall had started off a pretty girl with a brilliant smile and turned into a sour-faced, plain-looking woman. How had that happened?

Bernie was three-quarters of the way down the hall when she stopped in front of one of the photos. "Libby, come here."

Libby walked over. "What's up?"

Bernie pointed to a goofy-looking kid mugging for the camera. He was sitting at a picnic table in what looked like Highland Park. "Isn't that Manny?" she asked Libby.

Libby squinted. She bent over to take a closer look. "It sure is," she said after a minute had gone by. *Boy has he changed,* she thought again, *and not for the better.*

Bernie studied the other people in the photo. There was Clara Randall sitting at the edge of the picnic table with her hands folded on the table, and between her and Manny were a stiff-looking, sour-faced, well-dressed, middle-aged couple. She pointed to them. "I'm betting they're his parents. Manny looks just like them."

"Dad would know," Libby observed. "Too bad we can't ask him."

Bernie ignored the comment. "They don't look like much fun, do they?"

"I think you can safely surmise that anyone who names their kid Raymond Manford probably isn't," Libby replied. She studied the couple's faces. "I bet they expected great things from their son."

"Maybe if they had expected less, they would have gotten more," Bernie observed.

"That certainly wasn't the principle Mom operated under."

"No, it wasn't, was it?" Bernie said softly. Her sister, being the older one, had definitely borne the brunt of her mom's expectations.

She was thinking about that while Libby gently nibbled on the inside of her cheek and studied the pictures on the wall. "He looks familiar," she said, pointing to a slightly older kid standing in back of Manny.

He looked familiar to Bernie too. She just couldn't put a name to his face. "We should get going," she said after glancing at her watch. "The less time we're in here, the better. How about you take the rooms on the right side and I'll take the ones on the left?"

"Works for me," Libby told her. She shook her head. She was still thinking about the kid in the picture with Manny. "I know I know that guy from somewhere."

"It'll come to you," Bernie reassured her as she started toward the second bedroom on the left-hand side. The cat jumped down and followed her.

Including Clara Randall's, there were five bedrooms in all on the second floor and one bedroom in the attic. It turned out that of the remaining bedrooms on the second floor, one was being used as a sewing room, while the next three rooms had no furniture in them at all. They were chock-full of racks of clothes and shoes and various accessories.

"Holy cow," Libby said, emerging from her first room and joining Bernie. "And I thought you shopped a lot." She gestured to the room she'd just been in. "There must be ten racks of coats and pants and suits in there."

Bernie surveyed boxes of shoes stacked up against the wall and arranged by color and type. The middle of the room was filled with three racks of skirts and dresses, while shelving filled with sweaters and blouses and handbags lined the other walls.

"It looks as if Clara Randall never gave anything away," Bernie said in a massive understatement.

Then she walked over and opened the closet door. It was packed with old clothes neatly hung on pink quilted hangers. The scent of lavender mixed with the smell of mothballs assaulted Bernie's nose. The cat must not have liked it, because she scampered to the other side of the room. She sniffed at the baseboards while Bernie quickly thumbed through the clothes. The dresses were from places like Saks and Lord & Taylor and Bergdorf's.

"Definitely oldies but goodies," Bernie observed, shutting the closet door behind her. "There's a lot of money here," she said, referring to the clothes, as she and Libby walked back out into the hallway.

Libby shook her head. "I can't imagine staying in a house like this by myself," she said, interrupting Bernie's train of thought. "It's too big. It would give me the heebie jeebies."

Bernie smiled. That had been one of her mother's expressions. "Me too, but Clara must have liked it this way. She could certainly afford to move," Bernie said as she slowly made her way back out into the hallway. The cat followed. "I guess she needed room for all of her stuff."

She reached down and massaged her ankle. It was throbbing by now. The more she was on it, the more painful it became. She ignored the ache and limped toward the door to the attic. It was midway down the hall and qualitatively different from the other doors upstairs. This one was new. The other doors were solid oak; this was hollow core, and even though it had been stained, it didn't match the others.

"I bet Clara Randall got this at Home Depot," Bernie said as she grasped the doorknob and pulled.

The door opened easily and the cat scampered up the stairs before Bernie could stop her.

"Great," Bernie said, looking at the dark stairwell. She put out her hand and felt around until she found a light switch and turned it on. She sighed as she studied the stairs. They looked steep and the treads of the two middle ones were sagging.

"I'll go if you want," Libby offered. "You can stay here."

"No. I can do it," Bernie said, gritting her teeth. After all, she'd been the one who had insisted on this. She grabbed hold of the banister and pulled herself up one step at a time. Libby came up after her to make sure her sister didn't fall.

The cat was sitting on a bed when Bernie got up there. It was one of those futons that converted into a bed. The bed was unmade, a bath towel was thrown on a chair, there was a backpack on the dresser and magazines on the floor, as well as empty candy wrappers, movie ticket stubs, and clothes.

"Someone is living up here," Bernie said as Libby picked up a pair of jeans and held them up. "The question is: is it Manny?"

"These look like they could fit him," Libby said.

"They are really big," Bernie allowed.

Libby peeked inside the waistband. "The waist size is forty-two. I'd say that's pretty big."

"Me too." Bernie watched Libby going through the jean's pockets. She found some loose change, a crumpled up Snickers wrapper, and a receipt from the local CVS for a bottle of aspirin, but that was it.

"There's nothing of interest here," Libby noted disappointedly.

Bernie grunted "We're not done yet," she observed.

Then she walked over to an old, battered desk set off in a corner. She ran her finger over a stack of old newspapers, then picked up a chess book lying next to them and opened the cover. There was Manny's name written in the corner in blue ink. "This is his room," she said, holding up the book for Libby to see.

Libby smiled. "Well, at least we're right about that." And she bent down and looked under the futon.

Meanwhile, Bernie went through Manny's dresser drawers. Aside from some underwear, socks, T-shirts, and a couple of hoodies, there wasn't much in there. Whereas Clara Randall had way too much, Manny Roget had practically nothing.

"You know what I don't see?" Bernie told Libby when she'd finished going through the drawers. "I don't see a laptop, or a tablet, or anything of that nature."

"Maybe whoever killed him took it," Libby posited.

"Maybe," Bernie said as she walked over to the mesh basket that was full of clothes and began rummaging through them. A few minutes later, she held up a laptop. "Or not. It was buried under some T-shirts," she explained.

"Odd place for it," Libby observed.

Bernie grunted a response. Then she sat down on the futon, opened it up, and tried to log in, but she couldn't. It was password protected. Bernie cursed under her breath and began trying different combinations of Manny Roget's name, but nothing worked, and after five minutes of trying, she gave up and put the laptop back where she'd found it.

In the meantime Libby had opened up Manny's backpack. It was empty except for a couple of energy drinks, three packs of gum, and a folder containing order forms and a book of receipts, both of which had the word *Arf* printed on them. "Look at what I found," Libby cried, holding up the folder for Bernie to see.

"I think we have a theme going here." Bernie held up a large black T-shirt with the logo *ARF* written on it, which she'd found on the bed buried under a pile of smelly sweatpants. *Begging for More* was written underneath it. "You know what this means, don't you?"

"Offhand, I'd say it means that Manny was selling Ellen and Lisa's products," Libby said.

"And the contestant wins the prize," Bernie said. Then she snapped her fingers. "Hey. I think I know who the guy in the pictures is. The one you were talking about. It just came to me."

"Who is he?" Libby asked.

"You're not going to believe this."

"Try me."

"It's Bruce, Ellen's husband."

Libby crinkled her nose. "Seriously? Are you sure?"

"Maybe sixty/forty percent sure," Bernie replied. She was about to say something else when the doorbell rang.

She and her sister froze.

They could hear the door open.

Someone yelled, "Hey, Miss Randall, are you home?"

Chapter 18

"Told you we shouldn't be doing this," Libby hissed at Bernie as she threw the Arf T-shirt back on the bed.

"Miss Randall," the voice called again.

Bernie recognized the voice. She held out her hands, palms down. "Calm," she told Libby.

"Calm down?" Libby's voice rose, despite herself. "Are you nuts?"

"No. It's Ethan," Bernie said.

"You're sure?" Libby demanded.

"I'm positive."

Libby took a deep breath. This was bad, but it could be worse. "What the hell is he doing here?"

"Haven't got a clue. Let's go ask him. Well, we don't want him to come up the stairs, do we?" Bernie said in the face of Libby's hesitation.

"No, we definitely don't want that," Libby agreed.

"You go first. It's going to take me longer. Go," she said, giving Libby's shoulder a gentle shove.

"I'm going," Libby said. The last thing she wanted was for Ethan to see Clara Randall lying there like that. He'd probably have nightmares for weeks. She knew that she would have at his age. She turned and hurried down the stairs. "Ethan," she yelled, "stay where you are. I'll be right down."

Bernie grabbed the T-shirt Libby had been holding up and the folder she'd found and stuffed both of them in her bag. "Okay," she said to the cat. "Let's go."

The cat looked at Bernie and yawned.

"Seriously," Bernie told her. "We have to leave."

The cat yawned some more. Bernie went over to pick her up but the kitten growled at her. Bernie threw her hands up. "Okay. Suit yourself." And she turned to go. At which point the cat jumped off the bed and scampered down the stairs ahead of Bernie. "I bet you think you're funny," Bernie told her as she went by. The cat meowed her reply.

Ethan was in the hallway when Libby came down the stairs. "What are you doing here?" he asked.

"I could ask you the same question," Libby replied.

Ethan wiped a drop of rain off his cheek. Libby could see that his hair was damp and his polo shirt was wet. He sneezed. Then he said, "I came to see if Miss Randall would pay me the money she owes me."

"For what?" Libby asked.

"For cutting the grass." He caught sight of the tabby coming down the stairs and knelt down. The cat made straight for him and started purring.

"Boy, Miss Randall is going to be pissed when she sees the cat inside."

"Does the cat have a name?" Libby asked.

"I don't know," Ethan said. "I don't think so. Old Lady Randall just calls her the cat. She lives out in the garage. Miss Randall said she doesn't want fur on her rugs."

"Really?" Bernie said, who'd just joined them. "That's not very nice."

"That's what I told Miss Randall," Ethan said.

"And what did she say?" Bernie asked.

"That the cat was lucky she didn't take it to the ASPCA and have it put down. She didn't even want to keep the food in the house. Said it attracted mice."

"We found a whole bag of food in the kitchen," Bernie told him.

Ethan hitched up his shorts. "Well, she changed her mind when the raccoons came into the garage, ripped open the cat food, and ate it."

Bernie nodded. "Makes sense to me." Suddenly she realized that her throat was feeling scratchy. She hoped she wasn't getting a summer cold. They were the worst. "I'll be back in a second," she told Ethan and Libby.

"Where are you going?" Libby asked her.

"To the kitchen to get a glass of water to take my zinc with."

"That doesn't work," Libby said.

"I guess we'll find out," Bernie told her, and

she limped off leaving Libby to deal with Ethan.

Libby turned toward Ethan. "Did you ever see the man who was living here?" she asked.

Ethan shook his head. "I never saw anyone here except for Old Lady Randall. But I'm not here that much."

"When was the last time you saw her?"

Ethan considered the question for a moment before answering. "Maybe a week ago. She was supposed to pay me then for mowing the grass, but she told me she didn't have any cash on her and that I should come back. I rode my bike over here yesterday and knocked on the door but she didn't answer, so I figured I'd try today." He sneezed again. "How come you're asking me all these questions? Is something wrong?"

"You could say that. Miss Randall had an accident," Libby said as gently as she could.

Ethan's ears perked up. He leaned forward. "What kind of accident?"

"A bad one."

Ethan blinked. "You mean like the kind that makes you dead? That kind of accident?"

"Yes, Ethan. That's exactly what I mean."

His eyes widened. "Were you upstairs investigating?"

Libby nodded.

"Wow. That is so cool. Not about Old Lady Randall, of course," Ethan said hastily, realizing what he sounded like. "So what are you going to do now? Look for more clues? I can help you, you know."

"We're going to call the police," Libby said.

"Can I go upstairs first?" Ethan asked.

"No," Libby said.

"But I've never seen a dead person," Ethan protested.

"You will soon enough," Libby told him.

"Please?"

"I said no."

"Why not?"

"Because I said so," Libby told him, her mother's words flying out of her mouth.

She was in the middle of calling the police when Bernie rejoined them.

"Okay. I'm all set," she said.

Ethan tugged at Bernie's sleeve. "Does this mean I won't get paid?" he asked, looking mournful.

Libby and Bernie exchanged glances.

Libby patted his head. "Maybe we can work something out," she told him.

Chapter 19

Bernie, Libby, Ethan, and the cat watched the rain drizzling down on the geraniums as they waited on the porch for a Longely squad car to arrive. Fifteen minutes later one did. This time things went better. The fact that it was Chris Bright, a regular who bought coffee and scones from A Little Taste of Heaven at least four times a week, helped.

"Unbelievable," Chris said once he was on the porch. "What is it with you two and dead bodies?"

Bernie smiled. "Just lucky, I guess."

Chris smiled back. He took out his notebook and pen. "Tell me the story," he instructed.

So Bernie did. More or less. The trick to being a good liar was sticking as close to the truth as possible. She began by explaining to him that they'd had an appointment with Clara Randall concerning a party she'd been thinking of giving—a small untraceable lie—and that she and Libby had become alarmed when they'd rung the bell and no one answered the door. Then they'd become even more alarmed when they'd peeked through the front door window and saw the mail lying on the floor.

They were about to call the police—"honest" Bernie said when Chris raised an eyebrow—but they thought they heard a noise. A noise that in retrospect turned out to be the cat, but at the time sounded like Miss Randall in distress. Naturally, they rushed inside to see if anything was wrong.

"Naturally," Chris echoed gravely.

Bernie smiled placidly and continued. "Once we were in the hallway we realized that the noise we'd been hearing was coming from upstairs, so we ran up there. The noise was even louder when we reached the landing."

"Then what?" Chris asked.

"Then we looked and saw that the door to the first bedroom on the left was open, so we went inside. That's when we found Clara Randall lying on the floor with her cat meowing beside her. One look at all that blood and we knew she was dead."

Libby nodded. "But I took her pulse just to make sure."

"Did you touch anything?" Chris asked.

Both Libby and Bernie shook their heads.

"No. Absolutely not," Bernie said. "We didn't stop to look at or touch anything in Miss Randall's room. We know better than that. Really!" Bernie put a lot of indignation in her voice. "Chris, I'm shocked that you would even suggest such a thing."

Chris suppressed a smile. "Go on."

"As I was saying," Bernie said, "I was about to call the police when we heard the downstairs door open and Ethan came in. He too was looking for Miss Randall, isn't that right, Ethan?"

Ethan nodded.

Chris looked at Ethan. "Is that what happened?"

"Yes," Ethan whispered, looking down at the floor.

"Why were you looking for her?"

"Because she owed me lawn-mowing money."

"Anyway," Bernie said, resuming her tale. "Then we called you and here we all are."

Chris looked at Bernie. "That's it?" he asked.

"Absolutely," Bernie replied.

"Nothing else to add?"

"Nope."

"Nice story."

"It's not a story," Bernie protested.

"I meant that in the metaphorical sense." And Chris called it in.

Then they all waited.

Ten minutes later the crime scene guys and Lucy arrived simultaneously. The crime scene squad went in the house and Bernie told the exact same story she'd told to Chris to Lucy.

Lucy glared at her. He put his hands on his hips. Bernie decided he'd gained more weight.

"You expect me to believe that?" he growled.

"It's the truth," Bernie said, looking as pious as she possibly could.

"You don't know the meaning of the word," Lucy snapped.

Bernie didn't say anything. She watched the rain dripping off the eaves of the porch.

Lucy came a step closer and stuck his neck out, making him, Libby decided, look like a turtle.

"For openers," he said to both Libby and Bernie, "I can't conceive of Clara Randall giving a party. The concept is ludicrous. She never had any visitors. She didn't like people."

Bernie refrained telling Lucy about Manny staying in the house. She figured he'd find out soon enough. Instead she said, "Evidently, Miss Randall was having a change of heart. Believe me"—Bernie rested her hand on her own heart—"I was as surprised as you were by the request. But she seemed serious about it."

"So she called you?" Lucy asked. His tone was one of casual interest.

Bernie avoided the trap. Although she didn't think Lucy would go so far as to subpoena her phone records, she figured it was better to be on the safe side.

"No," Bernie said. "Actually she didn't. She flagged us down when we were driving by her house."

"What kind of party was it?"

"Nothing elaborate," Bernie said. "She wanted to do something for the neighbors. She told me she wanted it to be a surprise."

"I see." Lucy laced his fingers together and cracked his knuckles. One of his more annoying habits. He nodded at the road. "This is a little out of the way for you, isn't it?"

Libby jumped in. "It is, but we like to change things up from time to time."

Lucy turned to Libby. "So you agree with everything that your sister said?"

Libby nodded. "Why wouldn't I?"

"Why indeed? I can think of plenty of reasons."

"How do you want us to respond to that statement?" Bernie asked.

Lucy cracked his knuckles again instead of answering. A minute went by.

Finally Bernie pointed at Ethan and said, "I think we should get him home, don't you? His parents are probably worried about him by now." Not only did Ethan need a ride, but Bernie figured it would be a good opportunity to have a chat with Ellen and Bruce.

"Great," Ethan said. He gestured to the bike lying on the front lawn. "I rode over here. What about my bike?"

"Not a problem. We'll take it with us," Libby said. Then she went down the stairs, picked the bike up, and started walking it to the van. Bernie and Ethan followed. It wasn't until they'd finished loading the bike in the back and closed the doors that they realized that the cat had jumped into Mathilda.

"You can't come," Libby told her.

She meowed, walked over to Ethan, and curled up in his lap.

"You can't leave her," Ethan protested.

"We can't bring her," Libby replied.

"We'll deal with the cat later," Bernie told her sister. "Right now we need to get going before Lucy changes his mind and arrests us."

"Why would Lucy arrest you?" Ethan piped up.

"I didn't really mean that," Bernie lied. She

realized she'd have to be careful about what she said around Ethan.

"Then why did you say it?" Ethan demanded.

"I wondered that myself," Bernie replied.

That pretty much put the kibosh on the conversation for a few minutes and no one was talking when they pulled out into the road and turned left to go to the Hadleys' house. It was still drizzling and Libby turned on the windshield wipers. Two blocks down Ethan spoke.

"Would he arrest you because you lied?"

"I didn't lie," Bernie said indignantly.

"Yeah, you did," Ethan replied. "You told me you guys were upstairs investigating, but you told the police you weren't. Isn't that a lie?"

"Not really," Bernie said.

"Then what is it?"

"A linguistic quibble."

Obviously Ethan wasn't buying it, because the next thing he said was, "My parents say lying is wrong."

"It is," Bernie replied. "Most of the time."

Ethan digested that for a moment. Then he said, "Kind of like when I told Mom that Matt wasn't at the Freeboughs' party when he was. I mean, like he was just there because Kara was crying and called him up and said he had to come, otherwise she was going to take all these pills, but if I told Mom and Dad, Matt would have been grounded for like a century."

Bernie smiled. "Yeah. Kinda like that."

"I don't get it," Ethan said.

"Get what?"

"Why one kind of lie is okay and the other isn't."

"If it's any comfort to you, Ethan, neither do I," Libby said as she turned the speed of the windshield wipers up.

Everyone was silent until they reached the Hadleys' colonial. Ethan was quiet because he was overwhelmed, and Bernie and Libby were quiet because the things they had to discuss, they couldn't talk about in front of Ethan.

Chapter 20

It was raining harder now and Libby pulled up as close to the Hadleys' front porch as she could get.

Ethan looked at the cat. "I can't take her. My dad's allergic."

"It's okay," Libby said soothingly. "We'll take care of her."

"You're not going to take her to the ASPCA, are you?" Ethan asked, panic in his voice.

"No, we won't," Libby said. Of course, that's exactly what she'd been thinking they'd do.

"Because they'll kill her."

"She could get adopted," Bernie pointed out.

Ethan eyes began to mist.

"Fine," Libby said. "We'll find a home for her."

"We will?" Bernie asked, surprised.

"Yes, we will," Libby said firmly before she got out. Then she went around to the back of the van and got Ethan's bike out, while Ethan ran onto the porch and rang the doorbell. The cat surveyed the activity with interest.

Ethan's dad opened the door a moment later. The sounds of a video game spilled out.

"Where the hell have you been?" Bruce asked his son. "You're late for dinner." Ethan started to stutter out an answer, but before he could complete his sentence Bruce caught sight of Libby. "Why are you here?" he demanded, his expression hardening. "What's going on?"

Ethan started biting his nails.

"Well?" Bruce said, looking from Libby to Ethan and back again. "Someone answer me."

"I'll explain," Libby told Ethan. She leaned his bike against the wall. "You go inside."

"This better be good," Bruce said to his son as Ethan scooted by him, giving his dad as wide a berth as possible.

"It's not Ethan's fault that he's late," Bernie said, making her way slowly up the stairs. Looking at Bruce's face, she decided she'd been right. Bruce was the kid in the photograph. He'd been considerably younger and skinnier and he'd had all his hair back then, but it was the same person.

"Really." Bruce crossed his arms over his chest and planted his feet in the doorway. "Goody. Another voice heard from. Ethan can speak for himself."

Looking at him, Bernie decided that Bruce Randall was one of those men who'd peaked in high school. He was big with a tendency toward a gut. When Ellen had met him, he'd been a blond, blue-eyed, star high school linebacker, but that had been a long time ago.

"Clara Randall is dead," Bernie announced as she searched Bruce's face for a reaction.

There wasn't one.

"And what does that have to do with Ethan being late?" Bruce asked.

"He went there to collect his lawn-mowing money and came into the house at the same time we were discovering her body upstairs. So we had to wait till the police arrived. Once they came, we gave Ethan a lift back."

"I see," Bruce said.

"Don't you want to know how Clara Randall died?" Libby asked.

"I presume from old age," Bruce said in a dry tone of voice.

"Not exactly. She had an accident or someone hit her on the head," Bernie told him.

Bruce shifted his position. "That's a big difference. Which is it?"

"We don't know yet, but in the meantime we need to talk to Ellen and you," Bernie said.

Bruce's frown got deeper. "And why would that be?"

"Because the dead man in the motel was Manny, more formally known as Raymond Manford Roget, and he was living in Clara Randall's house."

Bruce shrugged. "And?"

"The name doesn't ring a bell?" Bernie asked.

"Should it?" Bruce shot back.

"Considering he worked for your wife, I would think it would." She pulled the Arf T-shirt she'd taken from the attic out of her bag and waved it in Bruce's face.

"I wouldn't know," Bruce said. "I don't have much to do with my wife's business. That's her thing, not mine. Anyway, he could have gotten that shirt in a store."

"They're not available retail." Bernie tucked a wisp of hair back in her ponytail. "Anyway, I find it hard to believe you don't know what's going on, considering your wife's business operates out of your basement," Bernie said.

Bruce glared at her. "*Did* operate out of the basement, and for your information, I'm at work when Ellen and Lisa are baking. In addition, Lisa takes care of all of the deliveries. So, if you have any questions, I suggest you talk to her."

"We will," Libby said. "But right now we're

talking to you. So you didn't know this Manny?"

Bruce snorted. "I just said that."

"Because hanging on Clara Randall's wall is a picture of him and you together at a picnic in Highland Park."

Bruce shook his head. "Sorry, it doesn't ring a bell."

Bernie lifted an eyebrow. "Seriously?"

Bruce spread his hands apart. "Hey, that was a long time ago."

"So you do remember," Libby said.

"I remember going to picnics there when I was a kid. That's what we used to do on Sunday afternoons. There were always lots of kids hanging around. So maybe Manny was one of them. So what? And now if you'll excuse me, I have to go."

"Fine, but we'd still like to speak to Ellen," Bernie told him.

"You can't. She's out," Bruce told them.

"Out?"

Bruce crossed his arms over his chest. "That's what I just said. She's out doing an errand."

"She's not answering her cell."

"That's because she left it in the house."

"Oh," Bernie said. Ordinarily Ellen never went anywhere without it, but then these weren't ordinary times. "Okay, then. Just tell her my sister and I were here."

"I don't think I'm going to do that," Bruce said.

Bernie could see the vein in Bruce's neck start to pulse. "And why is that?"

"Because of the kind of friend you turned out to be," Bruce said, pointing to Bernie.

"You're wrong. She's a good friend to Ellen," Libby told him.

"I don't think so. Your sister is the one who put the ransom note idea in my wife's thick skull. If she hadn't done that, none of this would have happened. Your sister ruined our lives."

"My sister was kidding when she said that to your wife," Libby told Bruce. "She never expected her to follow up on it."

"That's not what my wife says," Bruce retorted.

Bernie jumped into the conversation. "Well, Ellen is wrong," she said.

"So now my wife is a liar on top of everything else?"

"I didn't say that," Bernie cried.

Bruce didn't reply. He just slammed the door in her face.

"That man's a jerk," Libby said as she walked down the porch steps. "How can anyone be married to someone like that?"

Bernie came down the steps after her. "I don't know, but they've been married for a long time, so there's got to be something there."

"How about inertia?" Libby got the keys for the van out of her backpack and she and her sister got into the van. The cat sat in Bernie's lap.

"Bruce is big enough, you know."

Libby put the keys in the van's ignition. Mathilda coughed twice and started up. "Big enough for what, Bernie?"

"To have killed Manny."

The cat meowed and Bernie automatically began petting her.

"But why would he, Bernie?" Libby asked as she drove onto Sycamore Street. "What motive would he have?"

"I have no idea, but he knew where Ellen was going to be. In fact, he's the only one who did."

"That we know of. Maybe Ellen told someone else about her plans."

"That's possible," Bernie conceded. She thought for a minute. "She might have told Lisa. They talk a lot."

"Well, they are in business together."

"And then Lisa could have told someone else. . . ."

"Also possible." Libby slowed down to let a car pass.

The cat began to purr.

"We have to talk to Lisa, but before we do that, we have to figure out what we're going to do with Cindy."

Libby briefly took her eyes off the road to look at her sister. "Cindy? Who is Cindy?" she demanded.

"She's the cat, of course."

"Why Cindy?"

"Because she reminds me of Cinderella."

Libby scrunched up her nose. "Because?"

Bernie shrugged. "I don't know. She just does. Do you have another suggestion?"

Libby thought for a moment. "No. Not really."

Bernie scratched the cat behind her ears. "Then Cinderella it is. Home, James."

"Dad will be so pleased," Libby noted.

"Can you think of another place?"

Libby considered the possibilities. None presented themselves. "Not really." Marvin had an allergy to cats and Brandon rented a "no-pets-allowed" flat.

"It's just until we find her a new home," Bernie assured her sister. "After all, we did promise Ethan."

On the way to the flat, they stopped at a pet store and picked up a litter box, a small bag of litter, and some canned and dry food.

"You know," Libby said at the register, "maybe Bruce is covering for Ellen."

Bernie snorted at the idea. "That I doubt," she said. "If anything, he probably set her up."

Chapter 21

Sean looked at Cindy and Cindy looked at Sean. "Why is she here?" he asked.

Libby explained.

Sean leaned forward. "Clara Randall is dead?"

Bernie nodded. "She either fell or was hit over the head. Given the circumstances, Libby and I are going with getting hit over the head."

Sean sighed. "It must have been quite a blow. I thought she was too mean to die."

"Evidently not," Bernie said as the cat jumped into Sean's lap, curled up, and closed her eyes.

"Make yourself at home, why don't you?" Sean said to Cindy.

Cindy opened her eyes for a minute and closed them again.

"She likes you, Dad," Bernie said.

Sean looked decidedly unthrilled.

"Dad, she's just here till we find her a new home," Libby said hastily. "She'll help with the mouse problem."

"We don't have a mouse problem," Sean said, giving Cindy a tentative pat on the back. "I guess we can all manage for a while, the key concept here being *a while*." Then he changed the subject. "Was there a weapon?" he asked, getting back to Clara Randall's death.

"Not that Bernie or I saw," Libby replied. "I figure someone pushed her, she hit her head on the bedpost, and it was bye-bye, Clara, off to the promised land."

"She could have just gotten dizzy and fallen," Sean said.

"She could have," Bernie agreed, "but the door was open."

"Did the lock give any evidence of being jimmied?" Sean asked.

Bernie and Libby exchanged glances. They hadn't looked. Libby closed her eyes and thought back.

"I don't think so," she said when she opened them. "At least there was nothing there that caught my attention."

"Meaning either Clara Randall left the door open, which is unlikely, or whoever did this had a key." Sean gave the cat another pat.

"They could have gotten the key from Manny," Bernie suggested. "I'm sure he had one since he was staying there."

Sean steepled his fingers together. "Could it have been a robbery?"

Bernie replied. "I guess it could have been, but it sure didn't look that way to me. If it was, whoever did it knew exactly where what they wanted was. There was nothing out of place down- or upstairs."

"And you said Manny was living there?" Sean asked.

"His stuff was there," Bernie said. She got up, took out the Arf T-shirt, and showed it to her dad. "He had this in his room, plus a book of order forms and receipts with Arf printed at the top."

Sean scratched his chin. "Did you find anything else?"

"Not really. A couple of chess books, some clothing. It didn't look as if Manny had much in the way of possessions. We did find his laptop, but we didn't find his wallet or his phone. I figure someone took them."

"That's a good guess," Sean said. "The question is whether they took those items because there was something that pointed to the killer's identity or did they take them to sell or for their own use?" He was about to add something else when his cell rang. The cat startled. As Sean leaned over and picked it up off the table next to him, Cindy jumped off his lap, onto the floor, then onto the arm of the sofa.

Bernie and Libby watched while their dad nodded his head and said, "Yeah, you don't say," and "Interesting."

"Well?" Libby said after Sean had hung up. "What's going on? What's so interesting?"

"That was Clyde," Sean said. "He thought we'd want to know. According to the ME, it seems as if our friend Manny Roget had spent some time in a cold room, a very cold room, before he ended up on the bed in the motel. At least that's what a preliminary autopsy indicates."

"So what's the timeline?" Bernie asked.

"The ME is saying probably within the last twenty-four to forty-eight hours," Sean said.

"That's a fairly wide time frame," Bernie noted as Cindy yawned, jumped off the sofa and back on Sean's lap, where she circled around three times and lay back down.

"She really does like you," Libby observed.

Sean frowned. "Well, I hope she's not going to get too comfortable, because she's not going to be here that long." Nevertheless he began petting her.

Bernie tried not to smile. Instead she bent over and started massaging her ankle. Even though the swelling was going down, it still felt better when she had it propped up. "So," she hypothesized, "first Manny gets killed, and then whoever does that takes his keys and goes to Clara Randall's house to find something. He lets himself in, closing the door behind him, and goes up the stairs. Clara is just coming out of the bathroom and she sees him and screams, and this person goes in, and either accidentally or on purpose pushes her and she hits her head on the bedpost and dies."

"That's certainly a plausible scenario," Sean commented. "Clara as collateral damage. I wonder what he was looking for."

"If what I'm saying is true," Bernie said.

"There is that," Sean agreed.

He gazed out the window. It was still pouring. The streets were empty, except for a few people running for cover. The streetlights were coming on and they reflected on the pavement. A gust of wind whipped the branches of the ash tree in front of the shop. Hopefully, the storm would blow through in another hour or so.

"I don't suppose you'd like to go out," Sean asked Cindy.

She didn't bother replying.

"Just like a woman," he said, and petted her some more. Cindy began to purr. It was a deep purr that filled the house. "You know what I would do," Sean said after another minute had gone by. "I would talk to Ellen and see who else she told her plan to."

"That's what we were planning to do, Dad," Libby said. "But first we have to find her."

"Ask her husband," Sean suggested.

"We did," Bernie said. "He says she's out doing an errand."

"What kind of errand?"

Bernie shook her head. "He won't tell me or he doesn't know, and even if he did know he won't tell me. I'm not on his good side at the moment. He blames me for what happened."

"They don't have a good marriage, do they?" Sean commented.

Bernie snorted. "That's putting it mildly," she said.

"Bruce Hadley." Sean said the name slowly. "I heard something about him recently. I just can't remember what it was."

"Maybe Clyde would know," Libby suggested.

"Maybe," Sean said, and reached for the phone to call him at home. This time the cat didn't move. "He doesn't," he informed his daughters after he'd spoken to him.

"Maybe Brandon does," Bernie suggested, ringing him up. The call went to voice mail but he called her back five minutes later.

Bernie could hear voices intermingled with the sound of the TV and the clinking of glasses in the background. "Busy night?" she asked.

"Busier than I would expect considering that it's a weekday," Brandon answered. "So what's up, Tiger Lily?"

Bernie gave him the condensed version.

"Bruce Hadley, hunh?" Brandon said. "Yeah, he's in some deep doo-doo." And he told Bernie what he knew.

"So what did he say?" Libby asked Bernie after Brandon had hung up.

Bernie sneezed. She hoped the zinc worked and nipped the cold in the bud. "Evidently Bruce's business is in trouble," she replied. "He's behind on his state and federal taxes as well as being three months behind on the taxes for his apartment building. The county is about to sell it to the Land Trust."

"No wonder he hasn't been paying any attention to Ellen," Libby observed. "I'd say he's been a little preoccupied."

Bernie shifted her position. "I wonder if Ellen knows. Somehow, I'm guessing not."

"How could she not?" Libby demanded.

"Maybe because Bruce hasn't told her," Bernie replied.

"More to the point, how does Brandon know?" Sean asked, interrupting.

"The way he always knows everything," Bernie replied. "He overheard it. Bruce's partner was in RJ's for a drink last week. Brandon heard him talking to one of his friends."

Sean continued to pet Cindy. "It's interesting information; in fact it might help rule him out."

"How so?" Libby asked. "I'd think the opposite."

Sean paused for a moment to organize his thoughts, then started talking. "According to Brandon, Bruce needs money, agreed?"

Libby and Bernie nodded. "Agreed," they chorused.

"So in that case it would behoove him to take out a big insurance policy on Ellen and kill her and collect the money—theoretically speaking."

"He could have. We don't know that he hasn't," Bernie pointed out.

"That's true," Sean said, "we don't. But Ellen isn't dead, Manny Roget is, and Ellen is being framed for the murder. She's on the verge of expanding her business, so having her arrested is not going to be in Bruce's interest. In fact, just the opposite is true. If Ellen goes to jail the family loses a second income stream, not to mention the attendant legal fees."

"I can see why Bruce is so pissed," Bernie allowed.

The cat got up, stretched, turned around, lay back down on Sean's lap, and began butting her head against his hand. Sean absentmindedly rubbed the tips of her ears as he continued speaking. "It seems to me we have two questions here. The first is, who benefits from Manny Roget's death? And the second is, was Ellen selected as the fall guy or was this happenstance?

"Did someone just happen to see your friend leaving the motel and think, oh there's a good place to park a body? I would say the probability of that happening is fairly low. All things being equal, we might want to start with Manny. Why did he come back? More importantly, why did Ellen pretend she didn't know who he was?"

Sean shook his finger at Bernie and Libby. "If you ask me, that's the crux of the matter. Answer that and you'll have the answers to everything."

Then, before Sean could say anything else, the downstairs door opened and shut and footsteps came thundering up the stairs. Cindy jumped off Sean's lap, scampered into Bernie's bedroom, and hid under the bed.

"Who's that?" Sean demanded as Matt and Ryan Hadley came bursting through the door.

They were both soaked to the skin.

"We found something," Matt cried, shaking the water out of his hair like a puppy dog.

"Yeah," Ryan added. "You gotta see this."

"This had better be good," Bernie said, pointing to the clock on the wall. "Do you have any idea what time it is?"

"We do now," Ryan chirped.

Chapter 22

Y ou're not helping your cause," Sean growled. "But . . ." Ryan began.

Sean glared at him and Ryan stopped talking and looked down at the floor.

"Do you not believe in knocking?" Sean asked him. "Calling would be even better. Do you just barge into people's houses whenever you feel like it? You should be glad I didn't shoot you!"

"Sorry." Matt looked sheepish.

"Me too," Ryan said.

Matt wiped drops of rain off his face with his forearm. "It's just that this is important."

"It really is," Ryan said, backing his brother up. "It couldn't wait."

"At least pull your shorts up," Sean instructed. "They're down around your knees."

Ryan scowled, but he did what Sean asked.

Libby got up, went to the bathroom, got two towels, and offered them to the boys. "Here," she said. "Dry yourselves off. Now, what's this all about?" she asked when they were done.

"We found something," Matt repeated. "Something important."

"And what would that be?" Sean asked skeptically.

"It's in these e-mails. Lisa, my mom's partner, is telling her something bad is going to happen if she doesn't go along with the deal. That's important, right?"

"It could be," Sean conceded.

Matt unzipped the backpack he was carrying, took out a sheaf of papers, walked over, and handed them to Bernie. "I figure that Lisa killed that guy and tried to pin it on my mom. Just read these and you'll see why I'm saying that."

"You will," Ryan said. "For sure. No question about it."

Bernie looked at the papers in her hand. As far as she could tell they were printouts of Ellen Hadley's e-mail correspondence. "How did you get these?" she asked Matt.

Matt and Ryan looked at each other and shrugged.

"Seriously," Bernie said.

"It was easy," Matt replied. "We just logged in and printed them out."

"So your mom's account isn't password protected?" Libby asked.

"No. Yes." Matt and Ryan spoke simultaneously.

"Which is it?" Bernie asked them.

"It isn't," Matt said.

Bernie looked at Ryan. "Is it?" she inquired.

Ryan bit his lip. He looked down at the floor, unable to meet her eyes. "Yeah," he muttered.

"That's what I thought," Bernie said. "So you hacked in? Answer me," she demanded when Ryan didn't reply.

"More or less," Ryan conceded.

Libby leaned forward. "Is it more or less?"

"More," Ryan conceded.

"Are we in trouble?" Matt asked. "Are you going to tell our mom?"

"No, on both counts," Bernie said, the answer coming out without her thinking about it. As far as she was concerned, that was the least of Ellen's problems at the moment. "So which one of you did it?"

Ryan and Matt exchanged more glances.

Ryan raised his hand. "I did."

"Are you good?" Bernie asked.

A small smile played around the corners of Ryan's mouth. "Very," he said proudly.

"Bernie," Libby cried. She saw where this was going.

Bernie ignored her and focused her attention on Ryan.

"Why do you want to know?" Ryan asked.

Bernie shrugged. "Just curious."

Ryan yanked up his shorts again. "I can get into pretty much anything."

Bernie smiled. "Good to know. The way things are going, we may need your services."

"Seriously?" Matt asked.

"I was kidding," Bernie said.

"No you weren't," Ryan replied.

"You're right. I wasn't," Bernie said.

"Sweet," Ryan said, beaming.

"Excellent," Matt replied. "You know we'd do anything for Mom."

"You should probably tell her that," Bernie said.

"Bernie," Libby repeated, more loudly this time.

This time Bernie turned and faced her sister. "Why not?" she said to Libby. "I figure we can use all the help we can get."

It was not a statement Libby could dispute.

Matt interrupted. "Excuse me."

Both Bernie and Libby looked at him. He shuffled his feet.

"I don't mean to be rude or anything," he said.

"But?" Libby asked.

"I was just wondering if you had any more of that stuff you gave us the last time. It was so good."

"Stuff?" Bernie asked.

"Food."

Libby grinned. "I think we can find something

for you guys. Do you want brownies, blondies, or lemon squares?"

"We'll take whatever you want to give us," Matt said.

"Everything my mom bakes tastes like dog biscuits," Ryan said as Libby got up. "And Dad made this awful spaghetti with green globs in it for dinner. It was disgusting. Nobody could eat it, not even Dad."

"You mean pesto?" Bernie asked.

"Yeah," Ryan said. "What's wrong with mac 'n cheese?"

Bernie chuckled as she watched them go out the door. She could hear them on the stairs as she called Ellen. Ellen didn't pick up. She texted her. No response. Ellen was certainly back by now.

"Answer," she muttered under her breath before she left her a message. She was beginning to get seriously annoyed. And worried. Bernie just hoped that Ellen hadn't done anything stupid, or stupider, than she already had.

Bernie and Sean were reading through Ellen Hadley's e-mails to Lisa when Libby came up twenty minutes later bearing a pitcher of iced mint tea made with real mint, a plate of thin-sliced chocolate chip banana bread, plus a saucer of milk for Cindy.

"What did you give the kids?" Bernie asked as Libby set the tray down on the coffee table and put the saucer on the floor. Cindy emerged from the bedroom, ran over, and started drinking. Evidently she'd forgiven the boys' interruption.

"I boxed up eight brownies, three lemon squares, and the five blondies we had left from this morning. I told them to save some for Ethan, but I'm betting they'll be gone before they get home."

Bernie thought of what they'd eaten when they'd come over the last time. "I'd say that's a good bet," she agreed, while Libby poured everyone a glass of tea and passed around the banana bread.

"So what did you find?" Libby asked after she sat down.

Sean took a sip of his tea, then put it down on the side table. "Let me just say that I think the boys have exaggerated somewhat." He held out the sheaf of papers to Libby. "Here—take a look."

Libby took them and began reading. The e-mails went from Ellen saying she didn't think that renting another work space was such a good idea, to her saying she'd be damned if she was going to be run out of her own business. For her part, Lisa said she wasn't going to be held back by someone like Ellen and it was her business as much as Ellen's, a fact that Ellen disagreed with in no uncertain terms.

I INVENTED THE RECIPES. I NAMED THE BUSINESS. ME. NOT YOU.

Lisa responded with STOP LISTENING TO YOUR HUSBAND. HE'S DEAD WEIGHT.

Ellen wrote back WHAT ABOUT YOURS?

The last three e-mails had been in capital letters.

"Hardly a basis to say that Lisa is our killer," Libby said. "Besides"—she closed her eyes, trying to picture Lisa Stone—"isn't she a little wisp of a thing?"

"Yeah," Bernie said. "If she weighs a hundred pounds she weighs a lot. But look at the fifth e-mail in. The one that begins 'I see no need . . .'"

Libby found it and read it. "'Lisa, I see no need to hire anyone to sell our products. I think we can do that ourselves.'" She put the paper back. "Manny? Is that who you think she's referring to?"

"I'm thinking yes."

Libby checked the date on the e-mail. It was six months ago. "So Lisa was the one who hired him, not Ellen?"

"So it would seem from the e-mails," Bernie said. "But that still doesn't mean Ellen didn't know who it was when she saw Manny lying on the bed."

Libby waved her hand around. "Of course she did. Even if she didn't recognize him from back in the day, even if she knew him by a different name, she had to have known who he was. He was delivering orders for them, for heaven's sake.

At least, that's what it says here," and she nodded at the papers Matt had given her.

Bernie searched for her phone and called Ellen again. The phone rang for a while before it went to voice mail. "Call me," Bernie said. "Call me whenever you get this message." Then she hung up.

"Maybe she really doesn't want to talk to you," Libby observed.

"I guess not," Bernie said. "She's probably too upset."

"Either that or she needs time to come up with a really good explanation."

Bernie sighed. She was thinking it, but she wasn't going to say it. "We should talk to Lisa Stone," she said instead.

"Yes, we should," Sean agreed. "What do we know about her anyway?"

Libby thought for a moment. Then she said, "We know that she never comes into the shop."

"Besides that," Sean said.

"We know that she's rich. Or rather that her husband is," Bernie added.

"And that they moved back here from the city about five . . ."

"Ten," Bernie corrected.

"Fine, ten years ago to be with Lisa's mom."

Sean snapped his fingers. "Mindy Wood. She died in a car accident. A hit-and-run. They never found out who did it."

"I remember it being very sad," said Bernie. She had a vague recollection of the event. "We also know that the Stones have two young children."

"What does the husband do?" Sean asked.

"Jeremy? I heard he's in real estate," Bernie replied. "Though I'm not really sure exactly what he does in it. I know Lisa used to do some sort of public relations stuff for one of the big firms in the city."

"Are Lisa and Ellen good friends?" Sean asked.

"Wrong tense. They were before they went into business with each other," Bernie answered.

Sean grunted. "Not an unusual situation."

"Maybe she knows where Ellen is," Bernie said.

"Ellen will be in touch," Libby reassured her.

"I know," Bernie replied. "I just hope she hasn't done anything else stupid."

"Like what?" Libby asked.

Bernie shrugged her shoulders. "I don't know. She's just so impulsive."

"She'll be fine," Libby said.

"Probably," Bernie replied, hoping that what her sister was saying was true.

Bernie's nervousness morphed into restlessness. She began tapping her fingers on her leg. She wanted to call Lisa, but she didn't have her phone number, or her husband's for that matter, and there was no listed house number. Not that she was surprised. Landlines were becoming a thing of the past.

She turned to Libby. "How about going for a ride?" she asked.

"Now?" Libby's voice rose. She was ready to go to bed.

"Of course now. Don't you want to hear what Lisa has to say?"

"I do—tomorrow. She's probably getting ready to go to sleep. Like all sensible people," Libby couldn't resist adding. "Anyway, this isn't about Lisa, is it? It's about Ellen. I thought we agreed she's going to be fine."

Bernie made a face. "We did, but I'd just like to make sure she's okay. It's not like Ellen to be out of touch like this."

"Maybe the police have finally picked her up," Libby suggested.

"Clyde would have let us know," Bernie countered.

"Then maybe she lost her phone. Or it lost power. Or how's this? Maybe she just doesn't want to talk to you right now."

Sean leaned forward. "Bernie, if you're really that concerned, I can take you," he said.

Libby looked from her sister to her dad and back again. No way was her father driving at night in the rain. "I'll go," she grumbled. "But I think it's going to be a waste of time."

As it turned out, Libby was right. They drove by Ellen's house, the Riverview, RJ's, and Lisa's house for good measure, as well as Skylar Park, but they didn't spot Ellen's car anywhere. *But at least we tried,* Bernie reasoned as they drove home with the raindrops pelting the windshield and the wind tossing the magnolia blossoms onto the ground.

Chapter 23

It was one o'clock in the afternoon the following day when Bernie and Libby left A Little Taste of Heaven and set out for Lisa Stone's house. The sisters had intended on getting an earlier start, but the dishwasher had backed up and they'd had to wait for the plumber to come, as well as deal with a rush order for several strawberry cream pies. The good news was that it had finally stopped raining, leaving the streets and the grass glistening. The bad news was that no one had heard from Ellen. Or if they had, they weren't telling Bernie.

On the way to Lisa Stone's house, Bernie spotted a rainbow over the Hudson River. "Look," she said, pointing at it.

"That's nice." Libby barely glanced at it as she kept driving. She just wanted to get this interview with Lisa Stone over with and get back to the shop. She had too much to do.

Ten minutes later, Libby pulled onto the winding road that led to Lisa Stone's residence.

Sited on top of Fortescue Hill, the house had been built in the forties and was, as the real estate people liked to say, "loaded with charm." It was fieldstone on the bottom and wood on top, with window boxes filled with pansies and greenery on the lower levels. A trellis with deep red climbing roses ran up in a narrow band on the left side of the house.

"Nice," Bernie said as they drove up to the house past banks of daylilies and ferns.

"If you care for perfection," Libby said sourly.

She did not do well on three hours' worth of sleep. She parked as close to the house as possible before getting out and climbing the stairs. Bernie joined her a moment later. Inside they could hear the sound of a Spanish soap opera on the television. Bernie rang the doorbell. A moment later, a heavyset Hispanic-looking woman dressed in jeans, a black T-shirt, and sneakers came to the door. She was holding a dust rag in one hand and a bottle of furniture polish in the other.

"Yes?" she asked in heavily accented English. When Bernie explained what she wanted she shook her head and replied that neither Mr. or Mrs. Stone was here.

"And Ellen?" Bernie asked. "Ellen Hadley?"

The woman looked at her for a moment. Then said, "Who this?"

"Mrs. Stone's business partner," Bernie replied.

"Ah," the woman said, her expression revealing nothing. "*Claro*."

"*Claro* what?" Bernie asked.

The woman looked at her as if she didn't understand what Bernie was saying, although Bernie had a feeling that she did.

"Ellen Hadley *está aquí*?" Bernie asked, using her high school Spanish.

The woman shrugged her shoulders.

"*Es importante*," Bernie said. The feeling she had about this woman became a conviction. Not only did this woman understand English, she knew something about Ellen Hadley. Bernie was positive of it.

"I go now," the woman said, but she didn't move. Instead she smiled and looked Bernie up and down.

"*Un momento*," Bernie told her, having gotten what the woman wanted.

The woman crossed her arms over her chest and waited.

Bernie turned to Libby. "How much money do you have on you?"

Her sister's eyes narrowed. "Why?"

"How much?"

"A couple of hundred."

Bernie held out her hand. "Give me a hundred."

"Are you kidding me? No."

"I'll pay it back," Bernie said. She raised her hand. "I swear."

"Use your own money."

"I forgot my wallet in the flat."

Libby made a face. "How convenient."

"Please," Bernie begged her sister, as the woman in the doorway looked with interest at the scene unfolding on the doorstep.

"All I can say is you'd better give this back to me," Libby said as she dug into her wallet and handed Bernie five twenty-dollar bills.

"Ellen Hadley *está aquí*?" Bernie asked again, holding out a twenty-dollar bill.

The woman thought for a moment. Then she switched the furniture polish to her left hand, held out her right hand, and said in unaccented English, "I'll take the five twenties if you please, and by the way, your Spanish is terrible. It's *estuvo* not *está*. That is if you're talking about the past tense, which I take it you are."

Bernie handed the money over. "Everyone's a comedian."

The woman counted it and slipped it in her jeans pocket. "Thank you."

Now it was Bernie's turn to cross her arms over her chest and wait for the woman to begin. After a minute she did.

She said, "Your friend was here about three in the morning. She rang the bell and woke everyone up. There was this big fight between Mr. and Mrs. Stone and your friend."

Bernie uncrossed her arms and leaned forward.

"What were they saying? What was it about?"

The woman pointed to the garage. "I live on the second floor, so I didn't get most of it, although they did wake me up with their shouting. The only thing I did hear was Ellen yelling something about Manny's wife and that she knew that this would happen, and Mr. Stone was screaming it was none of Ellen Hadley's business, and Mrs. Stone was crying and telling everyone to calm down. Then the boys came down and wanted to know what was going on, and Mrs. Stone took them off to bed, and that was the end of that."

"And afterward?" Libby asked.

"I'm not sure," the woman said. "I heard the front door to the house slam, and then I heard a car take off. I presume it was Ellen Hadley's. Then nothing." She shrugged. "I turned over and went back to sleep."

"Are you sure you heard right about Manny's wife?" Libby asked her.

The woman nodded. "Pretty sure. It's not as if I was right there. And now if you'll excuse me, I have to finish my work before the señora of the house returns." This time she turned and went inside.

Chapter 24

Manny married," Bernie mused out loud as she and Libby climbed back into Mathilda.

"Interesting." Bernie closed the van door. It stuck a little and she reminded herself to get that taken care of. "Not that there's any reason he shouldn't be. Maybe that's why he came back after all these years."

"If that woman is telling the truth," Libby said.

"Why shouldn't she be?"

Libby snorted. "Because she lied."

"About what?" Bernie protested.

Libby pulled out of the driveway. "Not speaking English when she did."

Bernie rolled down the window. It was getting warm out. "I'd call that playing the game."

"And I'd call it lying by omission. Well, at least we know where Ellen was at three this morning." Libby slowed down to let a doe and two fawns cross the road.

Bernie watched them disappear into a grove of birch trees. She knew they were annoying, that they ate everyone's plants, but she loved to watch them anyway.

"The question is where is Ellen now?" She'd tried calling her earlier in the day and gotten no response.

"Probably sleeping," Libby guessed.

"But where?" Bernie said. They'd already driven by Ellen's hangout places and there'd been no sign of her.

"Hopefully Lisa will know," Libby said.

"Hopefully," Bernie said as she got out her cell, called their dad, and asked him to check out Manny's marital status. After Bernie hung up, she rolled the window down some more, closed her eyes, and concentrated on the smell of lilacs permeating the air.

"What are you thinking about?" Libby asked after five minutes had gone by.

Bernie opened her eyes. "Nothing," she said, surprising herself with her answer. "Absolutely nothing. I'm just enjoying the sunshine and how sweet everything smells after the winter."

"It was long," Libby allowed.

"And brutal," Bernie rejoined.

"This is true," Libby said. It had been so bad it had gotten her thinking of moving to Florida.

There was no traffic on Route 76 at that time of the day and the sisters made it to Croton in a little under twenty minutes. Then they rode around for another ten minutes looking for the building that Lisa and Ellen had rented. They finally found it at the south end of the park hidden behind three warehouses, a storage unit, and a factory that made cardboard boxes.

"This must be it," Libby said, stopping in front

of an unnumbered, unmarked rectangular building constructed of cinderblocks and spray painted an ugly shade of gray. There was one vehicle, a Range Rover, parked by the door. Ellen's Subaru was nowhere in sight.

"I'm not sure I'd want to be here at night," Libby commented as she got out of Mathilda.

"I wouldn't want to be here day or night," observed Bernie. She pushed the van door open. "Too depressing. I'd want to shoot myself."

As the sisters got closer to the door, they could hear the sounds of hard rock blaring out of the building.

"Not the music I'd choose to bake to," Bernie observed as she knocked on the door.

When no one answered she opened the door and stepped inside. The space had been divided into a small, dimly lit hallway that led off into three work areas, two of which appeared to be vacant. The third space was occupied by Arf, as the hand-lettered sign tacked to the door made clear. This time Bernie didn't knock. She walked in. Lisa was standing over a prep table weighing out flour and pouring it into a mixer. Evidently, she and Ellen hadn't gotten a new one yet. Bernie looked around. The space was certainly larger than Ellen Hadley's basement. It was rigged out with three large commercial ovens, a dishwasher, two double sinks, and two large coolers.

"Nice setup," Bernie said to Lisa's back. "You

can certainly pump out a lot of product here."

Lisa whirled around. "Oh," she said when she realized who it was. "You scared me."

"Sorry, we didn't mean to," Bernie replied, noting as she did that Lisa looked as if she hadn't gotten much sleep the night before or the night before that either. Her blond hair had a cowlick sticking straight up in the back of her head, her skin looked blotchy because she wasn't wearing any makeup, and her clothes were rumpled.

"We're looking for Ellen," Libby said.

"Figured," Lisa said. "So is everyone. Why should you be different?"

"So have you . . . ?" Bernie asked.

"Seen her?"

"Yes."

Lisa weighed out two more scoops of flour and put them in the mixer. "Sorry, but I can't say that I have."

"Can you say that you haven't?" Libby asked.

Lisa put down the scoop she was using and dusted off her hands. "I don't think I have time for word games right now."

Bernie leaned against the prep table to take the weight off her foot. "Neither do we. So you would tell us if you'd seen her?"

Lisa's hand went up to her necklace, a large tear-shaped diamond on a gold chain. She began unconsciously moving the charm back and forth. "Of course I would."

"So you definitely haven't seen her," Libby said.

Lisa shook her head. She looked slightly annoyed. "That's what I just said, isn't it? How many times do I have to repeat that?"

"Or heard from her?" Libby continued.

"No, I haven't heard from her," Lisa said exasperatedly.

"That's too bad," Bernie replied. She was extremely impressed by Lisa's ability to lie. Nothing in her expression suggested she was telling anything other than the truth. If Bernie didn't know better, she'd believe her.

"Yes, it is," Lisa continued. "It would be nice if I did." She nodded to the prep table. "After all, these dog biscuits aren't going to bake themselves." She frowned. "Ellen knows we have a big order due. She knows this is make it or break it time for us. I can't believe she isn't here."

Bernie gestured toward Lisa's phone, then pointed to the overhead fan. "Do you think you could lower the volume? I'm having trouble hearing."

"Well, I'm not," Lisa said.

Bernie leaned over, picked up Lisa's phone, and turned the music off. The silence was overwhelming. "Well, I am," Bernie said.

Lisa let go of her necklace. "You can't do that," she squawked.

"I just did. We need to talk."

"Then make an appointment like any other

normal human being," Lisa spluttered. "You know, you just can't walk in here and invade my space."

Bernie smiled pleasantly. "That description seems a tad extreme."

"There's a law against that."

"I doubt it, but I could be wrong. There are laws against lots of things," Bernie observed.

Lisa sniffed. "I have a good mind to call the police."

"Go right ahead," Bernie told her. She could tell that Lisa's heart wasn't in the threat. "But consider this: if you answer our questions, we'll be out of here in a couple of minutes, whereas if you call the police it'll take a good deal longer. I can promise you I'll make sure of that. Think about it," Bernie urged.

Lisa spent a minute weighing her options. She took a deep breath and let it out, after which she repeated the maneuver a second and a third time. *She looks like a guppy,* Bernie couldn't help thinking.

"Fine," Lisa said when she had calmed down. "What do you want to know? I already told you I haven't seen Ellen."

"Funny," Bernie said, "but that's one of the reasons we're here. See, Libby and I heard she came by your house early this morning."

"Who told you that?" Lisa snapped, her eyes suddenly alert.

"Ellen told me," Bernie lied.

"I thought you said you hadn't heard from her."

"No. I've heard from her. I haven't seen her. There's a difference."

"A very fine one."

"So what were you two fighting about?" Bernie asked.

Lisa gave a mirthless smile. "If you spoke to her, then I'm sure you know, so why don't you tell me."

"You were fighting about Manny," Bernie said, repeating what the housekeeper had told her earlier.

Lisa didn't say anything, but she didn't have to, Bernie thought. This time her face gave her away. She blinked several times, then looked down at the floor and back again. Bernie could see she'd gotten it right.

Gratified, Bernie continued. "Ellen knew who Manny was, right?"

"Obviously," Lisa replied.

"Just checking." Bernie moved her ring up and down her finger. "So why did Ellen tell me she didn't know who he was when she saw him lying on the bed in the motel?"

"You'll have to ask her that question yourself," Lisa responded. "I have no idea. Who knows why Ellen does anything? I certainly don't."

"So your husband knew Manny," Bernie said, abruptly changing topics.

Lisa placed her hands on her hips and jutted her chin forward. "What if he did? What's your point?"

"Nothing," Libby said, stepping into the conversation. "We were just curious, my sister and I. How does Jeremy know him?"

Lisa shrugged. "It's a complicated story and I don't remember all the details."

Libby reached over and moved a spatula away from the prep table's edge. "How about the details you do recall?"

"I really don't remember any," Lisa hedged. "Like I just said, you'd better ask Jeremy."

"We intend to," Bernie said. She continued playing with her ring. "I guess I was surprised to see Manny back, considering the way he left. I mean if it was me, I don't think I'd want to come back here. Too many bad memories."

"Neither would I," Lisa conceded. "But I guess everyone's different."

"I'm surprised you hired him given the circumstances. I'm not sure I would have," Bernie said.

"Well, I don't think he did what they said he did," Lisa replied. "I think he was framed by Melinda and Kitty, and anyway, that was a long time ago."

"Is that what Ellen thinks?" Libby asked.

Lisa shrugged. "I have no idea. Not that it matters. She wouldn't have wanted to hire anyone even if he was the Angel Gabriel himself."

Bernie laughed. "Really?"

"Yes, really. She's the kind of person who never wants to move forward. She always sees the glass as half empty instead of half full." Lisa put her hands on her hips. "Tell me that isn't true."

"It is," Bernie admitted. "Ellen definitely has her issues. As do we all," she hastily added.

"Exactly," Lisa said, warming to the topic. "I mean it's one thing being friends, but it's another trying to run a business together. Ellen never sees the larger picture."

Bernie made a face. "Eventually she does, but it takes a while. Libby and I are trying to help Ellen out but—"

Lisa interrupted. "I don't envy you."

Bernie sighed. "It's been tough," she admitted, feeling disloyal.

Lisa shook her head and put on a more sorrowful than angry face. "Ellen is her own worst enemy. Always has been as long as I've known her. But I don't have to tell you that. If you come to a turn in the road and going east is the good choice and going west is the bad one, Ellen will always go west."

Bernie bit her lip. What Lisa was saying was true. Nevertheless that had nothing to do with what she and Lisa were discussing now. "Speaking of bad choices, did Ellen tell you about her plan?"

Lisa cocked her head. "Are you talking about a business plan, because Ellen doesn't have one. I can tell you that right off the bat. She's more of the 'I'll-bake-and-they-will-come' school of business."

"No," Libby said. "My sister is talking about her plan to kidnap herself. Did she mention that to you?"

Lisa snorted. "Oh God. That stupid thing! I told her not to do it. I told her to go to Barneys and get a whole new wardrobe if she was feeling that way. That would certainly get Bruce's attention. . . . It always gets Jeremy's, but she wouldn't listen. Like I said, she really is her own worst enemy. What more proof do you need than that?"

"Do you know if Ellen told anyone else?" Bernie asked. She started playing with the spatula again and made herself stop.

"Of course she did," Lisa replied. Her hand crept up to her diamond teardrop charm again. "You know how Ellen is. She gets upset, she just starts yakking away. She told everyone. The question is who didn't she tell?"

"Everyone?" Bernie repeated. "Could you be more specific?"

Lisa dropped her hand to the prep table and began tapping her fingers on it. "Well, I know that she told me. I know that she told the woman who does her nails."

"How do you know that?" Libby asked.

"Because we both go to Kim and when I went in there, Kim told me she thought that Ellen's kidnap plan was one of the stupidest things she'd ever heard and heaven only knows who she told. Given Ellen, she could have told the crossing guard at the school or the cashier at Whole Foods."

Libby unwrapped a square of seventy percent dark chocolate that had been manufactured in Brooklyn and popped it in her mouth. Suddenly she realized she was hungry. Possibly because she hadn't had any lunch.

"So Bruce could have known about Ellen's plan?" Libby asked.

Lisa gave Libby an incredulous look. "Of course, Bruce knew about Ellen's plans."

"Why are you so sure?" Bernie asked.

"Because my husband told him, that's why I'm so sure," Lisa replied.

Chapter 25

Bernie's eyes widened. "Wow."

She was stunned. So for that matter was Libby, who wondered if she'd heard right. When she looked at her sister she could see Bernie was thinking the same thing.

"Why would Jeremy do something like that?" Libby asked after a couple of seconds had elapsed.

"Why?" Lisa repeated. Her voice rose slightly. "What do you mean *why?* It's obvious."

"Not to us," Bernie said, pointing to herself and her sister.

"Because I told him to." Lisa slowed down her speech as if she was talking to a four-year-old. "Jeremy and I discussed it and we both came to the same conclusion. We thought that what Ellen was about to do was wrong and we thought that Bruce should have a heads-up. I know he tends to be a little on the . . . bossy side . . . but he's going through a rough time now and the last thing he needed was something like this."

Libby shifted her weight to her other foot. "So how did Bruce react when Jeremy told him?"

"Jeremy said he was pissed. Wouldn't you be?"

"For sure," Bernie answered. "Did he say anything?"

"Jeremy said Bruce told him that he was going to teach Ellen a lesson she'd never forget."

"Well, Bruce certainly managed to accomplish that with Manny," Bernie observed.

"Don't be ridiculous," Lisa shot back. "Bruce would never do something like that. Cut off Ellen's credit cards, yes; kill someone and leave their body on the bed for her to find? No. Absolutely not. We're not talking about the Mafia here."

Bernie shrugged. "I don't know. Maybe Manny and Ellen were having an affair and Bruce found out and, as you said, decided to teach Ellen a lesson."

"Ellen and Manny an item?" Lisa scoffed. "No way. She doesn't like beards or tattoos or men with earrings. They're a turnoff to her. She's a total prep when it comes to guys. You know that."

"Except for Damion," said Bernie. "The professional wrestler."

"I'd forgotten about him," Lisa admitted.

"She was with him for a couple of months."

"I don't think it was that long," Lisa said.

Bernie was about to reply when Libby jumped into the conversation. "You're missing the point," she said to Lisa. "The point is that whoever killed Manny and planted him in the bed had to have known that Ellen had left the room."

"If Ellen's telling the truth," Lisa said.

"We're assuming she is," Bernie informed her.

"Fine then," Lisa said. "Maybe putting Manny there was a totally random act."

"And maybe," Bernie said, "there really is a pot of gold at the end of the rainbow and the cow jumped over the moon."

Lisa glared at Bernie. "So you're suggesting it wasn't?"

Bernie nodded. "That I am."

Lisa put her hand up to her throat. "But that would mean that Manny was killed by someone who knew where Ellen was and wanted to frame her," Lisa protested in an amazed tone of voice.

Bernie managed to keep herself from saying, *I'm shocked, simply shocked and appalled.* Instead she said, "Exactly. That's the assumption we're working on."

"And you"—Libby nodded in Lisa's direction—"your husband, and Bruce did know."

Lisa made an incredulous face. "You're suggesting that Jeremy and I had something to do with Manny's death?"

"My sister isn't suggesting anything," Bernie told her. "She's just pointing out a fact."

"It's not a fact," Lisa countered. "It's a supposition. There are lots of other people who could have known about Ellen's plan."

"So you've said," Bernie replied.

"I'm serious," Lisa said.

Bernie crossed her arms over her chest. "So am I."

She didn't say anything else. Neither did Libby. The three women stood there listening to the *beep beep* of a truck backing up. Finally Lisa couldn't stand the silence anymore.

"I don't know who else knew about Ellen's plan," she said. "But I do know this. Jeremy had nothing to do with what happened. He had no reason to kill Manny and neither did I. I mean do either of us look like someone who would be capable of killing somebody?"

"Possibly. Murderers come in all shapes and sizes," Bernie replied.

Lisa raised an eyebrow. "Really?"

"Yes, really," Bernie said. "I should know."

"Yes, I guess you would," Lisa conceded.

"That's true of friends too," Bernie continued.

"Meaning?" Lisa asked.

"Well, there are friends and then there are pretend friends."

"Are you suggesting I'm the latter?"

"You said it, not me."

"I take it we're talking about Ellen."

"Who else?"

Lisa batted her eyelashes, giving a good imitation of someone being unfairly accused. "I've always been her friend," she protested.

"I don't know," Bernie said. "From where I stand, I'd call what you did selling her out."

Lisa's expression hardened. "If I were you, I wouldn't be so judgmental."

Bernie leaned forward. "So you still consider yourself Ellen's friend?"

"Yes. Definitely, even though we've been having a few business disagreements."

"Then why did you tell Bruce about Ellen's plan?"

"I didn't. My husband did."

Libby made a rude sound. "Please. Give me a break. Unless my mind is going, you just told Bernie and me that you told Jeremy about Ellen's plan, and that you both discussed it and you decided that Jeremy should tell Bruce. Is that correct?"

Lisa started to nibble on one of her nails, realized what she was doing, and touched her necklace again. "Truth?"

"Truth would be refreshing," Libby said.

Lisa bit her lip while she paced back and forth in front of the prep table. "I did tell Jeremy I thought it would be a good idea to tell Bruce what Ellen was planning," Lisa said, coming to a stop. "Now I wish I hadn't, but I just thought Ellen needed a wake-up call. I told her not to do what she was planning. I told her several times. I begged her not to. I begged her to talk to Bruce. I begged her to go back into therapy. It never occurred to me that something like Manny would have happened. Not in my wildest dreams. Do you believe me?"

"Yes," Bernie said, although she wasn't completely convinced.

Lisa sighed in relief. "Is there anything else you want to know?"

"About Manny," Bernie said.

"Yes," Lisa asked. "What about him?"

"Why did you hire him?" Bernie asked. She'd found that sometimes if she asked the same question again she'd get a different answer. This time she didn't.

"I already told you we needed someone and he was there," Lisa promptly answered. "If we're going to expand we need someone to fill orders, run errands, do deliveries." Lisa looked at Libby and Bernie. "You two of all people should realize that."

"I understand completely," Libby said. "But I

think what my sister is asking is how did Manny show up on your radar?"

Lisa smiled. "He'd gotten in touch with my husband. They'd had lunch together or something the day before. I think Jeremy said he wanted some advice."

"About what?" Libby asked. Jeremy seemed out of Manny's pay grade.

Lisa shrugged. "I don't know. I didn't ask, but at dinner that night I mentioned that we were thinking of hiring someone; Ellen wanted to volunteer her sons." Lisa rolled her eyes. "I didn't even want to think about that, so when Jeremy mentioned that Manny was looking for a job, I said okay. He had a driver's license and he seemed nice enough. I figured he could do the job, he was available, so it was a good fit."

"He wasn't working at the time?" Bernie asked.

"Not as far as I know," Lisa answered. "He told me he'd been striping but he'd been laid off."

Bernie cocked her head. "Striping?"

"Painting stripes on the roads," Lisa explained.

"Did you ask him for references?" Bernie continued.

Lisa shook her head. "No. Jeremy knew him. What more did I need? I called Manny up right away. Then I called Ellen up to tell her the good news. Let me tell you she was not happy."

"So how does your husband know Manny?" Libby asked.

Lisa shook her head in disbelief. "You're kidding me, right?"

"I wouldn't be asking if I knew," Bernie replied.

Lisa's hand crept up toward her necklace again. "He and Jeremy are brothers-in-law, or ex-brothers-in law, I should say."

"Really?" Bernie said. Whatever she'd been expecting, it wasn't this.

"Yup. This was a long time ago. Manny married Daisy when they were both out in Colorado. The marriage didn't last very long, but Jeremy told me he wanted to help Manny out for old time's sake."

"As simple as that," Bernie said.

"Yes. As simple as that," Lisa answered.

"What did Ellen say about Manny?" Libby asked.

"I already told you. She wanted to hire her son. She said he'd work for free. She didn't think hiring someone was necessary, but then she never wants to spend money. We'd still be in her basement if I hadn't forced her to sign the lease for this place."

"Have you ever thought that maybe she's right about keeping things small?" Bernie asked.

"She's not," Lisa replied with utter conviction in her voice. "You grow your business or you die. The trick is to be able to expand and be bought out by some big corporation. That's the way things go these days."

"That's not what Ellen wants," Libby said. Even

she knew that. She reached into her pocket, brought out a square of chocolate, and popped it in her mouth. The chocolate had almost melted and Libby realized that soon it would be too hot to carry chocolate around.

Lisa made a dismissive noise. "That's because she's back with the dinosaurs."

"By those standards I guess we are too, but we're doing pretty well," Bernie replied. "I mean we're not going anyplace. We've stayed the same for years."

Lisa smiled. "But you have options," she pointed out. "You could expand or franchise."

"We don't want to," Libby replied. "We'd lose the whole character of the place if we did."

Bernie nodded her head in agreement.

"Which is fine if that's what you want," Lisa said in a patronizing tone. "Don't get me wrong. But Ellen and I want to go somewhere."

"Define somewhere," Libby demanded.

"In all the supermarkets," Lisa said. "We have a good product and it deserves to be on all the shelves."

"You mean *you* want to go somewhere." Bernie put air quotes around the word *you*. "Ellen maybe not so much."

Lisa put up her hand. "Oh no. She wants to, that's her dream. She just doesn't want to do what it takes to get there. She prefers to stay at home and fantasize about being rich and famous instead of getting out there and getting her hands dirty."

"That may be," Bernie said. "But I can tell you she's not very happy with the move."

"She'll come around and see this is for the best," Lisa said. "Like I said before, Ellen doesn't like change."

Bernie couldn't argue with that because it was true.

Lisa looked from Bernie to Libby and back again. "Any more questions before I get back to work?"

"Yes, one," Libby said. "For the record. One more time. Ellen definitely knew who Manny was?" She just wanted to make sure that Bernie couldn't argue with her later about that.

"Of course Ellen knew who Manny was," Lisa replied exasperatedly. "I already told you that twenty times."

"Four," Libby said.

"Whatever. How could Ellen not know? Manny came to her house. She gave him his deliveries. She paid him."

"Bruce said that you were in charge of deliveries," Bernie said.

Lisa shook her head. "I don't know where he gets that from. We both were."

Bernie nodded. Then she leaned over the prep table, turned Lisa's music back on, and thanked Lisa for talking to them. "Come on," she said to Libby. "I think we've heard enough."

"I knew it," Libby said when they walked outside. She shaded her eyes from the sun's glare. "I knew Ellen was lying to us."

"She probably had a reasonable explanation," Bernie replied.

"Like what?" Libby demanded. "Short of saving us from the clutches of a serial killer, I can't think of any."

Bernie was about to answer when her phone vibrated in her bag. She dug it out, read the text, then showed it to Libby.

"Come on," she said to her sister as she texted Ellen back. "Let's go before she changes her mind and takes off again."

"Well, I for one will definitely be interested in hearing what she has to say," Libby said as she climbed into Mathilda. "I'm going to love listening to her explain why she did what she did."

"You and me both, kiddo," Bernie replied with feeling. "You and me both."

Then she called her dad and asked him to find out what he could about Daisy Stone.

Chapter 26

F ifteen minutes later, the sisters were down at the other end of Skylar Park, the far end, the end that most people in Longely don't go to. As Bernie put on her sunglasses, she pondered why she didn't come up to this end more frequently. She really did like it a lot better. She liked the solitude and the sound of the waves slapping the shore. She liked watching the seagulls wheeling above the water.

This end didn't have benches for sitting or trails for walking, or fields for soccer or baseball. This end of the park was mostly boulders and scrub grass and trees interspersed with clumps of dandelions, daisies, violets, and drifts of speedwell. Wild turkeys lived here as well as a colony of feral cats and the occasional raccoon. Bernie had spotted a couple of eagles riding the thermals the last few times she'd been here. She'd been told they had an aerie not too far away.

Another reason no one came to this end of Skylar Park was that it was difficult to get to. You had to drive down a rutted, narrow access road and pull over onto the dirt to park. The road abutted a steep slope, which turned into a scree of pebble-sized rocks that led down to the marshy banks of the Hudson River. Ellen was standing on the gravel contemplating the river's debris-clogged dark waters when Libby and Bernie arrived. She could hear Mathilda coming and turned, waiting for the van to appear. She hugged herself as she watched Libby park the van and the sisters get out and scramble down the side of the hill.

"That was fast," she said to them when they reached her.

Bernie bent down and rubbed her ankle. The walk down the hill had irritated it. She decided she needed to wrap it again to give it more support.

"We didn't want you to disappear again," Libby explained. Ellen looked exhausted, Libby decided. She looked as if she was having trouble staying on her feet.

Ellen shrugged.

"What's the shrug supposed to mean?" The question came out harsher-sounding than Libby had intended, but she was tired too, and when she got tired she got irritable.

"It means I'm sorry if I've caused you any trouble."

"As well you should be," Libby told her, trying for a lighter tone.

As she studied Ellen, Libby realized that she looked more than exhausted. She seemed flattened, deflated, as if her will and energy had run out somewhere down the line.

Bernie took a step forward. "Why haven't you answered my calls?" she demanded.

"I needed time to think," Ellen stammered.

"About what?" Bernie said.

Ellen looked at her. Her eyes were glazed over and dull. "You know. About stuff. About the Riverview Motel."

"You mean about what happened to Manny?" Bernie asked.

"Yeah, Manny," Ellen said quickly—maybe a little too quickly, Bernie decided.

"You still could have called," Bernie told her. "We've been worried about you. Really worried."

"She's been worried about you," Libby couldn't help saying. "I've just been really annoyed. What the hell were you thinking, taking off like that? Bernie sprained her ankle chasing you and I got grabbed by your husband. He scared me half to death."

"Libby," Bernie said, warning her to be quiet.

Ellen held out her hand. "It's okay," she told Bernie. Her voice grew a little more animated. She turned to Libby. "You have every right to be angry," she said to her. "I just wanted to tell you guys why I did what I did. I wanted you to know."

"You mean why you ran away?" Bernie asked.

Ellen bit her lip. "Yes."

"Tell us," Bernie urged.

Ellen looked out over the water. "It's just so hard for me to talk about."

Bernie waited, not saying anything. Finally, after a couple of minutes, Ellen began.

"When I came back and saw Manny on the bed just lying there," she said, "I panicked."

"I can see that," Bernie said. A dragonfly buzzed around her head and she waved it off.

"My first thought was that you'd help me . . . you know . . . get rid of him . . . bury him or something." Ellen's voice faltered. She rubbed her shoulders. She was wearing a light cotton T-shirt and shorts and the breeze that had sprung up was making her feel cold. She wished she was wearing her jacket, but it was in her car, and she didn't have the energy to climb up the hill and go get it.

"So you told us," Libby said. Her tone of voice was not friendly.

"I'm truly sorry about that," Ellen told Bernie and Libby. "I was scared. I don't know what I was thinking. Then after I said it, when I saw your reaction, I realized how wrong I was to even think that."

"Why did you keep insisting you didn't know who Manny was?" Bernie asked.

Ellen laughed bitterly. "I think I thought that if I didn't admit I knew Manny, this thing wasn't happening. It would go away." She hugged herself tighter and walked in a tight circle to keep warm.

"So why did you run?" Libby asked.

"Because I heard you talking about calling the police. I just couldn't deal. It's like I've been dropped into the middle of a nightmare and I can't wake up."

"That's for sure," Bernie allowed. "So who do you think put Manny in the bed?" she asked.

Ellen turned and studied a tugboat going down the river. It was pushing a barge heaped with coal. "I don't know."

"Maybe someone who knew what you were going to do," Libby suggested.

"I've thought of that," Ellen admitted.

"Lisa tells me you told everyone," Bernie informed her.

Ellen turned back and faced Bernie. "No. I just told you and her."

"And the manicurist," Bernie said.

"That's true," Ellen admitted. "But I'm not sure she counts. Her English is very bad."

"Well, Lisa told her husband and Jeremy told your husband."

"That's what she told me when I was at her house the other night," Ellen said. She started biting her cuticles. "That's the thing, the awful thing." Ellen fell silent.

"What's the awful thing?" Bernie prompted.

"Everything. That this is all my fault," Ellen whispered. She covered her face with her hands and started to cry.

"Was that because you slept with Manny?" Bernie asked. The time for subtle was past.

Ellen raised her head. "It wasn't like that," she protested.

"So what was it like?" Bernie asked.

"We were friends. Good friends."

"Friends with benefits?" Libby said.

"No," Ellen cried. "Not at all. We liked the same things. He made me laugh."

"Unlike Bruce," Bernie observed.

Ellen didn't say anything.

Bernie crossed her arms over her chest and studied her friend.

"Why are you staring at me like that?" Ellen demanded.

"Are you sure you didn't sleep with Manny?" persisted Bernie.

Ellen looked away.

"You did, didn't you?" Bernie said.

Ellen's face fell. "Once. Just once," she whispered in such a low voice that Bernie had to lean in to hear her.

"Did Bruce know?" Libby asked.

Ellen shook her head. "Absolutely not."

"You're sure?" Libby demanded.

"Yes," Ellen said, but her voice wavered.

The three women were quiet for a moment. A tugboat guiding a barge down the river tooted its horn.

"Ellen, do you think Bruce killed Manny?" Bernie asked suddenly.

"No. No, I don't," Ellen cried.

"But you suspect it," Bernie said.

The fact that Ellen didn't reply told Bernie all she needed to know. Instead, Ellen studied the rocks under her feet. The wind had picked up and Bernie could see the goose bumps on Ellen's skin. Bernie tried to hug her, but Ellen waved her off. She sniffed and wiped her eyes with the back of her hands. Then she started to talk.

"I knew we shouldn't have hired Manny. I knew it. We didn't need him. I knew things wouldn't turn out well. Sometimes you just have this feeling in your gut and you have to go with that." Ellen made a fist and lightly hit herself in her stomach. "I told Lisa that, but she wouldn't listen. She never listens to anything I say. Just because she was this big PR person down in New York she thinks she knows it all. But she doesn't. If Manny hadn't come back none of this would have happened. There was no way we could keep them apart."

"Them?" Libby said. "Who are them?"

But instead of replying, Ellen bit her lip and turned to the river. She'd begun crying again. Tears were rolling down her cheeks. "It's all such a mess," Ellen said. "I can't believe things have gotten so out of hand."

"What's gotten out of hand?" Libby demanded.

Ellen just shook her head.

Libby threw up her hands in disgust. "Why did you ask us to come if you won't talk to us?"

Libby bit her lip and turned to watch a yacht tying off on a buoy two hundred feet from shore. At this moment she reckoned that Ellen had to be one of the most annoying people on the planet.

"Bruce wants me gone," Ellen said suddenly. "He doesn't love me anymore."

"Why are you saying that?" Bernie asked her friend.

Ellen looked away.

"Because he forgets your birthday?" Bernie said. "Lots of men do that. It's just not as important to him as it is to you."

"It not that," Ellen replied.

"Then what is it?" Bernie demanded. She was running out of patience. All this drama was exhausting her. "Just tell me why you said what you did."

Ellen began wringing her hands. "Because I heard Bruce on the phone. He was saying, 'This would be a good time to get rid of her.' Is that good enough for you? Is it?"

"Ellen, how do you know he was talking about you?" Bernie asked.

"Because he was. He was." Ellen balled up her hands into fists and stamped her feet. "I could tell. You have to believe me. You do."

Libby snorted in disgust. She found her mind wandering to her to-do list as she watched two gulls squabbling over a sub roll they'd found on the shore.

Ellen took two deep breaths, straightened up, and stepped away from Bernie. She cupped her hands, covered her mouth and nose with them, then brought them back down. "He was sleeping with Lisa," Ellen said. "My partner. My friend." She took another deep breath and let it out. "There. I've said it."

"Super," Libby said to no one in particular.

"Who would have thought we had our own little reality TV series going here? Maybe we could call it *Longely Housewives*?"

"Are you positive?" Bernie asked, ignoring her sister.

She hadn't detected even an iota of anything like that going on when she and Libby had talked to Lisa, but maybe that was because Lisa was just a good actress. Maybe that's why Lisa was so down on Ellen. Maybe it was because she felt guilty taking over Ellen's business and her husband in one fell swoop.

"Yes," Ellen whispered, her eyes misting up again. "And you know what's even worse? I deserve it. I deserve whatever I get."

"Well, you certainly are your own worst enemy," Libby observed, thinking about what Lisa had said. "That's for sure."

Ellen started sobbing again.

Chapter 27

S ean put down his newspaper and glanced up at the clock on the wall opposite him. It was a little after three in the afternoon and his daughters were supposed to have been home slightly over an hour ago.

"What do you know, they're back," he said to Cindy as Bernie and Libby walked through the door of the flat. Not that he was keeping track or anything.

The cat meowed in response.

"That took a while," he told Bernie as she closed the door.

She took a step and almost tripped over Clyde's fishing tackle, which was leaning against the wall. "Jeez. What is this doing here?"

"Clyde dropped it off for me."

"I see that. Can I put it somewhere else?" Bernie asked.

Sean shrugged. "Be my guest."

Sean watched as Bernie relocated the fishing gear to the far corner by the window. At least, Bernie reckoned, it would be out of the way there. Not for the first time she wished they lived in a slightly larger space.

"So how did it go?" Sean asked her.

"Could have been better," Bernie replied. "A lot better."

Sean decided that both his daughters looked hot, tired, and extremely annoyed.

"Problems?" he asked.

"Frustrations," Libby said.

Sean folded his newspaper and prepared to listen. "Tell the old man."

"After we eat," Libby announced. She trudged downstairs to rustle up a late afternoon snack for everyone.

"Bring up the deviled eggs if there are any left,"

Bernie yelled to her sister as she plopped herself down on the sofa.

Cindy jumped off Sean's lap, jumped up on the sofa, and began rubbing herself against Bernie's leg.

"It was that bad?" Sean asked.

Bernie began stroking Cindy's ears. "I wouldn't say bad, I'd say Libby and I are annoyed, hampered, impeded, and flummoxed."

Sean laughed. "It's nice to know your education hasn't gone to waste."

Bernie nodded at Cindy "She probably knows what happened."

"Too bad she's not telling," Sean said, and he went back to glancing at the local paper, not that there was much of interest there, just notes from the garden club, a description of a high school soccer game, a report about a proposed property tax increase, and a long letter about a speed trap on Route 79.

Ten minutes later, Libby reappeared upstairs bearing a tray filled with a plate of deviled eggs, a bowl of homemade fruit salad, sliced cinnamon and raisin bread with butter, ginger snap cookies, and iced coffee for them, and a bit of poached salmon and some milk for the cat.

A bolt of lightning zigzagged through the sky as Libby set the tray down on the coffee table. "At least we didn't get poured on," she commented as the heavens opened up and raindrops began pelting down.

"This is true," Bernie said.

She levered herself up and closed the windows, while Libby dished out the food. The cat jumped off the sofa and began to lap up the salmon. No one talked for a few minutes. The girls were too busy concentrating on eating and Sean was waiting to hear what they had to say.

"So, Dad," Bernie said after she'd eaten two and a half deviled eggs, "any luck finding out whether or not Manny married and divorced Daisy Stone?"

"Nope," Sean replied. He got up and carefully spooned some fruit salad onto his plate. "Not that that means anything, my computer skills being what they are. Clyde said he'd ask his nephew to take a look, so I guess we'll have to wait and see."

"How about locating Daisy Stone?" Bernie asked. "Did you have any more luck with that?"

Sean snorted. "Do you know how many Daisy Stones are out there?"

"A lot?" Libby hazarded.

"That is a major understatement. I need a DOB."

Bernie finished off the last half of her third deviled egg. "I'll put it on the to-do list."

"The ever-expanding list," Libby commented as she contemplated the slice of cinnamon and raisin bread she'd put on her plate and wondered how melted squares of dark chocolate would taste on it. Pretty good, she imagined. Add a sprinkling of sea salt and it would probably be delicious.

Sean took a bite of his fruit salad, then gestured to the salad with his fork. "What herb do you have in here?"

Libby answered. "Lemon verbena. You like it, Dad?"

Sean nodded. "Very much. It's a nice change from mint." He went back to eating.

For the next five minutes the only sound in the room was the sound of the rain on the roof and the cat lapping up the milk. Then the cat jumped back up on Sean's lap, and as if on signal, Libby and Bernie began filling Sean in on what had happened that afternoon.

Sean put down his fork, laced his fingers together, and listened intently. When his daughters were done, he leaned over, snagged a ginger snap, and nibbled on it while he considered what he'd been told.

"So where did Ellen go after you finished talking to her?"

Bernie propped up her leg on the corner of the coffee table and massaged her ankle. She knew she should get some ice on it because it was a little swollen again, but she was too lazy to move. "First she said something about driving around, then she said something about going back to the Riverview, then she wanted us to drive with her to the police station while she turned herself in."

Sean leaned forward. "So she confessed to killing Manny?"

"No, she didn't. What she says is this is all her fault—cosmically speaking."

Sean shook his head in disgust. "Whatever you do, keep her away from Lucy. He'd have her in cuffs in a New York minute and it'll be hell getting her back out. You know how he is when he fixates on things."

Libby licked a dab of butter off her finger. "I know. Hopefully we got her to understand that."

"I think we did." Bernie stirred a lump of sugar into her iced coffee.

Libby had made the iced coffee with coffee ice cubes and Bernie decided there was a big difference between using those and regular ice cubes. Definitely worth the effort, in her opinion.

Sean finished off his cookie and had a sip of his coffee. "So where is Ellen now?"

Bernie took another swallow of coffee and put her glass down. She was struggling to keep her eyes open. Hopefully, the coffee would help. "She's at the Riverview Motel. I think."

Sean raised an eyebrow. "What?"

"I know," Bernie said.

"Given the circumstances, I would think that would be the last place she'd want to go," Sean observed. "Did she say why?"

"Something about not causing her family any more grief."

Sean made a rude noise. "That's garbage."

"I know. Then she told us she wanted to

commune with Manny's spirit and apologize to him."

Sean made an even ruder noise. "You know what I'm thinking?"

"That she's finally gone off the deep end and is making stuff up?" Libby asked. "That she needs serious tranqs?"

"Pretty much. Or she's searching for something."

"Her mind?" Libby quipped.

"That's probably it," Sean allowed. "Either she's really screwed up or a lot smarter than we give her credit for."

"I'm going with screwed up," Bernie said.

"Ditto," said Libby.

Chapter 28

As Sean ate a ginger snap, he recalled that Rose had always called Ellen fragile. Maybe she was right. Of course, what had happened to her was enough to unhinge anyone. One thing was for sure, Sean decided as Cindy turned around on Sean's lap and settled back down, Ellen definitely wasn't presenting herself in the best possible light murder-suspect-wise.

"Why does she do that?" he asked as he automatically began petting the cat again.

"Because she's a cat and that's what cats do," Bernie said. She finished off a piece of the cinnamon toast. She hadn't realized how hungry she was. Maybe that's why she was feeling so tired. Or maybe she was feeling so tired because she felt as if she was running around in circles. "So, Dad, what do you think about what Ellen said?"

"You mean about Lisa and Bruce?" Sean guessed.

Libby and Bernie both nodded.

"It's possible it's true; of course anything is possible." Sean started to get up. The cat meowed and jumped down. "What?" he said to Cindy, who was looking at him reproachfully from the floor as he spooned some more fruit salad onto his plate. "Am I merely here for your convenience?"

"That would be a yes, Dad," Bernie answered.

"Which is why I never wanted a cat," Sean noted as he sat back down.

"Well, you've got one now," Libby replied as Cindy immediately jumped back up on Sean's lap and made herself at home.

"And whose fault is that?" Sean asked.

Bernie moved her leg to a more comfortable position. "Mine, of course. Everything always is."

"I'm glad we're clear on that," Libby quipped as she reached over for a ginger snap. The extra butter she'd added had made the cookies a little more crumbly and she decided she liked them that way. She liked the contrast between the sharp flavor and the soft texture although, she reflected, she supposed you couldn't call them snaps anymore. "At least it's not a mini potbellied pig."

"Yeah, but we could eat that," Sean said.

"Dad," Libby wailed. "Eat Hilda! What an awful thing to say."

Sean grinned. He liked the fact that he still had the power to get Libby going.

Bernie coughed and Sean and Libby looked at her.

"Can we get back to Ellen?" she asked.

"By all means," Sean said. He extended his hand. "Please continue."

"With pleasure," Bernie said. "Personally, I'm having trouble believing what she was telling Libby and me. I talked to Brandon and he hasn't heard anything about Bruce and Lisa having an affair. In fact, he hasn't heard anything about Bruce having an affair with anyone; all he's heard about Bruce is that he's in deep financial doo-doo. Jeremy, on the other hand, seems to be doing well. Brandon said that rumor has it that he's involved in some big real estate deal."

"Like what?" Sean asked.

Bernie shook her head. "Brandon doesn't know. He said he'd keep an ear out for more info about Jeremy and Bruce. Considering he works in gossip central, I figure if he doesn't hear about it, there's nothing to hear about, if you know what I mean."

"Marvin hasn't heard anything either," Libby said.

"Because people talk at funerals?" Bernie asked.

"More than you would think," Libby replied hotly. "Don't be such a snot."

Bernie put her hands up in a gesture of surrender. "I wasn't being sarcastic. I was asking."

"Sure you were, Bernie."

"I was. I swear."

"Then the answer is yes," Libby told her, mollified.

Sean cleared his throat and his daughters turned to him. "Did either of you talk to Lisa?" Sean said. "Did you ask her?"

Bernie nodded. "We most certainly did. After we said good-bye to Ellen, I called up Lisa. I have to say she sounded pretty surprised when I asked her about her and Bruce."

"She could have been pretending," Sean said.

"She could have been," Bernie agreed, "but she sounded pretty convincing. She said that Ellen had finally gone over the edge, or words to that effect."

Sean bit into a strawberry. "And what did Bruce and Jeremy say?"

"We don't know," Libby and Bernie chorused at the same time.

Bernie took over. "We have calls in to both of them, but neither of them have called back, not that I'm surprised. Actually, I'll be surprised if they do call. I'll tell you one thing though. Those are going to be interesting conversations," she reflected.

"Might I suggest," Sean said, "that's the kind of conversation you have in person. You want to be able to see their reactions when you ask the question."

Bernie and Libby both nodded.

"That's what we figured," Bernie said.

"Also," Sean continued, "you might want to mention Daisy to Jeremy and see if he knows where she is." He speared a piece of melon with his fork and ate it as he watched another flash of lightning bisect the sky. "After all, she is his sister."

"And if he doesn't?" Bernie asked. "Or if he does and won't tell us?"

"Try Lisa," Sean suggested. "She might have her sister-in-law's address and be more likely to give the information out, being less protective and all."

"Anything else?" Libby asked.

"Since you asked," Sean said, "it might be interesting to see if you can find out a little more about Manny. Like, for starters, why did he come back to Longely? I can't believe it's nostalgia given the way he left. There has to have been a fairly compelling reason, since this place holds nothing but bad memories for him." Sean put his fork down on the plate and drummed his fingers on the arm of his chair. Cindy opened one eye and closed it again. "And then there's the question of what Manny's been doing since he came back, aside from working for Ellen and Lisa, that is. Maybe that would prove a fruitful avenue to go down."

"We'll ask around some more," Libby told him. "But so far we haven't come up with anything. As far as I can tell, no one seems to have had any contact with Manny except for Ellen and Lisa, their families, Miss Randall, and the guy who's helping out at the Riverview Motel, and he just knows Manny to play chess with."

"One thing is for certain," Bernie added, "Manny didn't go to RJ's when he was alive. Brandon's never seen him." Bernie shifted her leg. "He asked the guys on the other shifts and got a negative. He even asked some of the bartenders at Cliff's, Shifty's, and the Blue Elephant," she said, naming the other most popular bars in town, "and no one remembers serving Manny."

"Maybe he didn't drink," Libby said. "Or maybe he liked to drink at home."

"Or maybe he was keeping a low profile," Sean said. "But if Manny's been back here for a while, someone has to know him. This is too small a town not to be noticed. For starters, how did he make his living? Unless he was on disability, of course."

"Well, Lisa said he was on a striping crew before he worked for Arf," Libby noted.

"Good. That's a start." Sean rubbed his hands together. "See if you can find those guys."

Bernie took out her phone and looked up striping on the Web. There was a long list of companies, none of them local. She showed the list to her dad. "I think that might be hard to do."

"Maybe a little," Sean conceded. "Okay. Then start with Clara Randall's neighbors and see what they have to say. After that, I'd work my way out to the closest fast-food shops and gas stations."

Libby reached up and massaged the crick she'd developed in the back of her neck. "What do you think, Bernie?"

Bernie startled. She'd been staring out the window. "Sorry. What did you say?"

Libby repeated what her dad had just said.

Bernie nodded her head. "It seems like a good idea."

"You don't sound that enthusiastic," Sean observed.

"I am," Bernie said with as much eagerness as she could muster. "I really am. I'm just tired. It's been a long day."

But Bernie was lying. It was true she was tired, but that wasn't why she hadn't been listening. She'd been mulling over an idea that had popped into her head a few minutes ago, an idea she knew her dad and Libby weren't going to approve of. For a moment, she debated telling them and then decided against it. Why cause trouble and get everyone all riled up? No, she'd keep her idea to herself for the time being and save herself the ensuing drama.

She figured that she and Libby would go talk to Clara Randall's neighbors like her father had suggested and then, when they were done with that, they'd trot across the street to Clara Randall's house and scoop up Manny's laptop. If the police hadn't taken it already, that is. Of course, that was a big *if*.

Chapter 29

Y ou're nuts," Libby exclaimed, looking slightly aghast. She was standing on the sidewalk across from Clara Randall's house facing Bernie. Due to the weather, they were the only people out on the street. Everyone else was tucked up in their houses instead of doing spring stuff like yard work and washing cars.

"No. I'm not," Bernie replied. She'd just explained her idea to · Libby and gotten the reaction she'd expected.

It was seven o'clock in the evening. The sky was still a gun-metal gray, but at least it had finally stopped raining, although it looked as if it was going to start again any minute. It was still wet out though. Water was pooling in the gutters, beading on the blades of grass, and dripping down from the tree branches. Bernie brushed a drop of water off her nose, spotted an earthworm on the sidewalk that had been flushed out of the ground by the rain, bent down, picked it up, and put it back on the lawn.

"For good luck," she explained to Libby even though Libby hadn't asked her why she was doing it. "Maybe there's something on Manny's laptop that can tell us something," Bernie continued. "And at this point we need everything we can get."

"Agreed, but even if there is, I'm sure the police have the laptop in their possession," Libby said as she looked at the crime scene tape festooning Clara Randall's house. She couldn't help thinking that with the tape the house reminded her of a badly wrapped package.

She and her sister had just spent the last hour and a quarter following their dad's suggestion. They'd gone up and down a two-block area knocking on people's doors and asking about Manny Roget. Half the people hadn't been in and the ones who had been in hadn't had much to say. Yes, they'd seen Manny Roget from time to time going in and out of Clara Randall's house, but most of them had never spoken to him.

Evidently, he was a man who kept to himself. Only three of the people they'd talked to had exchanged greetings with him. All three said he seemed pleasant enough. Maybe a little on the shy side. How long had Manny Roget lived in Clara Randall's house? No one Bernie and Libby talked to knew precisely. The estimates they'd gotten ranged from three to seven months.

The only thing everyone agreed on was that Manny hadn't been there when the big nor'easter had come barreling through around Thanksgiving. They were sure of that because otherwise he would have been outside helping drag the tree branches off the lawns along with everyone else and they would have remembered that. He was not, everyone agreed, an inconspicuous person.

"We need to see what's on that computer," Bernie reiterated.

"Then we should have taken it when we had the chance," Libby pointed out. She stuck her hands in the pockets of her old, battered L. L. Bean rain jacket, realized there was a hole in both pockets, and took her hands out. "But we didn't and now the police have it."

"You don't know that," Bernie countered. "What if the CID missed it? They could have. Basically, they were dealing with Clara Randall's homicide scene, not Manny's. They probably just gave his room a quick look through, if that. After all, I put the laptop back in the laundry basket. It was hard to see, so it could still be in the house. It certainly won't hurt to look."

"Yes, it most certainly will," Libby said. She folded her arms across her chest. The wind was picking up and blowing the branches around, sending down scatters of raindrops. It looked as if they'd just caught a lull and the rain would be coming back soon, Libby thought. She reached back and pulled up her hood. She didn't like getting her head wet. "What happens if we get caught in the house?" she demanded. "What then? I don't even want to think about what will happen if we are. Dad will have a coronary."

"We're not going to get caught," Bernie assured her. "We can go in through the back. No one can see us there. The fence and the garage provide the perfect cover."

Libby snorted. "I don't care. Even if what you say is true, which I'm not sure it is, I don't think it's worth the risk."

"Then stay here," Bernie told her. "I'll be in and out in no time."

Libby screwed her face up. "I'm serious about not going."

Bernie put the hood up on her Burberry as well. "I'm not forcing you, but I just want to remind you that we promised Ellen's sons we'd get to the bottom of this."

"I haven't forgotten," Libby said stiffly. "I just don't think that breaking in to Clara Randall's house is the way to accomplish that goal. Even if the computer is there, we won't be able to get the information off it. Remember, it's password protected."

"Don't worry. I haven't forgotten," Bernie said. "So?"

"So now we know someone who might be able to get around that small little obstacle."

"You mean Ryan?"

"No. Tom Hanks."

"Seriously."

Bernie laughed. "Who else? I'm sure not talking about Brandon or Marvin." They were nearly as bad on a computer as she and Libby were.

"First of all, Ryan probably can't do it," Libby replied, her voice rising slightly.

Bernie frowned at her sister. "Why do you always have to be so negative?"

"I think *realistic* is the word you should be using," Libby retorted. The truth was she was having deep misgivings about asking Ryan to hack into Manny's computer. It seemed wrong to her on a number of different levels. "And even if he can, I'm not sure it's the right thing to do."

"I disagree. Anyway, he wants to try," Bernie said.

"How do you know that?" Libby demanded.

"Simple," Bernie replied. "Because I asked him."

"When?"

"Earlier, when you were in the bathroom getting ready to go out."

"He could go to jail," Libby protested.

"No, he can't, Libby. He's too young. I checked. The most he'll get is probation. He really wants to do this. He told me this is his way of making up for being an ungrateful little brat."

Libby's eyebrows shot up. "Those were his words?"

"Not exactly, but close enough." Bernie leaned against a lamppost to take the weight off her ankle. The swelling had gone down, but every time she stood or walked on it, it started to ache again. "I think we owe it to Ryan to give him the opportunity to square things up. We should let him try."

"If the laptop is there."

"Which we won't know until . . ."

Libby put up her hand to stop Bernie talking. "All right. You win." She didn't have the energy to argue anymore. "Let's just make this fast."

Bernie hugged her. "You're the best big sister ever."

Libby untangled herself from Bernie. "No. Just the stupidest."

Sometimes being the older sibling sucked, Libby decided. How had Bernie convinced her to once again do something they shouldn't be doing? She didn't know. But this she did know. If they got caught Libby knew that the major blame would fall on her shoulders because it always did. Her dad would tell her that she was the older one and hence should know better. And truth? You know what? He was right.

Chapter 30

Libby was thinking about what her father would say if he knew what they were doing as she and Bernie quickly crossed the street and walked down the driveway to Clara Randall's house.

"What if someone sees us going in?" Libby asked. She could feel her heart rate kicking up.

"No one can see us," Bernie assured her, nodding at the fence and laurel bushes with her chin. "Our hoods are up and there's no line of sight from the other houses into the backyard."

"But if someone does see us and call the cops?" Libby persisted.

Bernie pointed to the garage. "Then we'll say we just came back to get the cat food for Cindy."

By now the sisters were standing in front of the house's back door. Bernie tried the door handle. The door was locked. Not that she'd expected anything different.

"Stand in front of me," she commanded Libby.

Libby sighed and did as she was told while Bernie went to work with Brandon's lock picks, the ones she'd borrowed when she'd locked herself out of her house and had "forgotten" to return.

"You can always work as a B and E guy if the store ever closes down," Libby cracked as she stood guard.

Her sister grunted and kept on twisting the picks in the lock. The hood was making her perspire, but she didn't want to take it off in case anyone was watching. A strand of hair fell across her face and she blew it away. She had to admit she really wasn't very good with the picks. She was just borderline competent, if that. Why wasn't there an app for this? That's what she wanted to know. Heaven only knows, there was an app for everything else under the sun.

"What's the holdup?" Libby asked after another minute had gone by.

"No holdup. It just takes me a little while," Bernie said between gritted teeth. She supposed if worst came to worst she could always break a window and get in that way, although that would attract attention from the police, something she was trying to avoid.

"Come on," Libby hissed.

"I'm doing the best I can," Bernie snapped. She applied more pressure to the pick. A moment later she felt something give and then the tumblers clicked. "We're in," she told Libby as she straightened up and pushed the door handle down. "I hope."

The door swung open. Bernie pumped her fist in the air. "Yes," she crowed. Then she covered her mouth and looked around. Fortunately, no one was there to hear her.

A moment later, Libby and Bernie walked inside.

"What do we say if the police come now, Bernie?" Libby asked. The cat food alibi now being off the table, since they were inside the house.

"We don't say anything, Libby. We run."

Libby pointed to Bernie's ankle. "You're barely back to walking."

"Don't worry," Bernie said as she walked through the kitchen. "It's not going to come to that."

"That's what you always say," Libby muttered as she closed the door behind them.

"And I'm right ninety percent of the time," Bernie rejoined.

"It's the other ten percent that worries me," Libby said as she looked around the kitchen.

The room was smudged with patches of black dust the CID had left behind when they'd dusted for fingerprints. So were the living and dining rooms. The downstairs looked as if someone with coal dust on their hands had finger painted on the walls and the furniture. Clara Randall, Libby reflected as she headed for the stairs, would not have been pleased. She would not have been pleased at all.

Libby started up the stairs. The fifth step let out

a loud squeak when she stepped on it, making her gasp in surprise.

Bernie laughed. "Nervous?" she asked.

"Not at all," Libby answered. "I just wasn't expecting that. The stairs didn't squeak the last time we were here."

But Libby had lied. She was nervous. She didn't know whether it was because she was anxious about the cops coming or was just anxious about being in the house, period. The moment she'd walked in she'd felt a strange vibe, almost as if Clara Randall was watching them and blaming them for what had happened—although why Clara Randall would think that Libby didn't have the slightest idea. She wasn't going to tell her sister about what she was thinking though. She'd just make fun of her.

When she and Bernie got to the second-floor hallway, they looked around. The Fu Dogs were there as were the photos on the walls. There was no black dust on the walls or in the other bedrooms except for an errant smudge now and then. On the other hand, the police had obviously gone through Clara Randall's bedroom with a fine-tooth comb. They'd dusted the bed, walls, and dressers for prints and removed the bedding and a good part of the carpet. The room looked bereft. It was hot up there and with the windows shut tight the smell of Clara Randall's death lingered in the air like a bad memory. And there was another smell too. A familiar one, although Libby couldn't identify it.

She sniffed. "What is that odor?" she asked Bernie.

Bernie shook her head. "I don't know. Maybe it's better not to speculate."

"No. It's something else."

"Let me know when you figure it out," Bernie said before turning and walking out the door.

Being in there depressed her. She couldn't help remembering Clara Randall splayed out on the floor. It wasn't the way she would have wanted to go. Stupid comment. Who would? Libby followed Bernie out, making sure to walk around where Clara Randall had lain. The sisters slowed down a little to look at the pictures as they headed toward the door to Manny's room.

"I wonder who's going to take these," Bernie asked, referring to the photographs.

"I don't think anyone is," Libby said. "Clara Randall didn't have any family. Or at least none from around here."

"Sad," Bernie said.

"Very," Libby agreed. "At least Mom had Dad and us."

Bernie nodded as she stopped in front of the door to Manny's room. The walls and the floor were clean. No one had dusted for fingerprints here. She was right. This was how she had thought it would be. The evidence technicians had confined themselves to the scene of Clara Randall's death even though it was obvious to her that the two deaths were related.

She opened the door and slowly went up the stairs using the banister as leverage. The room looked the same way it had when she and Libby had left it. She went over to the laundry basket and peered inside. Yup. The laptop was still lying on its bed of dirty sweatpants. Another win for her!

"See," she said to Libby as she lifted it out. "I'm going to call Ryan and ask him to meet us somewhere so I can give this to him."

Libby didn't answer. She was standing off to one side looking out the window.

"What's up?" Bernie asked, joining her.

"That." Libby pointed to a blue Ford SUV with tinted windows slowly cruising down Clara Randall's driveway. As Bernie and Libby watched, the Ford turned around, drove back up the driveway, turned left, went down the street, came back up, and parked across from Clara Randall's house.

Libby pressed herself against the wall and took a deep breath to try and calm herself down. She didn't think whoever had been driving the vehicle could see her from the street, but she wanted to make sure. "Do you think that's an unmarked vehicle?" she asked anxiously.

"No," Bernie replied immediately. "I don't. An

unmarked vehicle wouldn't have those windows. They're illegal. Anyway, why would they be staking out this house?"

Why oh why, thought Libby, *do I let Bernie get me into these messes when I know better? What is wrong with me?*

"How about because they got a call from one of the neighbors about an intruder?" Libby snapped back.

"Think for a minute," Bernie told her sister. "If the Longely PD got a call like that they would have sent a squad car over and a cop would be downstairs banging on the front door and shining a light in the windows."

"So who is it then?"

"I have no idea. Can you see in?" Bernie asked Libby.

Libby peeked out. "No, I can't."

"Well, neither can I, so I'm not even going to begin to speculate."

"What do you think he—"

"Or she . . ."

"Whatever. Wants?"

Bernie clicked her tongue against her teeth. "Not a clue. If I don't know who he is, how am I going to know what he wants?"

"Well, I don't like it," Libby said, still studying the vehicle. "The windows freak me out."

"Me too," Bernie agreed. "Although maybe they're not as dark as they look."

"You're kidding me."

"It could be the angle we're looking at them from. It's possible," Bernie said defensively when Libby rolled her eyes. Bernie tapped her nails against her thigh while she thought about alternative explanations. "Maybe the SUV being here is just a random thing. Maybe whoever is driving is waiting for someone else. Or maybe they pulled over to have a chat on their phone. Maybe they got this car at an auction from a drug dealer and haven't gotten around to changing up the windows."

Libby snorted. "Talk about reaching."

Bernie leaned against the wall. "I'm just exploring possibilities."

"Okay," Libby said. "Call me crazy, but I wouldn't describe driving up and down Clara Randall's driveway as random. Whoever is in the SUV is definitely studying the house. Or waiting for us to come out. Either way is not good."

Bernie brightened. She had another idea. "How about this? Maybe it's a real estate agent wanting to get a jump on selling the house."

"That's a little better," Libby said, forced to admit that what Bernie had said made some sense. "That's slightly plausible. But what if it isn't? What if it's someone else? What if they are waiting for us to come out? What do we do then?" Libby asked. "We can't wait all evening for him or her to go away."

"We could go out and ask him what the hell he's doing," Bernie suggested.

"That's funny considering we're not supposed to be in the house at all."

"Then how about this?" Bernie said. "We'll give him ten more minutes and if he isn't gone we'll go out the back way."

"That's not going to help," Libby protested. "Whoever is in that SUV will still see us walking down the driveway."

"Not if we go through the hole in the fence . . ."

Libby furrowed her forehead. "What hole?"

"There's a loose plank on the far right."

"I didn't see it."

"Well, it's there," Bernie replied. "We can slip through that and circle around to Boyton," Bernie said. "Then you can get Mathilda and pick me up there. It'll be faster than me trying to walk." *At least,* she thought, *we parked the van around the corner. Thank God for small favors.*

"What if the SUV is in the driveway when we go outside?" Libby asked.

"What if the hand of God comes down and squashes us? What if we have a tornado? What if a flood washes us away?" said Bernie, waving her hands in the air. She was losing patience.

"I'm sorry," Libby said. "I don't see this as a great plan."

Bernie put her hands on her hips. "I'll be happy to entertain options. . . . Well?" she said when

Libby didn't reply. "I'm waiting for suggestions."

Libby looked at the floor. Much as she hated to admit it, she couldn't think of an alternative.

"Just as I thought," Bernie said.

"There's no need to be so smug," Libby said.

"I'm not being smug," Bernie told her. "I'm being factual."

The ten minutes went by slowly. Libby kept peeking out the window to check on the status of the blue Ford SUV while Bernie sat on the futon and tried to access Manny Roget's laptop.

"Total fail," she said in disgust after she'd tried every combination of Manny Roget's name that she could think of. It would be interesting to see how well Ryan would do. She turned the laptop off and stood up. "It's time to go."

"Maybe we should wait a little longer," Libby ventured.

Bernie shook her head. "For what? Whoever is in the SUV doesn't look like they're moving anytime soon, and as you said, we can't stay here forever." She put the laptop in its case, the case in her Louis Vuitton tote—bought used at a shop in the West Village—opened the door to Manny's room, and headed down the stairs.

"I told you we shouldn't be doing this," Libby grumbled as she followed Bernie. "I told you something bad would happen."

"Nothing bad has happened," Bernie replied as

she walked down the hall to the staircase that led to the first floor.

"Yet, Bernie. Yet."

Bernie laughed. "Think of it as an adventure, Libby."

"I don't like adventures," Libby whined.

"No kidding."

The sisters were now in the kitchen. Bernie looked out the kitchen window. The driveway was clear.

"And that," Bernie added as she opened the back door, "is the crux of your problem."

"My only problem," Libby snapped back, "is listening to you."

"Ah, but if you didn't, think how dull your life would be."

Libby wanted to say, "I like dull." But she didn't. There was no point. It would only continue the conversation.

Chapter 31

A minute later, Bernie and Libby were out of the house and through the gap in the fence. Libby pointed to a tear in her rain parka once they were on the other side. She'd caught her sleeve on a nail that had been sticking out of the wood.

Bernie was not sympathetic. "You need to throw that thing away, Libby," she said. "You needed to throw it away five years ago."

"It's my favorite raincoat," Libby squawked.

"A, it's a parka, not a raincoat; and B, I wouldn't brag about it if I were you," Bernie told her, eyeing the light green garment with distaste. "I can give you a raincoat of mine if you want. The navy one."

Libby didn't reply. She was too focused on getting to the van. As she hurried along she kept imagining that the blue SUV was going to come roaring out of one of the driveways in front of her, blocking her way, even though the streets and sidewalks were empty except for a group of giggling teenage girls ahead of her. By the time Libby had covered the three blocks to Mathilda, it had started raining again. Libby climbed in the van, put the key in the ignition, and turned it. Mathilda coughed three times and started up.

"Good girl," Libby murmured, patting the dashboard.

Then she put Mathilda in drive and went to pick up Bernie. But she wasn't on the corner.

"Damn," Libby said, cursing out loud. "Where are you?" Her heart started racing again.

A moment later, she spotted her sister standing under the branches of a large elm tree and slammed on the brakes. Mathilda squealed to a stop.

"I didn't want to get wet," Bernie explained as she climbed in. She closed the door and fastened her seat belt. "Any problems getting here?"

Libby shook her head. "For once, everything went smoothly."

"Excellent." Bernie pushed her hood down and stifled a sneeze. "What do you say we take a look and see if the SUV is still parked in front of Clara Randall's house?"

Libby took her eyes off the road and looked at her sister. "Are you planning on getting out and knocking on the SUV's door?"

"Why are you asking?"

"Because if you are, the answer is no. It's just asking for trouble."

"Then I'm not."

It had started raining harder. Libby reached over and turned on the windshield wipers.

"Don't you want to know who's inside the SUV?" Bernie asked.

"Of course, I do," Libby replied.

"And how would you propose we do that if we don't knock on their door?"

Libby thought for another minute. "We could follow them and see who gets out."

"I guess we could," Bernie conceded.

"Good." Libby drove around Boyton, made a right onto Ash, then another left. "I don't think the SUV is here," Libby said as she started up Clara Randall's block. "I don't see it. Do you?"

"No." Bernie scanned the street. "I don't." The blue SUV was nowhere in sight, which disappointed her. "Whoever was in it must have taken off."

"Probably because he knew we were gone and

there was no point in waiting around," Libby suggested.

"Which means that he saw us leave and didn't try and intercept us."

Libby frowned. "So he wasn't interested in us after all?"

"Maybe." Bernie rubbed her chin with her finger. "Maybe this whole thing was random after all."

"It didn't feel random to me," Libby said.

"Me either," Bernie allowed.

"I could feel his eyes watching us."

"Let's not go overboard here. On the other hand," Bernie ruminated, "if whoever it was, was watching us, we have a whole new set of problems."

Libby slowed down. "How so?"

"Because that means that the person in the SUV knew we were going to Clara Randall's house, and the only way he could have known that is if he followed us there."

"Or," Libby said, "he could have just seen us go in."

"He was just passing by and went, 'Wow, there are the Simmons girls. I think I'll stop and see what they're doing'? Doubtful."

"There's no need for sarcasm," Libby huffed. "I meant maybe he was staking out the house independently of us."

"And he left because he didn't want us to see who he was," Bernie said.

Libby nodded. "Exactly."

"It's plausible," Bernie conceded. "But why would he be staking out the house?"

"I don't know," Libby admitted. Another idea occurred to her. "Or maybe he wanted us to see him," she said. "Maybe he wanted to scare us off."

"Off what?" Bernie asked.

Libby shook her head again. She didn't have an answer. They were now in front of Clara Randall's house. Libby had just pulled into the parking space the SUV had vacated, when it pulled up behind them.

"Jeez," Libby said, taking a deep breath. "This is so not cool."

"That's it. I'm done. I'm going to settle this right now," Bernie said, and she started opening the van door.

"Don't," Libby cried. "You'll get yourself killed. Let's get out of here."

But it was too late. Bernie was already out of the van, walking toward the SUV. Libby cursed and followed her. What was wrong with her sister? That's what she wanted to know.

Libby was just behind Bernie as Bernie lifted her hand to rap on the window, but before she could, the window opened. *This is it,* Libby thought. She couldn't help it. She froze and closed her eyes. All she knew was that if her sister was going to get shot, she didn't want to see it. Then she heard a familiar voice and opened her eyes. It was Ellen.

Libby's pulse rate jumped. Ellen wasn't going to get arrested because she was going to kill her first.

"What is wrong with you?" Libby yelled at Ellen. "You scared us to death."

Ellen shrank back from the window. "I didn't mean to," she stammered.

Bernie turned toward Libby. "Calm down," she told her.

"Calm down?" Libby's voice rose even louder. "Calm down? I thought you were going to die!" She turned on Ellen. "What the hell were you doing spying on us like that?" she demanded.

"I . . . I wasn't. I thought I saw you both going into Old Lady Randall's house, and I wanted to know what was happening." Ellen sniffed.

"Nothing is happening," Bernie said, seeing no reason to tell Ellen about Manny's computer at this juncture and open up a whole new can of worms.

"Then what are you doing here?" Ellen asked.

"Just tying up some loose ends," Bernie answered truthfully.

Libby tapped on the door of Ellen's SUV to get her attention. "How about finishing telling us why you parked across the street," she said.

"Ah . . . sure," Ellen replied. "I . . . I drove up the driveway, but you weren't there, so I decided to park on the street. Then I got tired of waiting and drove off, but as I was going down Westcott I saw you and decided to ask what you guys were doing." Ellen turned to Bernie. "I didn't mean to scare you. Honest, I didn't."

"I know." Bernie reached through the open window and patted Ellen's hand. "It's okay."

"It isn't okay," Libby said, still pissed. "What about this car?"

"This car?" asked Ellen, looking confused.

"It's got tinted windows."

"I don't understand," Ellen said.

Bernie intervened. "I think what Libby is asking is how come you aren't driving the Subaru? My sister thinks that the tinted windows mean you were trying to hide your identity."

"But I wasn't," Ellen protested. "Al lent me this because he's keeping the Subaru for a couple of days because he needed to order parts for the exhaust system." Ellen started to cry again. "Oh my God," she moaned as she covered her face with her hands. "All I do is cause trouble for everyone. I can't do anything right. I'm so, so sorry."

"It's okay," Bernie told Ellen as Libby stalked to the van and slammed the door shut. The thud echoed down the street.

"No, it isn't," Ellen wailed. "Libby hates me."

"She'll get over it," Bernie told her. "My sister doesn't like being wrong." She spent the next five minutes comforting Ellen.

"Aren't you embarrassed about the way you overreacted?" she said to Libby after Ellen had driven off.

"I didn't overreact," Libby snapped back. "You agreed with me."

Bernie wanted to tell her she hadn't, but instead of risking an argument, Bernie dug her phone out of her bag and called Ryan to tell him they had Manny's computer.

He answered on the first ring and suggested he meet Libby and Bernie for a handoff at the Starbucks located a half mile from where they were.

"You're on," Bernie told him before hanging up and telling Libby where to go.

Libby nodded and turned down Levitt Street. She didn't say anything for the next five blocks. At Midler she turned to Bernie and said, "How come you didn't tell Ellen about Manny's computer?"

"Given Ellen's mouth, I just figured that the less she knows at this point, the better."

"Makes sense," Libby said, and she went back to looking at the road.

Chapter 32

It was getting on dusk, the hour when cars without their headlights on blur and dissolve in the grayness and people are settling in for the evening. When Libby pulled into Starbucks the lot was almost empty. During the day, it would be jammed with vehicles jockeying for space, with people getting their caffeine jolt before they got on or off Metro-North, but at night the place was practically deserted.

Bernie sat there for a moment listening to the rain splattering on Mathilda's hood. Then she tucked her tote under her raincoat. "Ready?" she asked Libby.

"When you are," her sister replied, turning the motor off. "I still don't think I overreacted," she said.

"Fine. You jumped to a conclusion," Bernie told her.

"A legitimate one."

"Can we drop it?"

"If you insist," Libby said, still feeling aggrieved.

The sisters put up their hoods and made a dash for the door. A Joan Baez tape greeted them as they walked inside. Bernie immediately spotted Ryan and Matt standing by the counter. Of course, they were easy to spot since there were only six other people in there. *Not the best place for a meeting,* Bernie couldn't help thinking as she walked toward them.

"Can I get you anything?" Bernie asked when she reached them. She'd been planning on handing the laptop over and leaving, but now she figured she had to at least treat the kids to something to eat and drink.

Ryan nodded. "I'll take a piece of cheesecake and a brownie."

"And I'll have a piece of cheesecake and the half moon cookie," Matt said, pointing to the last one in the display case. "And a venti latte."

"Me too," Ryan said.

Bernie added two coffees for herself and Libby to the order and paid the cashier, a girl who looked as if she'd been on her feet way too long. Then they collected their beverages and Libby led the way to a four-person table situated by the window.

"We saw my mom," Ryan announced as he put ten packets of sugar into his coffee and stirred the mixture with his plastic fork.

"Funny, so did we," Libby said, restraining herself from saying, "Why don't you have a little coffee with your sugar?"

"She came by the house earlier." Ryan turned his head away but not before Bernie saw his eyes beginning to mist.

"Don't be such a dork," Matt said to Ryan, hitting his younger brother on the back of his head with the flat of his hand. "Ryan's upset," Matt explained to Bernie and Libby, "because the parents were fighting again. Really fighting about what Mom did, and then Ethan got in the middle of it and told both of them that if they got divorced, even if Mom did go to jail, he'd never speak to them again."

Bernie took a sip of her coffee and put it down. It was overbrewed. The coffee had been sitting for too long. But then what did she expect at this time of the night? She should have ordered decaf. That way they would have had to make a fresh pot.

"So what did your parents say?" Bernie asked.

"Dad told Ethan to zip it and Mom started crying and ran out of the house."

Ryan blinked several times. "Is she going to jail?"

"I hope not," Bernie told him.

"That's why you want me to look at Manny's computer, right?"

Bernie nodded. "Yup. You're our main man."

Ryan smiled and attacked his cheesecake, while Matt licked the icing off his half moon cookie, then started on the cookie itself.

A thought occurred to Libby. "Did you tell anyone about the laptop?" she asked anxiously.

"No." Matt looked confused. "Should we have?"

"No. Don't tell anyone," Bernie said quickly. "No one needs to know."

Ryan and Matt looked at each other. Both shrugged at the same time.

"Fine," Matt said.

"Works for me," Ryan added. He took another large bite of his cheesecake, swallowed, and sipped his coffee. "Can I see it?"

"By all means." Bernie took the laptop out of her tote and handed it across the table. She watched as Ryan opened the case and took the laptop out.

"Cheap piece of crap," he muttered to himself

as he turned it on. "I don't know why people get this kind of stuff."

"You think you'll be able to get in?" Bernie asked him.

"Probably," Ryan said.

"Because I couldn't," Bernie told him.

Ryan favored her with a look that clearly said, why am I not surprised?

Bernie drew herself up. "I know a little," she retorted, defending herself.

"If you say so," Ryan said dismissively.

Bernie opened her mouth and closed it again. He was right, and anyway, she wasn't about to get in a pissing contest with a teenage boy. "Remember," Bernie said instead, "no one can know you have it. We can get in a lot of trouble if anyone finds out."

Ryan glared at her. "I'm not an idiot, you know."

"I didn't think you were," Bernie said.

"So you'll call us?" Libby asked.

"As soon as I have something," Ryan said. He was studying the screen and didn't bother to look up. "Come on, baby," he crooned to it. "Let me in."

"Call us even if you don't have anything," Bernie said.

Ryan didn't answer her.

Matt shrugged. "That's what he's like when he does this kind of thing," he said. "Totally focused. Don't worry. I'll call one way or another."

It was raining even harder now. Torrents were

pouring out of the sky, turning everything watery when Libby and Bernie stepped outside.

"I feel like Noah in the flood," Libby grumbled as she tossed her coffee cup in the trash. She hadn't wanted it in the first place; neither had Bernie, who did the same.

"I guess we'll see what Ryan comes up with," Bernie said to Libby as they hurried over to Mathilda. She cursed as she stepped in a puddle that had formed on the tarmac and went into water past her instep.

"All I can say," Libby said, walking around another puddle, "is that I hope whatever Ryan finds is worth it."

"At least we'll have something," Bernie replied, "and in my book something is better than nothing."

Libby muttered something under her breath, but Bernie didn't bother to ask her what she'd said because she was pretty sure she already knew. She was just getting in the van when she got a call on her cell from Jeremy Stone.

"Lisa's husband wants to talk to us," she told Libby after she'd hung up.

Libby sighed. "No rest for the weary."

"Or the wicked," Bernie added. "He wants to meet us at the Roost," she said, naming a dive bar on the far end of town.

Libby started Mathilda up. The engine coughed twice and turned over. She didn't like rain or damp or cold. Basically, she drove best when it was sunny and the temperature ranged from seventy down to forty.

"I wonder why he picked there."

"My guess?" Bernie replied. "Because he doesn't want to be seen talking to us."

"That would be mine too," Libby said.

Bernie smiled. It was nice when she and Libby agreed on something.

Chapter 33

The Roost, popularly referred to as Ed's after its owner, was a strictly-for-the-locals kind of bar. Situated at the wrong end of Main Street, it was a small place with windows that were so crusted over with dirt that you couldn't see through them and a neon sign that had lost all but two of its letters years ago. There were iron bars on the front window and the door, and when you opened the door the odors of stale beer, cigarette smoke, and unwashed bodies drifted out.

There was a pool table in the back that no one used and a foosball table next to it that was similarly ignored. It was dark inside, the TV being the only spot of color in the place. Mostly everyone who came in during the weekdays sat at the bar watching the flickering image on the TV while engaging in some serious drinking. The decorations on the walls, coated with smoke and grime and grease, had faded long ago, becoming virtually invisible over the years. It was one of those places that should have been torn down but somehow never was.

"At least Ed's is empty," Libby said, as she parked on the street in front of the place. On the weekends, the sidewalk out front was jammed with motorcycles, the beer flowed, and the police were called so often they might as well have had a station there.

"Thank God for small favors," Bernie commented as she put up the hood on her raincoat and got out of Mathilda. She wasn't in the mood to deal with members of the Riders at the moment.

She and Libby ran for the bar. They could see Jeremy Stone sitting at one of the tables across from the bar nursing a beer when they walked in. They took off their rain gear and hung their coats on the coatrack next to the door. As she did, Bernie decided Jeremy looked as out of place here as an Hermès bag in Walmart. He was wearing an Armani suit, a blue shirt with a white collar and matching French cuffs with gold cuff links in them, handmade Italian loafers on his feet, and a Rolex on his wrist.

Bernie and Libby nodded at him and went up to the bar. The bartender, a woman named Sandra, watched them from the stool she was sitting on. She was stringy skinny, had a face that had seen way too much of the sun, and bleached hair that looked like straw and was held back in a ponytail with a rubber band.

She didn't get up when the sisters approached, not that Bernie had expected her to. This was the kind of place where the regulars got good service and everyone else waited. Finally, after two minutes had gone by, she reluctantly put the magazine she was paging through down and strolled over.

"Yes?" she asked in a voice telegraphing a two-pack-a-day habit.

"Two beers," Bernie said. "Anything in a can." She didn't trust the glasses in this place.

Sandra shrugged, walked over to the cooler, got two Budweisers out, and sent them flying down the bar. Bernie caught them before they went over the edge and landed on the floor.

"Seven bucks," Sandra said.

Bernie fished a ten out and handed it to her. Sandra put the ten in the register, took out three ones, folded them up, and slid them down the front of her shirt into her bra.

"Yes?" Sandra growled at Bernie, who was staring at her. "You have a problem with something?"

"No," Bernie said. "Not at all. I'm just admiring your mind-reading ability."

Sandra frowned. "Meaning?"

"Meaning how did you know I was going to tip you three bucks?"

"Why?" Sandra asked, shoving the money down further into her bra. "You want it back?"

"No," Bernie hastily told her. "I definitely do not."

Sandra smirked. "That's what I thought."

"I figure you need all the help you can get." Then before Sandra could answer, Bernie grabbed the two beers and brought them over to the table where Libby and Jeremy were sitting. "Why did you pick here?" she asked Jeremy as she set the cans down.

"I liked it. It has a certain . . . ambience." Jeremy smiled. "And Sandra has my back, don't you, honey?"

"Sure do, Mr. Stone," Sandra said perfunctorily as she raised her eyes from the magazine she'd gone back to leafing through.

Or maybe Sandra doesn't have your back after all, Bernie reflected as she studied the expression on the woman's face.

"See," Jeremy said. "She's tough, you know."

"Of that," Libby said, throwing Sandra a look, "I have no doubt." In fact, she reminded her of a girl called Barbara Nelson who used to pick on her in third grade. "So are you two friends?"

Jeremy's answer was vague. "Something like that." Then he leaned forward. "I called because I want to get some things straight with both of you," he said, changing the subject.

"What a coincidence," Libby said, also leaning

forward. "We want to get some things straightened out with you too."

Bernie popped the tab on the top of her Budweiser beer and took a sip. She made a face and put the can down. Now she remembered why she didn't drink this stuff anymore. It tasted like warm piss. She'd definitely been spoiled by the microbrews.

"Indeed we do," she said, seconding Libby.

"Such as?" Jeremy asked.

Bernie extended her hand palm up and inclined her head. "Age before beauty."

Jeremy ran his finger around the top of his beer can. "Fine. If you insist, I will. First off, I don't know where Ellen gets off saying her husband and my wife were hooking up."

"I take it Lisa told you?" Bernie asked.

"She picked up the phone as soon as you left," Jeremy replied.

Bernie could imagine the phone call. "So, it's not true?" she asked.

"What do you think?" Jeremy replied, narrowing his eyes.

"Honestly, I have no idea."

Jeremy clenched his fist. "Why would my wife hook up with someone like Bruce?"

"I don't know. Because she was attracted to him?" Bernie said.

"She can't stand the man," Jeremy hissed.

"Maybe Lisa did it to piss you off," Libby

replied. "Or maybe she wanted to get Ellen back for something."

"Ab-so-lu-te-ly not," Jeremy replied. He sat back and took a deep breath and let it out. Libby could see him calming himself down. "My wife and I have an excellent relationship." Jeremy took a sip of his beer, made a face, and set the can down.

"So if we ask the neighbors we wouldn't hear any stories about fights between you and Lisa?" Libby asked, fishing around.

"Of course you would. Everyone has fights now and then."

"I think my sister is talking about the kind the police are called in on," Bernie said.

"Don't be absurd," Jeremy scoffed. "It's true Lisa and I have had some problems in the past," he admitted. "But we've put those behind us. I'll take an oath on that on my mother's grave."

"That's a little extreme," Libby replied.

"Why would Ellen say something like that?" Bernie asked.

"Because she's delusional," Jeremy said. He downed a big gulp of his beer. "The woman is crazy."

"Maybe a little emotional, a little overreactive," Bernie allowed, defending her friend, "but not crazy. Usually she has a reason for what she says. She doesn't make things up out of whole cloth."

"She did in this case," Jeremy said. "I can assure you of that."

Bernie decided not to argue the point.

Jeremy smiled a tight little smile and moved his Rolex up and down his wrist. The motion seemed to calm him. "I want to make sure you understand that, because I don't want that rumor spread around town." This time his tone was sincere.

"Then you should talk to Ellen," Bernie told him. "She's the one who's saying it, not us."

Jeremy shook his head. It was a more in sorrow than anger gesture. "I realize that. My wife always said she was a little too tightly wrapped. I know she doesn't like me. I know she's mad at Lisa, but this . . . this goes beyond the pale." He turned his hands palms up and held them out. "God only knows who else she's told.

"This is a small town and Lisa and I have to live in it," Jeremy continued. He stabbed the table-top with the tip of his finger. "I live on my reputation." He stabbed the table with his finger again to make his point. "The last thing I need is for my name or my wife's name to be the target of salacious rumors."

"Salacious. Nice word," Bernie commented.

Jeremy colored a little. "I'm serious here."

"We can see that," Bernie said, referring to herself and her sister.

"And while we're on the subject, I also don't

want to be dragged through the mud of a murder investigation by you guys."

"Dragged through the mud? Wow," Bernie said.

Jeremy leaned back. "I don't want you guys going around to our neighbors and putting ideas in their heads."

"And if the police talk to your neighbors?"

"That's not going to happen."

"But if it does?" Bernie persisted.

"I'll deal with it then." Jeremy smiled a real smile for the first time since Bernie and Libby had walked into the bar. "Good. I'm glad that's settled," he said, even though from Bernie's point of view nothing had been. He began to stand. "Then we're all through here."

"Not quite," Bernie countered.

Chapter 34

J eremy Stone glared at Bernie and Libby. *This,* Bernie thought, *is a man who is used to getting his own way.* She gave him her most charming smile.

"Now, it's my turn," she said.

Jeremy's expression darkened. "I thought we were done."

"And we will be soon," Bernie cooed. "But we have some questions—just a few—we need answered."

"And if I don't want to answer them?" Jeremy said.

Bernie leaned back in her chair and continued smiling. "One thing about our shop. Every time there's a homicide in Longely our business goes up. Do you know why?"

Jeremy shook his head. "Should I care?"

"Indeed you should. Here's the thing. People want to know what happened," she said. "Think of us as Twitter with coffee and muffins."

"Is that a threat?" Jeremy demanded.

"No," Bernie said. "It's a fact. People ask questions; they want answers. When they don't get them, they make up their own explanations."

Jeremy drummed his fingers on the table while he thought. "Okay," he said after a slight pause, while he perched on the edge of his chair. "I get it. What do you want to know? Within reason, of course."

"Good." Bernie ran her finger around the top of the beer can. "First off, we want to know about your sister, Daisy."

"What about her?" Jeremy demanded.

"Well, she was married to Manny, right?" Libby asked.

"A long time ago," Jeremy conceded.

"And then they got divorced?" Libby continued.

"So I was informed by a neighbor," Jeremy said.

Bernie leaned forward again. "Your sister didn't tell you?"

Jeremy shook his head. He looked sad. "My sister and I haven't spoken to each other for years and years."

"Why?" Libby asked.

Jeremy looked down at the table and back up. "We had a really bad fight before she ran off to Colorado. I reckon we haven't spoken more than once or twice since then."

"Do you know where she is now?" Libby asked.

Jeremy shrugged. "Your guess is as good as mine. I don't have the foggiest idea."

"Would anyone in your family know?"

"I'm it," Jeremy said. "My mother and father died years ago, and since they were only children, there really isn't anyone else." Jeremy took a sip of his beer and put his can down. "You still haven't told me why you want to know about Daisy."

Bernie took the beer tab from her can and started spinning it on the table. "We want to talk to her. We were hoping she could tell us a little more about Manny."

"Doubtful," Jeremy said. "From what I can gather, she and Manny haven't talked to each other in years. I was told it was a nasty divorce."

"Who told you?" Libby asked.

"The same person who told me they'd gotten divorced."

"Can we speak to him or her?" Bernie asked.

Jeremy shook his head, "I'm afraid not. He passed on a number of years ago."

"I see," Bernie said. "You know," she continued, "given the circumstances, I find it a little odd that Manny came to talk to you."

"I thought it was a bit odd too," Jeremy allowed. "But then Manny and I had a much better relationship than my sister and I did, not that that's saying much. Frankly, I was surprised to see him. I'd heard he'd died in a car crash." Jeremy leaned back in his chair and steepled his fingers together. "Is this helping at all?"

"A little. At this stage every crumb of knowledge helps." Bernie put the beer tab down.

Jeremy put his hands palms down on the table. "Are we done yet?"

"Not quite," Bernie said.

Jeremy tapped his watch face. "I have things to do."

"So do I," Bernie told him.

"Important things," Jeremy said.

"Fine," Bernie said. "But think about this. The more information we have, the faster we can wrap up this investigation."

Jeremy started drumming his fingers on the table again. "And I should care about that . . . why?"

"You should care about it," Bernie informed him, "because as much as you dislike Ellen"—she held up her hand—"and don't bother to deny it because it's obviously true—it's still in your interest to get Ellen off the hook and out of the limelight. I don't wish to point out the obvious, but you just told me you didn't want your family name dragged through the mud, and Manny *did* work for your wife's business. It makes people wonder. Need I say more?"

"Do the police know that?" Jeremy asked, looking a little more concerned.

"That he worked for Arf? Not unless Lisa told them."

"She didn't," Jeremy stated. "Have you?"

"Hardly," Libby replied. "Otherwise, you would have gotten a call from a detective by now. But it's probably only a matter of time before they find out."

Jeremy started twisting his Rolex around his wrist again.

"Good thing that's real," Bernie said, pointing at the watch. "Otherwise you'd have worn the plating off by now."

Jeremy sighed. After a minute of mulling things over, he said, "Fine. What are a few more minutes in the scheme of things anyway? There's really not much to tell. Manny looked me up because he was hoping I could find him a job . . . which, as you know, I did."

So far, Libby thought, Jeremy and Lisa's stories jibed, not that that was surprising. They'd probably talked things over by now.

"Simple as that?" Bernie asked.

"Yes," Jeremy replied. "As simple as that.

Manny called up and said he wanted to talk to me. Like I said, I was pretty surprised to hear his voice after all this time. Anyway, I took him to lunch down at Dad's Diner . . . I certainly wasn't taking him to the club. He looked in pretty bad shape when he walked into the place. In fact, I didn't recognize him at first, he'd gained so much weight."

"So then what?" Libby asked.

"We sat down and had a couple of sandwiches and he asked me if I knew of anyone who was hiring. I told him about Arf and he seemed to be all right with it, so later that evening I talked to Lisa and arranged for a meeting between the two of them."

"What else?" Libby asked.

"Nothing else. Then we ate lunch."

"What did you talk about?"

Jeremy scratched his chin. "Now that I come to think of it, we really didn't. He thanked me and told me he was going through a rough patch. By that time the waitress came with our sandwiches and we finished them and left." Jeremy thought for a moment. "I doubt we were in Dad's for more than half an hour. The service there is pretty fast, which was just as well because Manny seemed uneasy, like he wanted to get out of there." Jeremy drained his glass and stood up. "And that, as they say, is all she wrote. So, ladies, I bid you a farewell."

"One last question," Bernie said.

"Oh for God's sake, what?" Jeremy cried. "Enough is enough."

"We just want to know how Bruce reacted when you told him about Ellen's plan," Bernie said.

Jeremy shot his cuffs. "I wouldn't know because I didn't tell him."

"But Lisa said you did," Libby objected.

"That's because I lied," Jeremy said. "When it came down to it, I couldn't do it. I figured it really wasn't my place. I just told Lisa I had to keep the peace. But he might have known anyway. It was just a feeling I got when we were talking."

"How would he know, if you didn't tell him?" Bernie asked.

Jeremy shrugged. "Who knows who Ellen told? She could even have told Manny."

"Manny?" Bernie protested. "That makes no sense at all."

Jeremy shrugged again. "Maybe I'm wrong. Anyway, isn't it up to you two to make sense out of everything?" Jeremy asked Bernie and Libby before he walked out the door.

Chapter 35

It was business as usual at A Taste of Heaven, meaning the line was out the door, when Ryan and Matt walked into the shop at seven the next morning and asked to see Bernie and Libby.

"Hey, there are some kids to see you guys," Amber called into the kitchen before she turned back to the customer she was waiting on.

That was all she had time to say because it was the midmorning rush and she and Googie were swamped trying to fill the orders of the commuters who needed to make the 7:16 Metro-North into Penn Station.

"It's us," Ryan yelled over the din of the crowd.

"Figured," Bernie yelled back. "Come on back."

Amber jerked her head to the left. "That way," she said, directing the two brothers to the door on the left.

Libby looked up from what she was doing. "Could they have picked a worse time?" she muttered to her sister as she ladled raspberry muffin batter into three tins.

Not only was this one of the busiest times of the morning, but she and Bernie had overslept by an hour, so now they were behind on their lunch prep.

"Probably not," Bernie agreed. She was in the

middle of making a blue cheese and walnut potato salad. She'd eaten it down in a Gramercy Park bistro a couple of weeks ago and was anxious to see how it was going to do on A Little Taste of Heaven's menu.

She took the pot filled with new potatoes off the stove and poured the contents into a large sieve set in the kitchen sink. A plume of steam rose as the boiling water spilled out. Bernie gave the sieve a sharp shake to get the remaining liquid out, after which she conveyed the sieve to a second prep table, got a large bowl off the shelf, and dumped the potatoes onto a cutting board.

"Damn, they're hot," she said after she'd sliced a few. "I need asbestos fingers. Why aren't you doing this?" she asked Libby.

"Because I chopped ten pounds of onions," Libby reminded her.

"I guess this is better," Bernie conceded.

She hated chopping onions. By the time she was done the tears were running down her face. She'd tried freezing them and peeling them under water, but that didn't work, so then she'd tried the match trick. That hadn't worked either. Short of a scuba tank and a regulator, nothing that she knew kept the fumes out of her eyes and that, as one of her Cali friends used to say, was a little de trop. She'd done a quarter of the potatoes when Ryan and Matt marched through the door.

"I got it," Ryan announced. Then before Bernie

could ask him what he'd gotten, Ryan pointed to one of the chocolate chip muffins cooling on the rack on the prep table over by the far wall. "Can I have one of those?"

"Can I have one too?" Matt asked.

"By all means," Bernie said, avoiding Libby's scowl as the boys took two muffins apiece. "Now, what did you get?"

Ryan gave her a dumbfounded look. "The password to the laptop, of course."

"Of course." Bernie stopped slicing the potatoes and hit her forehead with the heel of her palm. "Sorry." How could she have forgotten about Manny's computer? There was way too much going on. Either that or she was definitely losing her grip. "So you unlocked it?"

Ryan grinned. "That's what I just said. It was a snap," he added, speaking through a mouthful of chocolate chip muffin. "I don't suppose you have any milk around here?"

"Just give me a sec to finish this up and I'll get you some," Bernie told him.

If she didn't finish the potato salad now before the potatoes cooled off, they wouldn't absorb all the dressing. As Ryan and Matt watched, Bernie sliced up the remaining potatoes and poured the vinaigrette she'd made with walnut oil, lemon juice, a touch of Dijon mustard, and salt and pepper over them. Then she quickly added the piles of chopped parsley, scallions, blue cheese, and walnuts she'd prepped earlier, reached into the bowl with her hands, and carefully combined the ingredients, taking care not to break the slices of potato. When she was sure all the ingredients were properly distributed, she covered the bowl with a layer of plastic wrap and put it in the cooler to meld.

One salad down and eight more to go, Bernie thought as she walked over to the three-basin sink and washed her hands.

"Now?" Ryan asked Bernie as she reached for a paper towel to dry them.

"Yes, now," Bernie replied, and she went out front to get Matt and Ryan a couple of pints of milk. "We have to get more whole milk from Lee's Dairy," she informed Libby on her way to the cooler. "We're almost out."

"I know." Libby didn't look up. She was carefully scraping the last of the raspberry batter out of the bowl and into the muffin tin with her spatula. "It's on the list."

Bernie was back from the front a moment later. "How long did it take you to unlock the laptop?" she asked Ryan as she handed the boys their drinks. They both opened up the bottles and proceeded to chug the milk down.

"Ten minutes," Ryan said when he was done. He wiped his milk mustache off his upper lip with the back of his hand.

"It took thirteen," Matt said.

"I still win the bet."

"By two lousy minutes."

Ryan shrugged. "Two minutes is two minutes. I said I'd do it in less than fifteen and I did, which means you still have to drive me to the mall."

Matt put the empty pint bottle on the corner of the prep table. "You know what I think?" he said.

"What?" Ryan asked.

Matt wagged a finger at his brother. "I think your watch is slow, that's what I think."

Ryan frowned. "See. I knew you were going to punk out, like you always do."

"Do not," Matt protested.

"Do too."

"Sez you," Matt said, punching his brother in the arm.

Bernie intervened. "That is enough!" she cried before the battle escalated.

The boys stopped talking and looked at her.

Ryan hitched up his pants. "Sorry," he mumbled.

"Me too," Matt said, reseating his baseball cap on his head.

"Apology accepted." Berne smiled. She turned to Ryan. "So you unlocked Manny's laptop in less than fifteen minutes?"

Ryan nodded.

"That's pretty fast."

"I was trying for ten."

Bernie grinned. "Boy, that makes me feel dumb," she said. "I don't think I could do it like ever."

Ryan's smile lit up his face. Bernie figured he didn't get too many compliments.

"It's really easy once you know the tricks," Ryan told her. "You want me to tell you how I did it?"

"By all means," Libby and Bernie said together. They looked at each other and laughed.

Ryan's smile grew so large it threatened to engulf his entire face. Then he went into a long, technical explanation of how he'd done what he had, of which Bernie and Libby understood maybe every tenth word, and that was because they were prepositions. When he was through, Ryan reached into his backpack, took out Manny's laptop, and ceremoniously handed it to Bernie. "Here you go," he said. "Nothing too interesting on it that I can see. It was pretty much all standard stuff. Yahoo. An AOL account, which I opened up for you too, by the way."

Ryan scrunched up his face. "I mean who uses AOL anymore? That's an old person's e-mail. He also had Excel, but nothing in it. There were no photos. He didn't even change his desktop settings. It's like it was when it came out of the factory." He rubbed his nose with his knuckle. "I gotta say this guy had the same taste in music as my mom and he played solitaire like she does. I mean WTF. Oops." He put his hand to his mouth. "Sorry about the language, but how lame is that? At least if he was playing Warcraft."

"So you could open all the apps?" Bernie asked him.

"Yeah," Ryan said. "I got 'em all opened. Nothing like using the same password for everything. I mean who does that?"

Bernie looked down at the ground. She did. Otherwise she couldn't remember any of them.

"And we'll be able to open them too?" Libby asked, referring to her and her sister.

Ryan gave her an incredulous look. "What would be the point of this if you couldn't?" And he gave them the password. "You wanna write it down?" Ryan asked.

Libby reached for a pen and a scrap of paper. If she didn't, she'd never remember it.

"After I opened everything up," Ryan said, "I took a look around. I was hoping I'd find some info on why this guy Manny was killed. Like that he was blackmailing someone or dealing drugs or that he was an international arms dealer. You know, something like that."

"And did you find anything?" Libby asked.

Ryan shook his head. "Not that I could see."

"I didn't see anything either," Matt added.

Bernie decided both boys sounded disappointed.

Ryan continued talking. "Most of the stuff I looked at was pretty boring," he confided. "It was all about real estate and things like that." He sighed and yanked up his pants, which were almost down around his thighs. "I just hope there's something on there that helps my mom."

"Me too," Bernie said. "Me too." The boys looked so crestfallen that Bernie added, "Thank you again. This is going to be an enormous help."

"Really?" Ryan asked, brightening.

"Yes, really," Bernie answered. She only hoped that was the case.

Chapter 36

Seen your mom again?" Bernie asked as she rested the Dell on the prep table and opened it. She couldn't resist taking a peek even though she and Libby had a ton of work to do.

"Yeah," Ryan said. "This morning."

Bernie looked up. "She's home?"

"No. She's still at that motel place, but she came back home last night and she and my dad shut themselves in the study and told us to go to bed. I guess she left after I went to sleep, but we got a text message telling us where she was and not to worry, but I don't know. She looks kind of weird. Her hair's all funny and she's not wearing any makeup or anything."

"Doofus, that's because we woke her up," Matt said.

"She said she wasn't sleeping," Ryan told his brother.

"She didn't say that."

"Yeah, she did. You were taking a piss."

"Oh." Matt stopped for a moment while he processed that. "Yeah. Well. Maybe."

"Definitely, dude."

Matt ran his hand through his hair. It looked as if it needed to be combed. "I wouldn't be sleeping either staying in that place."

"She's on the other side."

"So what? It's still the same place. I'd rather sleep on a park bench than stay in there. I think what happened affected her brain." Matt tapped the side of his head with his finger to emphasize the point. "Especially when she can be sleeping at home." Ryan turned to Libby and Bernie. "We brought her some cereal," he explained. "Lucky Charms."

"That was nice of you," Libby said.

"Yeah, well. She said she missed having breakfast with us," Ryan said. "I figured it was the least we could so, especially since this is our fault."

"It really isn't," Libby said.

"Yeah, it is," Ryan replied. "If we'd gotten her a birthday card none of this would have happened."

"Did Ellen say that?" Bernie asked.

"No. Dad did," Matt replied.

"No, he didn't," Ryan said.

"He did too. I heard him."

"That may be overstating things a bit," Bernie said, and she turned to Manny's laptop, effectively ending the conversation. "Let's take a look at this shall we?"

"Cool," Ryan said as he, his brother, and Libby crowded around Bernie.

"You're right, Ryan. This is pretty basic," she noted now that she'd taken a good look.

"That's what I told you," Ryan said. "There isn't even any porn." He sounded disappointed. "At least none that I can see."

Bernie laughed and opened up Manny's AOL account and took a peek. Ryan was right again. It was boring. Manny's e-mails were mostly junk mail—stuff about eating healthy, offers for miracle pills that helped you lose weight, exercise programs that promised to help you gain fifteen pounds of muscle mass in five days, offers for Viagra and penis enhancers, Groupon offers—stuff that went straight to Bernie's spam folder.

A little more promising were ads from firms touting various kinds of property investment schemes, stuff from Zillow, and two articles about a firm called Bruce and Calle, who were developing a parcel of land in Brooklyn.

"I guess Manny was interested in real estate," Bernie noted.

"I wonder why," Libby mused. "He didn't strike me as someone who had money to invest. He couldn't even afford his own place."

"Maybe he watched too many reality TV shows about flipping houses," Bernie said. "Maybe he thought this was how he was going to make his fortune."

"You going to call them now?" Ryan asked.

"Who?" Bernie asked, not getting Ryan's reference.

"That company that's selling stuff."

"You mean Bruce and Calle?"

Ryan nodded his head. "Yup. I looked them up. They're like this really big deal."

"I don't know what I'd ask if I did call them up," Bernie said.

Ryan shrugged. "Ask about Manny. I mean isn't that like a lead or something? They're always following up stuff like that on TV."

"It's really unlikely that Manny would have anything to do with them," Bernie observed. Then she looked at Ryan's face and changed her answer to, "I'll call if I need to," as she continued to scroll down Manny's e-mail.

She found more ads from real estate firms, most concerning parcels of land all over the United States, a shipping confirmation for an order containing a pair of jeans from the Big and Tall shop, and notification that three books on playing chess had been sent from Amazon. She checked the trash and spam. It was all junk mail and a few orders from Amazon. What there weren't, noted Bernie, were any e-mails from friends and family.

Bernie moved on and opened up Manny's Facebook account. Evidently, Manny had one friend—Daisy. No one else was listed. There was one post from a couple of months ago that read, SEE YOU. And that was it.

Bernie sighed and shook her head. "Too bad," she murmured. She'd been hoping for more.

"What's too bad?" Libby asked.

"That Manny didn't use social media," Bernie said.

"So?" Libby pointed to herself. "I don't have any social media accounts. What's wrong with that?"

"Seriously?" Ryan asked, clearly shocked. "You're not on Facebook or Instagram or Snapchat?"

"No, I'm not," Libby retorted. "Why? Is that a problem?"

"How do you talk to people?"

Libby put her hands on her hips. "The old-fashioned way. Face to face."

Ryan yanked his pants up. "That's so . . ."

". . . so what?" Libby demanded.

"Old," Ryan said.

Libby glared at him.

"Lots of my friends aren't on social media either," Bernie told Libby in an effort to make her feel better—even though all of them were. "It just would have made it easier for us to find out stuff about Manny if he was on some of the sites."

"Maybe that's why he wasn't on them," Ryan suggested as he yanked his pants up for the third time. The boy definitely needed a belt, Bernie decided. "Maybe he was on the down-low."

"Could be," Bernie concurred. It was certainly a possibility.

Libby snapped her fingers. Bernie, Ryan, and Matt turned to look at her. "You know, come to think of it, I don't think Manny had a cell phone."

"Everyone has a cell phone," Matt scoffed.

"I didn't see one in the motel room," Libby told Matt. She turned to Bernie. "Did you?"

"Now that you mention it, no, I didn't," Bernie replied. "And he didn't have one on him."

"Someone probably stole it," Ryan declared. "Those things are worth money. You unlock them and sell them on Craigslist."

Bernie tapped her fingers on the prep table. "Or the killer could have taken it."

"And sold it on Craigslist," Ryan interjected.

Bernie turned to Ryan. "How easy would it be to erase stuff off Manny's computer?"

Matt answered. "It would be a piece of cake."

"I checked and no one did anything like that," Ryan assured Bernie.

"And anyway," Matt continued, "if they were that serious they would have taken the hard drive out and run over it."

"Or wiped it clean and sold it," Ryan observed.

"Get real," Matt sneered. "The thing can't be worth more than thirty bucks."

"Hey, lame-o," Ryan said. "Thirty bucks is thirty bucks."

Matt snorted. "You've got money on the brain."

"So much for that idea," Bernie said, interrupting the two brothers. She closed the Dell. "Time to get back to work," she announced.

"That's it?" Ryan cried. "That's all you're going to do."

Bernie patted his shoulder. "I promise we're going to spend more time on this after the lunch rush."

Libby chimed in with a "we definitely will," which seemed to mollify Ryan. Bernie once again thanked Ryan and Matt for everything they'd done and was heading for the office, laptop in hand, figuring she'd stow it there, when she heard a commotion out front.

Amber was saying, "You can't go back there," and a man was replying, "Oh yeah? Watch me."

A few seconds later, Bruce burst into the kitchen. Amber was right behind him.

Chapter 37

Bruce took a look around, spotted Ryan and Matt, and headed toward them.

"Ethan told me you were here," he growled.

"You want me to call the cops?" Amber asked.

Bernie shook her head. "It's okay."

"Are you sure?" Amber asked.

"Yeah," Bernie told her. "I'm sure."

Amber looked dubious.

"Seriously," Bernie reassured her. "I've got this. Everything is under control."

"Okay," Amber said. "But Googie and I are out front if you need us."

Bernie nodded her thanks and told Amber to get back to work. Calling the police would only hype things up, instead of calm things down. Anyway, she was holding Manny's stolen Dell— not something that needed to be called attention to. Amber nodded and left and Bernie turned her attention back to Bruce and his sons.

"That little punk," Matt was muttering. He clenched and unclenched his fists as he turned to Ryan. "See. I told you we shouldn't have said anything to him. The kid's a total loser."

"No, he's smart," Bruce shot back. "You two are the losers."

Matt snorted. "Yeah. Well, we'll see how smart the little creep is when I—"

"When you do what?" Bruce demanded, interrupting his eldest son's rant.

Matt flushed. "Nothing."

Bruce took a step forward. "Listen to me carefully. I don't want you saying or doing anything to Ethan because he talked to me," Bruce warned.

Matt looked at his feet. "I wasn't gonna do nuthin'," he mumbled resentfully.

"You aren't going to do anything and I'm serious about this. Not a threat. Not a noogie. Not a finger on him. No hot sauce in his food. You got me?"

Matt nodded.

"And that goes for you too, Ryan."

Ryan scuffled his feet. "Yeah. I get it."

By now Bruce was almost nose to nose with his sons. "I'm dead serious about this. I want both of you to promise me that you'll leave your younger brother alone."

"Absolutely, dude," Matt said.

"Do not call me dude," Bruce said to Matt through clenched teeth.

"Sure. Whatever. How come you're always picking on me?"

"I don't," Bruce told him.

"Yeah you do. Like now. Why would I do anything to Ethan?"

Bruce wagged a finger under Matt's nose. "I haven't forgotten Ethan and the curfew incident, so don't try and play me," he warned. "I'm not your mother. Are we clear?"

Matt put his hands up in a gesture of mock surrender. "Crystal."

"I hope so."

Bernie watched Bruce scrutinize Matt's face. She reckoned Bruce must have believed him, because Bruce abruptly switched subjects, asking Matt what he and his brother were doing at the shop. Bernie decided it was time to get involved.

"They returned my laptop to me," she said, stepping forward.

Bruce scowled. "Really?"

"Yes, really. I asked Ryan to fix it. I had some sort of thing . . ."

"Virus," Ryan helpfully explained.

"Yes. Virus in it," Bernie said. "And he got it working again. I was very impressed. You should be proud of your son."

Bruce glowered. "I'd be prouder of him if he wasn't failing English and social studies and if he managed to get to class on time, so I'd stop getting calls from his school."

"Dad, you don't have to tell everyone," Ryan whined.

"If you're that embarrassed do your work and it won't be an issue," Bruce told him.

"Excuse me," Bernie said. She nodded at the laptop she was holding. "I'm just going to put this in the office so I don't get flour in it." Bernie knew it was irrational; there was no way Bruce could know whose laptop she was holding, but she still felt better with the computer away from Bruce's eyes.

"Do whatever you want," Bruce told Bernie, briefly looking at her before turning his gaze back to his sons. He began to lecture them.

"I've already warned you about getting mixed up in this stuff with your mother," he said. "I want you to let the police and the lawyers handle this." He rubbed his head. "I'm at my wit's end as it is. I don't need to worry about you two."

"Dad," Matt answered, contriving to look angelic. "That's why we're staying as far away as possible from the situation."

"Yeah," Ryan said. "You've made that really clear about our not getting involved."

"Good. Because I don't want any misunderstandings on the subject." Bruce indicated the door to the front of the shop. "Now, I want you two out of here. This is a school day."

"But, Dad," Matt protested. "We have plenty of time before the bell."

Bruce raised his hand. Matt stopped talking. "Do you want to lose your car?"

Matt looked down at the floor. "No," he mumbled.

"Then get out of here," Bruce ordered. "And I don't want to see you here again or that car of yours is gone. You can count on it."

Ryan frowned. "Not even to buy muffins?" he wheedled. "Or brownies? I like the brownies here. I mean since Mom's gone there's nothing to eat in the house. And anyway, these don't come out of a box."

"Out," Bruce bellowed.

"I'd appreciate it if you lowered your voices," Libby told him. "In case you haven't noticed, this is a place of business." She turned to Matt and

Ryan. "Guys," she said, "ask Amber for some brownies on your way out."

"And muffins?" Ryan asked hopefully. "Can we have a couple of those too?"

"Yes. And muffins. In fact, you can throw in some cookies too."

"That's not necessary," Bruce told her.

"I think it is," Libby replied. "You should feed them better." Now that she was looking at Matt and Ryan, she realized how skinny they were. "And get a couple of things for your brother as well," she added.

"Dad," Matt said.

Bruce glared at him. "What?"

"When is Mom coming back?"

"I don't know."

"Because," Matt said, "I'm saying to you what Ethan said to you before and I said to Mom this morning. If you guys get divorced none of us are going to speak to you again."

Then he and Ryan marched out of the back room before their dad could reply.

"Wow," Bernie said. "That's quite the ultimatum."

"They don't mean it," Bruce said.

Libby shook her head. "I wouldn't be so sure if I were you."

Chapter 38

Bruce waited until his sons were out the door before turning to Libby and Bernie. Then he said, "I told my kids and now I'm spelling it out for you. I don't want my sons here. I don't want them in the shop. I don't want them in your apartment. I don't want them near you. Period. Are we clear on that?"

"And if they do come around?" Bernie asked.

"I'll get a restraining order against you."

"Don't you think you're going over the top with this?" Libby asked. "That seems a little excessive."

"I don't think it's excessive." Bruce glared at her. "I don't think it's excessive at all. I can't deal with any more stuff." His voice rose. "At the very least, I need to know that my kids are where they ought to be."

Bernie rebuttoned the top button of her white cotton blouse. "I see."

"Do you really?" Bruce challenged.

"Yes," Bernie replied in a soft voice. "I think I do. Can I get you some coffee? You look as if you could use some."

In truth, Bruce looked as if he'd just rolled out of bed. He had a two-day growth of beard and hair that needed to be combed. There was a small coffee stain on the bottom of his pale blue polo shirt, his khakis were wrinkled, and the jacket he was wearing looked as if it had spent the night rolled up in a ball.

"Thanks, but no thanks," Bruce replied.

"Also, just so you know, you have a spot of toothpaste on your cheek," Bernie continued, indicating the spot by touching her own cheek.

"I don't care," Bruce informed her, rubbing the spot vigorously with the side of his hand. "We're not talking about my personal appearance here."

Bernie shrugged. "Fine. I was just trying to be helpful."

"Don't be," Bruce told her. "You've done enough of that already."

Bernie sighed. She was going from guilty to annoyed. "Are you talking about my suggestion to Ellen? I've already explained about that."

"No. I'm talking about the money you took from my kids. You should be ashamed of yourself."

Bernie stood straighter. "I'm not. On the contrary, I think hiring us makes your kids feel as if they're doing something to help their mom out, which they really need right now. In any case, Ellen asked them to come to us."

Bruce sawed the air with his right hand. "I don't care what my wife asked them to do. She's a total whack job. The fact that she got them involved in this proves how off her judgment is."

"Unlike yours?" Bernie asked.

"Meaning what?" Bruce demanded. "I wasn't the one who suggested she kidnap herself."

"I've already explained that a hundred times. It was a joke. A joke."

"Well, Ellen didn't take it that way."

"If I had known she would have taken it seriously, I never would have opened my mouth," Bernie protested.

"You should think before you speak," Bruce told her.

Bernie put her hands on her hips. "If we're passing the guilt around, let's talk about you. Let's talk about why Ellen did what she did. You forgot her birthday; you forgot her anniversary. You forgot Mother's Day."

"We got her a birthday present," Bruce protested.

"An iron? Seriously?" Bernie said. "All she wanted was some flowers. Hell, she probably would have been satisfied with a card. A hug. A thank-you. Anything. This was her way of asking for attention."

"Well, she sure got it," Bruce allowed.

"And how," Libby agreed. "Although I'm sure this is not the kind of attention she had in mind."

"Fine," Bruce said. "But things go both ways. What about me?" he demanded.

"What about you?" Bernie replied.

"You think I wouldn't like a little back rub when I get home or a little homemade goodie instead of a list of complaints. You think I don't have troubles?"

"I never said you didn't," Bernie said, remembering what Brandon had told her about Bruce's finances.

"My life is falling apart. I'm trying to support my family, and I'm exhausted when I get home," Bruce snapped. "Forgive me if I forget to ask Ellen how her day is going and I don't want to listen to a detailed recitation of her problems with the washing machine or that the mixer is broken. Forgive me if all I want to do is turn on the TV, have a beer, and watch some mindless junk for an hour before I go to bed."

"I understand you're tired, I understand you're stressed," Bernie said quietly. "But really, how much effort would it have taken to pick up the phone and call the florist?"

"I did that in the beginning. I did," Bruce replied in response to Bernie's skeptical look. "But whatever I did was never good enough. If I got Ellen daisies she wanted roses; if I got her roses she wanted daylilies. And you know what? It still isn't. There's always something wrong. You haven't lived with Ellen. You have no idea how demanding she can be."

"I agree she can be a little bit needy," Bernie responded. What else could she say? It was true.

"A little. Ha. That's a laugh."

Libby was about to say something when the

kitchen timer went off. She hurried over to the oven and peeked in. Then she lightly pressed the top of one of the muffins. It didn't spring back. Libby estimated that they had ten more minutes to go. She closed the oven door and reset the timer.

"So did you know about Ellen's plan?" Libby asked, fishing.

"How would I know?" Bruce demanded.

Libby shrugged. "I don't know. Maybe you heard about it."

"From who?"

"Possibly Manny," Libby said.

"Why would Ellen tell him?" Bruce asked.

"Because they were friends," Libby suggested.

Bruce laughed. "Well, that's not the impression I got from Manny. I mean honestly, I don't think they talked much."

"How come you think that?" Bernie asked, trying to keep her face expressionless. Talk about being clueless.

"Because he told me," Bruce said.

"You were friends?" Libby asked.

"We played squash together, so we talked the way that guys do."

"Squash?" Bernie repeated, genuinely surprised. Somehow, she couldn't see either Manny or Bruce playing that game.

"That's right," Bruce replied. "Why? Do you have a problem with that too?"

"No. Not at all," Bernie said hastily. "It's just that you guys don't seem like the squash types."

"And what type is that?" Bruce inquired.

"Easy. Rich, white, and privileged."

Despite himself, Bruce smiled. "Maybe that's true in other places but not at the Longely Y."

"But why squash?" Libby asked.

"It's good for losing weight." Bruce patted his belly unconsciously. "So we played once, sometimes twice a week."

"And did it work?" Libby inquired. She was always trying to lose twenty pounds.

"Yeah," Bruce answered. "It did. Manny lost about twenty pounds and I lost seven."

"Not bad," Libby allowed, picturing herself fitting into her old jeans. Then she remembered she was allergic to exercise.

"Did Manny have any friends there? Any enemies?" Bernie asked, bringing the conversation back to the investigation into Manny's death. "Did he play with anyone else?"

"Not that I know about," Bruce answered. "He came as my guest. Usually we played a couple of games and left. But occasionally Manny stayed behind. As to friends and enemies, not really. He pretty much kept to himself."

"Did he talk to anyone in the locker room?" Libby asked.

"He didn't change in the locker room. He had

his shorts on when he came. So did I, for that matter. Easier that way."

"And you never saw him speak to anyone when you were both there?" Libby inquired.

"Not really."

Libby cocked her head. "No one?"

Bruce scratched behind his ear. "Well, there was this woman. Sometimes he exchanged a few words with her."

"Does she have a name?" Libby asked.

"I think it was Sandy or Sandra. Something like that. I could be mistaken though."

Bernie and Libby exchanged looks.

"Was she thin and muscular with blond hair that looked like straw?" Bernie asked. "Very tan?"

"Yeah," Bruce said. "That's her. How did you know?"

"A lucky guess," Bernie said, thinking back to the interaction between Sandra and Jeremy at the Roost. She took a step forward. "Maybe you can help me understand something about Ellen," she said, switching the subject.

Bruce let out a mirthless laugh. "Then you've come to the wrong department, that's for sure."

"Do you have any idea why Ellen pretended she didn't know who Manny was?"

"Well, she told me she was scared and I believe it. Hell, if it was me I probably would have done the same thing," Bruce allowed.

Libby folded her arms across her chest. "Okay. I

understand Ellen's reason for not identifying Manny, but what was yours? Did you want to help your wife out? Or was it something else?"

"That's simple," Bruce replied. "I never saw him lying on the bed in the motel."

Bernie lifted an eyebrow in disbelief. "Say what?"

"No. It's true," Bruce insisted.

"I think my sister and I are having a hard time believing that," Libby told him. "You were there." She rubbed her upper arms. "Remember? Because I certainly do."

Bruce look abashed. "Sorry about grabbing you like that, but the cops and I had just gotten to the motel when you blundered out of the woods."

"You didn't have to dig your fingers in like that."

Bruce apologized again. "It's just that everything happened so fast," he explained. "The police got me while I was pulling up my driveway and told me that there was an incident involving Ellen. Then they drove me over to the motel. There was a squad car there already and I had just gotten out of the one I was riding in and was heading toward Ellen, when we heard something moving around in the woods."

"Me," Libby declared.

"Yeah, you," Bruce said. "Unfortunately." He scratched underneath his collar. "You're lucky Henderson didn't shoot you. I think he would have—he had his service weapon out—but I rushed out to grab you before he could. I guess everyone was really jacked because of the homicide. I never set foot in the motel room because I was too busy dealing with Ellen, and no one ever came around and showed me Manny's picture."

"So," Libby said after mulling over Bruce's replies for a moment, "you're telling me you didn't call the police?"

Bruce threw his hands up in the air. "Why should I have? I didn't even know there was a note. I never got into the house to read it. I gave it to the police later."

"So who alerted them, if you didn't?" Bernie asked. She could see Amber signaling her from the doorway. Bernie nodded and held out five fingers, signifying that she'd be out front in five more minutes. Amber nodded and left.

Bruce shrugged. "Your guess is as good as mine."

"Do you think Ellen killed Manny?" Libby abruptly asked Bruce.

Bruce slicked back his hair with the palm of his hand and swallowed. His eyes roved around the kitchen. Finally they came to rest on Libby. "Frankly, I don't know what to think anymore," he confessed. "All I do know is that I can't deal with this. I really can't. Not on top of everything else that's going on. And for what it's worth," he continued, the words spilling out, "you're probably not going to believe this, but I love my wife. I do. She just drives me nuts. You know how some people bring out the best in you?"

Bernie nodded.

"Well, Ellen brings out the worst."

"Maybe you guys need counseling," Bernie gently suggested.

"Well, we sure as hell need something," Bruce said. He gave a rueful shake of his head. "About my kids."

"Yes?" Bernie said.

"I'm trying to protect them."

"I respect that," Bernie told him, "but I don't think this is the way to do it."

"Maybe," Bruce said. Then he turned around and walked out of the kitchen.

"Do you think Bruce is telling the truth?" Libby asked Bernie after Bruce had left.

"Yeah, I do," Bernie replied.

"Tell me," Libby said. "I'm curious. Why didn't you ask Bruce about Ellen and Manny?"

Bernie thought about her answer for a moment. Then she said, "I guess I didn't want to make the situation worse than it already is."

"Last question," Libby said "So if Bruce didn't call the cops, who did?"

"I think I can make a pretty good guess on that," Bernie said as she went to talk to Amber, while Libby went to check on the raspberry muffins. They were perfect.

Chapter 39

It was a little after three in the afternoon and Bernie and Libby were parked along the side of the road outside Ellen and Bruce Hadley's house. The sisters watched as two does trailed by their fawns trotted down the street, nibbling at the hostas and laurel hedges as they went.

"You'd think we were in the country instead of a housing development," Bernie remarked as she checked her cell for the time. She reckoned she and Libby had a few more minutes to wait.

She took a sip of her coffee and ate the second half of her sandwich, which consisted of roasted vegetables with aioli on French bread. Then she rolled her window down another couple of inches to let the spring breeze in before turning her attention back to the Hadley residence. It was amazing how quickly, really only a matter of weeks, the greenery was threatening to overrun the house. Not that Bernie needed any more proof that Ellen was the one in the family who gardened or picked anything up.

The grass in the front yard needed mowing and weeds were beginning to run rampant over the flower beds. Bernie knew that by this time Ellen would have had her impatiens, marigolds, and petunias in the ground, but not now. Now Ellen was running around like a crazy person and the only things growing in the flower beds were dandelions, deadly nightshade, and speedwell, plus one lonely pansy.

The flower boxes on the bottom floor, which were usually filled with begonias and trailing ivy, were empty as well. A bike lay across the walkway, a basketball and a couple of empty soda cans sat on the bottom porch step, while two trash cans and a recycling bin sat on the curb, having yet to be returned to the garage.

"Ellen must have had a fit when she saw this," Libby stated, indicating the house with a sweep of her hand. Ellen was nothing if not house proud, to use one of her mother's favorite phrases, a phrase that did not apply to either herself or her sister, as her mother was fond of pointing out.

"I think she has more important things to worry about for the moment," Bernie noted, thinking about the conversation she, Libby, and Ellen had just had.

"She should come home," Libby said.

"She's going to," Bernie observed as she spied the yellow of the school bus coming down the road.

The bus turned on its flashing lights. A moment later, it glided to a stop, the doors opened, and Ethan got out. Bernie and Libby watched him trudge down the road toward his house. He was slouched over, his T-shirt pulled back by the backpack he was toting. His pants were at least a couple of sizes too big and looked as if they'd been rolled up in a ball and stuffed under the bed. The collar of his polo shirt was torn on the left side, and his socks were mismatched. Ethan's eyes were focused on the roadway and he was kicking a small rock with the side of his sneaker.

"Ethan," Bernie called out as he headed up the walkway to his front door.

Startled, he jumped, then stopped and looked at them. Bernie and Libby could see that he had deep circles under his eyes and a bug bite on his chin.

"Oh," he said. "It's you."

"Sorry to alarm you . . ."

Ethan stuck his chin out. "You didn't," he lied.

"Okay," Bernie said. "Then I'm not sorry."

"Are you here about Mom?"

"In a way," Bernie said.

Ethan blinked several times and swallowed. "Is she okay?" he asked anxiously. "She ain't in jail or anything like that, is she?"

"Isn't in jail," Bernie said, automatically correcting his grammar, "and she's fine." Which wasn't exactly a lie, Bernie decided, but it wasn't exactly the truth either, *fine* being a relative term. She and her sister got out of Mathilda. "But we have to talk."

Ethan looked down and dug a divot in the

ground with the toe of his sneaker. "My dad says I'm not supposed to go to your shop anymore," he announced when he looked up.

"I know," Bernie replied.

"He doesn't want me involved."

"I understand," Bernie said. "We just need one question answered."

Libby held out a white paper bag. "We brought you something from the shop."

Ethan brightened and shifted his backpack around. "Cookies?"

Libby nodded. "Chocolate chip and a couple of brownies."

Bernie pointed to her tote. "Plus, a pint of chocolate milk."

Ethan hurried over to where Bernie and Libby were standing, reached out his hand for the bag, then stopped himself as something occurred to him. "If Dad sees the bag, he'll think I've been to the shop."

"That's a possibility," Libby conceded. The last thing she wanted to do was get Ethan in trouble with Bruce.

Ethan's shoulders slumped, but then he had an idea and started smiling. "He didn't tell me not to talk to you though. He didn't say I couldn't eat anything outside the shop. He just told me I couldn't go inside your place."

Bernie laughed and asked him if he was going to be a lawyer when he grew up.

Ethan gave her a quizzical look. "What do you mean?"

"She means that's a literal interpretation of what your dad said," Libby explained.

"Then he should have said what he meant," Ethan told her.

"You're right," Bernie replied, pushing aside the small shred of guilt at what she was doing. "He should have."

Ethan grinned and indicated Mathilda with a nod of his head. "Maybe we can take a ride in the van and I can eat the stuff in there."

"Works for me," Bernie said. "What time is your dad supposed to be home?"

"Five-thirty, maybe six."

"This definitely won't take that long," Bernie assured him. "You'll be back before anyone knows you're gone."

Ethan nodded. "Can we go to Skylar Park? To the wild part?"

"Indeed we can," Libby replied.

"I like watching the birds."

"Your mom does too," Bernie observed as the three of them got in the van.

"My dad tricked me, you know," Ethan told Bernie and Libby, his jaw settling into a hard line, as he put on his seat belt.

"Tricked you about what?" Bernie asked.

"Tricked me into telling him where Matt and Ryan were this morning. I bet they're pretty mad at me," Ethan said as Bernie handed him the white bag.

"Well, I don't think they're exactly happy with you," Bernie cautiously replied as Libby started up Mathilda.

"It's okay," Ethan said with the sangfroid of the youngest brother. "They'll only hit me a little bit." And with that he started eating.

By the time they were halfway to Skylar Park, Ethan had finished off the cookies and the brownies and gulped down the pint of chocolate milk Bernie had gotten for him.

"Didn't you eat any lunch?" Bernie asked him.

Ethan shook his head. "Dad didn't make it."

"You could have made it yourself," Bernie pointed out. "A peanut butter and jelly sandwich isn't rocket science."

"I couldn't. We're out of peanut butter and bread," Ethan proclaimed, looking woeful. "And milk too."

Libby turned to Bernie. "The drive-thru? It's on the way."

"Definitely," Bernie replied. "You want a hamburger and a shake?" she asked Ethan.

When Ethan said yes, Libby made a sharp left. The drive-thru, officially known as the Liberty In 'n Out, had been in existence since 1962, and though it had changed hands several times, it still looked exactly the same. It also had the best fast food in town. Libby gave her order and five minutes later, with Ethan happily munching away, continued toward Skylar Park. By the time they arrived there, Ethan had finished everything Libby had ordered for him except for two fried onion rings, and those he crammed in his mouth as they got out of Matilda.

Bernie watched Ethan run to the shore, crunching on rocks as he went. The seabirds were wheeling and squawking above him. A stiff breeze was blowing and the smell of the Hudson came to them off the river. Ethan rubbed his arms to warm them, as Bernie and Libby joined him.

"My mom used to take me here all the time when I was little," Ethan reflected. "We used to bring bread crumbs and feed the birds."

"It must have been fun," Bernie told him as she put out her hand and drew Ethan closer to her. He was all skin and bone.

"It was," Ethan said. "She'd better come home."

"We're working on it," Bernie said. "That's why I have to ask you something."

Ethan tipped his face up and looked up at her. "What?"

"And, Ethan, it's important you tell me the truth."

He looked alarmed. Bernie gave his shoulder a reassuring squeeze.

"Did you call the police and tell them your mom had been kidnapped?" she asked him in her gentlest voice.

Ethan didn't answer, but the expression on his face told Bernie that he had indeed done exactly that. He buried his face in her side and Bernie rubbed his back.

"It's okay," she said.

"Everything. It's all my fault," Ethan sobbed.

"No, it isn't," Bernie assured him.

"It is," Ethan insisted.

"You're wrong," Bernie told him.

"That's not true," Ethan replied, the words coming out muffled because he was saying them into Bernie's shirt. He sniffed. "If it weren't for me, Mom wouldn't be going to jail."

Bernie gave up arguing with him and tried to console him instead. "She's not in jail yet," she told him. "And I'm going to make sure that doesn't happen."

Ethan lifted his tearstained face up to Bernie. "Promise?" he asked.

"I promise," Bernie said, even though she knew better than to give an assurance like that. But she did because she couldn't bear to see the expression on Ethan's face when she had hesitated.

"I didn't know," Ethan explained, his voice quavering. "I swear I didn't. I came home and saw the note on the table. It was addressed to my dad. I shouldn't have opened it. Ryan says I'm always getting into things that don't concern me, and he's right."

Bernie stroked his hair. "I know the feeling."

"I used Matt's trac phone to call the cops anonymously. It was so dumb."

"No, it wasn't," Libby said. She moved closer to Ethan and put her hand on his shoulder. "I would have done the same thing."

"You would?" Ethan asked.

"Absolutely," Libby answered with as much conviction as she could muster. "Short of being God, there's no way you could have possibly known what was going to happen."

"It's true," Bernie said when Ethan didn't respond.

"I suppose it is," Ethan finally said after a minute had gone by. "Still, I wish I hadn't."

"Of course you do," Libby said. "Given what happened, who wouldn't?"

As the three of them stood together watching the waves lap the shore, Bernie reflected that the Hadleys certainly had a lock on guilt. Everyone was taking the blame for what had happened at the Riverview. So if everyone was guilty, did that mean that no one was guilty? That's what Bernie wanted to know.

Chapter 40

Well, that clears up one mystery," Libby said as they headed for the Roost. "Now we know who called the cops. Not that that piece of information gets us very far."

"It gets us a little further down the road," Bernie replied.

"Like a quarter of a mile," Libby said.

"A little more than that," Bernie countered. "At least now we know that whoever killed Manny didn't call the police, and we know why Bruce didn't recognize Manny, and we know who Manny is. So that's an improvement."

"Okay." Libby stopped at the corner of Main and Front to let a jogger go by. "But here's what we don't know. We don't know why Manny came back to Longely, we don't know who killed him, or why whoever killed him left him on a bed in the Riverview Motel. We don't know why Ellen pretended not to know who Manny was, and let's not even discuss Miss Randall's homicide. We don't have a clue about that."

Bernie rubbed the back of her neck to try and relieve the crick she'd woken up with. "Yeah, we do. We know that the two murders are related. Solve Manny's and we'll solve Miss Randall's."

"This is true," Libby conceded. The jogger

nodded her thanks and Libby accelerated. "But that only makes things worse, since we now have two unsolved homicides. Really we don't have a whole lot more to show for the time we've put in than we did before we talked to everyone."

"A step anywhere is a step everywhere," Bernie intoned.

Libby snorted. "What's that supposed to mean?"

"I'm not sure," Bernie confessed.

"Then why'd you say it?"

"I just like the way it sounds."

Libby laughed as Bernie bent down and rubbed her ankle. Then she lifted up her leg and rested it on top of the dashboard. Bernie decided she probably should have waited a few more days before she put on her three-inch wedges, because her ankle was bothering her again.

"Okay then," Bernie said. "Maybe this is a better way to say what I meant. As Mom used to say, we're taking baby steps."

"If you ask me, we're crawling," Libby cracked as she parked Mathilda across the street from the Roost.

Ten Harley hogs were parked out in front of the bar.

"Great," Bernie said, looking at them gleaming under the streetlight. "Just what we need. Major attitude."

"You want to come back tomorrow afternoon

when the place is a little quieter?" Libby asked. "It might be easier to talk to Sandra then."

Bernie shook her head. Privately, she didn't think it would make any difference. "We're here already. Let's do this." And she got out of the van and limped inside with Libby trailing her.

Bernie wasn't a great fan of motorcycle gangs in general, but when she and Libby stepped inside she realized that they weren't talking about the Hell's Angels here. She knew most of the guys who were wearing leathers. Half of them were doctors, while the other half was evenly divided between lawyers, dentists, teachers, and accountants. More to the point, Sandra wasn't behind the bar. Bernie cursed under her breath. They couldn't seem to catch a break here.

"We're looking for Sandra," Bernie said to the bartender once she and Libby had made their way up to the bar.

"Well, I guess you're out of luck," the bartender replied.

Because of Brandon, Bernie probably knew half of the bartenders who worked in Longely, but she didn't recognize this guy. Bernie put him at around fifty, fifty-five. He was balding with a long, graying ponytail in back and a gut that puffed out his Hawaiian shirt in front. He had a big nose that twisted to one side and a thin line of a mouth. His arms and shoulders were powerful and his hands were huge. She had no doubt that he could take care of whatever came his way.

"Why is that?" Bernie asked. "Why are we out of luck?"

"Because she's not here," the bartender replied. "Obviously."

He seemed as surly as Sandra had been, Bernie thought. Maybe that was a requirement of the job. "I can see that. And you're . . . ?" Bernie said.

"Working."

"Ha-ha. Do you have a name?"

"Yeah." The bartender planted his hands on the bar and leaned forward. "It's Jack. My name is Jack."

"Thank you, Jack," Bernie replied. "Do you know where Sandra is?"

Jack looked around the bar first to make sure that no one needed anything before answering. "She took the night off," he told Bernie, his face expressionless. "Actually, make that she took the year off. She quit."

"Why?"

Jack shrugged. "Don't know, don't care. Not my business."

"I don't suppose you happen to have her address?" Libby asked him.

"Nope," Jack said.

"Or her telephone number?"

"Don't have that either."

"How about her last name?" Bernie said. "Do you have that?"

"We were never formally introduced," Jack said.

"Lovely," Bernie muttered as Jack walked down to the end of the bar and began to polish the beer glasses with a dirty cloth.

The question was how much did Jack want to pony up the information she needed? Twenty? Fifty? One hundred? Bernie had just decided to start with twenty when Libby began speaking to him.

"It's important," Libby told him.

Jack stopped polishing for a moment. "Why? Did she inherit a million dollars?"

"And if I said she did?" Libby asked.

Jack grinned. "I'd say you were lying."

"Could you be any more helpful?" Libby asked before Bernie could stop her.

"Not really," Jack replied.

"I was being sarcastic," Libby told him.

"You think I'm a moron," Jack growled.

"No. I think you're a jerk."

Jack cupped his hand to his ear. "What was that you said?"

Bernie kicked Libby before she could repeat her comment.

"She said you seem very busy," Bernie said to Jack.

He nodded and turned back to his polishing.

"That hurt," Libby complained as she bent down and rubbed her calf.

"It was supposed to. Let me handle this."

"You think you can do better?" Libby demanded.

"Well, I sure as hell can't do worse."

"Bet you ten you don't get any further than I did."

Bernie was just about to tell Libby the bet was on when someone tapped her on the shoulder.

Bernie spun around. Stu Hartley was grinning at her. He took one large coffee black, one corn muffin lightly toasted no butter, and an almond Danish. He was so punctual that Amber had his order ready to go when she saw him getting out of his Accord at six forty-five on the dot every Monday through Friday morning. An accountant, he commuted down to Loeb, Spenser & Brown, a high-end firm located on Madison Avenue. Usually, he wore a gray suit, white shirt, and gray-and-black-striped tie; tonight he was decked out in leather.

"I didn't know you rode," Bernie said, checking out his vest.

Stu gave a deprecating shrug. "I just got Jane."

Bernie furrowed her brow. "Jane?"

"The Harley next to the streetlight. That's what I'm calling her."

"Oh," Bernie said. "Why Jane?"

"She was my first true love, the one who broke my heart."

"I wouldn't tell my wife that if I were you," Bernie told him.

Stu shrugged. "I don't think she's going to care."

"Seriously?" Bernie asked.

A look of panic crossed Stu's face. "I shouldn't tell her?"

"Absolutely not. What does Esther say about the bike anyway?" Bernie asked. Somehow Stu's wife didn't strike her as the Harley-riding sort.

Stu gave Bernie a nervous grin. "Not much. Ha-ha." He tugged his vest down over his gut. "Actually," he confessed, "she doesn't know yet."

Bernie couldn't help herself. She laughed. She knew Stu's wife and she was not going to be amused. "Oh boy."

"Oh boy, is right," Stu allowed. "It'll be interesting when she comes back from her conference on Sunday. If you don't see me at the shop on Monday morning, call the police." He took a sip of his beer and put the can down. "I'll be buried in the backyard."

"What made you buy it?" Libby asked.

"Impulse," Stu replied. "I always wanted one and I was driving by the dealership in Eastwood and there she was gleaming in the window. I think I'm having a midlife crisis or something."

"I think maybe you are," Bernie agreed.

Stu leaned forward and clapped his hand on Bernie's shoulder. "Listen, I heard you talking to Jack and I might know where Sandy lives."

"That would be great," Bernie said.

Stu took his hand off Bernie's shoulder and

rubbed his chin. "I'm pretty sure she lives in the purple house with the lavender trim on the corner of Mission and Oak. You can't miss it."

Bernie raised an eyebrow. *Sandy,* she thought. Not Sandra. Interesting. Stu took another swallow of his beer. Bernie was amused to see he was drinking Budweiser. When she'd run into him at RJ's, it was the microbrews or nothing.

Stu explained. "Sometimes I go that way to get to the train station and I usually see her Civic parked in the driveway."

"Do you know why she isn't here?" Libby asked.

Stu leaned forward and lowered his voice. "I heard she was fired for being late too many times."

"That would do it," Libby said. It would certainly be grounds for letting someone go.

"Thanks for the tip," Bernie told Stu.

"My pleasure," Stu responded. "But I think she quit and people are making stuff up."

"We'll say a prayer for you," Libby told him. She knew Esther too. He was going to need it.

"To Stu," Bert Mendalbaum called out. He raised his can of beer. "L'chayim. May his wife not kill him."

"L'chayim," everyone bellied up to the bar responded as Bernie and Libby walked out the door.

When they were standing on the pavement,

Bernie called Brandon to see if maybe he knew Sandra's address or last name. Or anything. But he didn't.

"Not even her last name?" Bernie asked.

"I have a vague memory of it starting with a *P,* but I could be one hundred percent wrong. She doesn't hang around with anyone I know."

"Whom does she hang around with?" Bernie asked.

"I think she keeps to herself. Listen, gotta go," Brandon said. "Tony is a no-show and I'm in some serious weeds here." Then he hung up before Bernie could say anything else.

"Why do we want to talk to Sandra anyway?" Libby asked Bernie.

"Because," Bernie said lightly, running the tips of her fingers over the Harleys as she walked by them. Her old boyfriend had had a bike and sometimes she still missed riding on it. "Because she might be a lead, and even if she's not, we don't have anything to lose by talking to her."

"I guess it's worth a shot," Libby conceded. Although given her druthers, she'd rather be going home. She was tired and she wanted to go to bed.

Bernie nodded. "Exactly. We might as well try the address Stu gave us, and if that doesn't pan out I can come back to the Roost later by myself"— she emphasized the words *by myself*—"and see if I can get Sandra's info out of Jack."

"How much are you going to offer him?"

"I was thinking up to one hundred."

Libby smiled. "So I saved us a hundred bucks."

Bernie laughed. "Maybe you have." She looked at the moon overhead and felt the night breeze nibbling her arms. "Anyway, it's a nice night to go for a ride," she noted. "Maybe on the way back we can stop at Fannon's and pick up some ice cream for Dad and ourselves."

Libby perked up. Suddenly she didn't feel tired anymore. "Let's get coffee mocha chip. It's their best flavor, although"—she paused for a minute—"their banana chocolate chunk isn't too shabby either."

"We'll get a pint of each," Bernie happily said as she got in the van. *It's amazing what ice cream can do,* she thought. Just talking about it was putting her in a better mood already.

Chapter 41

Mission and Oak was on the far side of town. It had been a while since Libby and Bernie had been there, but they remembered the area being as close to slummy as anything in Longely got, which wasn't saying much. The houses here were smaller, two-story rental properties with no garages. Their postage stamp yards tended toward the unkempt and the landscaping mostly consisted of overgrown laurel hedges and impatiens.

But evidently things were changing, because this time when Libby drove by, Bernie spotted a few houses with new paint jobs, flower boxes, and extensive plantings, not to mention a couple of restaurants featuring organic ingredients, and an upscale food market advertising gelato—all signs that the far side of town was about to come up in the world.

"I wonder how Stu knows what Sandra's vehicle looks like," Libby mused as she pulled up in front of the house. "And he called her Sandy. She doesn't seem like a Sandy to me."

"The obvious answer comes to mind." Bernie replied. "Although for the life of me, I can't see her and Stu together."

Libby laughed at the idea. "Neither can I, but you never know. Look at Mom and Dad. I can't think of two more opposite people and they were really in love."

"Yes, they were," Bernie replied softly as she studied the driveway of the purple house. Even in the fading light the color popped, especially because the houses on either side were painted all white.

There was a car parked on the blacktop, but it wasn't a Civic. So either Stu was wrong or Sandra wasn't here. Well, there was only one way to find out. Bernie pressed her lips together as she contemplated the house Sandra was supposed to be living in. Constructed almost sixty years ago, the place had been conceived as a two-family colonial with one family living on the top floor and the other on the bottom. It must have been nice once, but over the years, time and weather had taken their toll. Paint was peeling off the windowsills, a couple of shutters were gone, the steps were listing to the left, and six heavy wooden posts supported the sagging wraparound porch on the second floor.

"I don't think I'd be sitting out there right now," Bernie remarked, indicating the small table and two chairs on the balcony.

"Me either," Libby agreed as Bernie scanned the windows for signs of life.

She couldn't see any lights or movement upstairs, but she did see a light shining through the curtains covering the window on the first floor. That and the car in the driveway led her to believe that someone was home.

Libby indicated the two entrance doors sitting side by side with a nod of her head. "I wonder which one is Sandra's."

Bernie pointed to the mailboxes. "Let's find out."

But they didn't. There was no name on either one. Bernie paused for a moment, then pressed the bell on the right underneath the sign that read JEHOVAH'S WITNESSES GO AWAY.

A moment later Bernie and Libby heard a cheery "I'm coming" and a moment after that the door was flung open and an elderly lady with flaming red hair, wearing a housecoat, a pearl choker, and bright yellow Converse sneakers confronted them.

"Yes?" she said, waving a cigarette holder around. A dribble of ash fell on her housecoat and she brushed it away.

Bernie started apologizing for the lateness of the hour, but the woman stopped her.

"Please," she said, "I never go to bed before four. All those years in the theater, you know." She peered at them through her glasses. "Do I know you?"

"I don't think so," Libby said.

"I think I do." The woman pushed her glasses up the bridge of her nose to get a better view. They were bright pink circles and covered half of her face. "Yes, indeed I do." She clapped her hands together. "You're Rose's girls, aren't you? I guess you don't remember me," she said when she saw the blank looks on their faces. "I'm Thelma, Auntie Thelma. Hollywood?"

"Oh my God." Libby's eyes widened as she recalled who the lady in front of her was. She put her hand to her mouth. "I remember now. You went off to Hollywood to be in the movies. You were supposed to marry Ronnie . . ."

"Zorn," Thelma said. "But I broke the engagement, and off I went to seek fame and fortune."

"And did you find it?" Libby asked.

Thelma grinned. "I never became a star, if that's what you're asking, but I got my SAG card and I've always worked steady, which, let me tell you, is no mean feat. I don't suppose either of you happened to see *Walk of the Zombies* or *Blood in the Sky* by any chance?"

Both Libby and Bernie shook their heads.

"No matter. Most people didn't, but I had starring roles in those." Thelma waved her cigarette holder around. "I never regretted going there for a moment or, for that matter, not marrying Ronnie Zorn. Rose was right. I was never cut out to be your typical hausfrau. But enough about me . . . I want to hear about you two," she said, shutting the door behind them.

Libby and Bernie spent the next half an hour perched on an ornate, carved, antique sofa, sipping iced tea out of jam jars, and catching up.

"Rose was such a wonderful lady. So talented. A regular domestic goddess is what she was," Thelma enthused. She giggled. "Unlike me. I used my oven to store my sweaters in." Thelma stabbed the cigarette holder in the air for emphasis. "Still do, for that matter. If you can't heat it up in the microwave I don't eat it." She pointed to her stomach. "I guess it works, because I still have my girlish figure."

She giggled again. "Well, as much as one can be girlish at my age." Thelma leaned forward. "You know," she confided, dropping her voice down to a stage whisper, "if it wasn't for your mom, I wouldn't have left Longely. She was the one who encouraged me to go to Hollywood to seek my fame and fortune. 'Thelma,' she said, 'you have to do what makes you happy.' And so I did."

"Well, she sure didn't say that to me when I headed out to the West Coast," Bernie recalled.

Thelma patted Bernie's knee. "You were her daughter. I'm sure she was scared you'd fall prey to evil influences—there's a lot of that out there."

"Maybe you're right," Bernie conceded, recalling Rose's words.

"Your mother was no fool," Thelma said.

"I never thought she was," Bernie replied.

Thelma beamed. "She was very proud of you, Bernie. You too, Libby." Then Thelma straightened up and looked from Bernie to Libby. "But enough of the past. What delightful mission has brought you to my humble abode? What can I help you with?"

Bernie got straight to the point. "We're looking for a woman called Sandra," she answered. "She works as a bartender at the Roost."

"Ah, yes." Thelma gave her head a little shake. "Poor dear."

"So you know her?" Libby asked.

Thelma clicked her tongue against her teeth. "I should hope so."

"Does she live here?" Bernie eagerly asked.

"Has for the last eight months," Thelma replied. She carefully took her cigarette out of her holder and stubbed it out in the ashtray on the coffee table. "Filthy habit, but I can't seem to give it up. Oh well." She gave a deprecating shrug. "Everyone has to die of something, right? Right?" Thelma repeated when neither Libby nor Bernie replied.

"Right," Bernie quickly said. "Does Sandra have a last name?"

"I take it you're asking me if I know it."

Bernie nodded.

Thelma snorted. "Of course I do. She's my upstairs tenant. Her name is Melon—as in the fruit." She sighed. "I probably should have asked more rent from her; she's paying practically nothing. I've always been bad when it comes to business. But given the flat's condition, I couldn't charge her the going rate. What do you think about the color, by the way?"

"Of the house?" Bernie asked.

"What else?"

"Quite eye-catching," Bernie said diplomatically. Which was true.

Thelma chortled. "That's one way of putting it. You should see it in the daylight. It positively sizzles. Let me tell you, the neighbors are not pleased, but I think it's good to expand people's horizons, don't you?" She sniffed. "They were quite unpleasant when I moved in."

"Is that why you chose those colors?" Bernie asked.

Thelma's expression reminded Bernie of, to use a phrase of her mother's, the cat that ate the canary.

"Let's just say," Thelma replied, "that it was an added benefit, but I chose those colors because I liked them. Also they were on sale, not a bad thing in my situation. Although I have gotten a call back for a toilet paper commercial and those do pay good money." Thelma looked pensive as she rat-tat-ted her fingernails, which were long and red, on the top of the arm of the love seat she was sitting in. Then she smiled and clasped her hands together. "However, I'm sure you're not interested in my employment opportunities or lack of them. So why do you ladies want to speak to Sandra, if I might ask?"

"Well, we're hoping she can help us with some information," Bernie replied.

"May I be so bold as to ask what kind of information you wish to solicit from her?"

Bernie and Libby looked at each other. They weren't quite sure how much they wanted to share.

Noting their reluctance, Thelma sat up straighter and smiled an utterly beguiling smile. "Oh, come on," she urged. "My life is utterly boring. Make an old lady's day."

Bernie and Libby couldn't help themselves.

They both smiled back. *The lady's a charmer,* Bernie thought. No doubt about that.

"Well?" Thelma asked. She leaned forward expectantly. "Is Sandra . . . involved in anything interesting?"

"Not really," Libby said.

Thelma's face fell.

"A little bit interesting," Bernie allowed.

Thelma's smile returned. "Does this have anything to do with Manny and Miss Randall by any chance?" she asked.

Bernie took a sip of her iced tea. It had a chemical aftertaste. She guessed it was one of those instant mixes. "How did you know?"

Thelma waved her hand in the air. "It's been all over the news."

"True," Bernie allowed.

Thelma's eyes glittered. "You're investigating?"

"More like poking around," Libby told her. In Libby's mind, investigating connoted warrants and wire taps.

"I see." Thelma clapped her hands. "What fun. How delightful." Then she realized what she'd said and put her hand to her mouth. "Oh dear. I sound dreadful. Absolutely heartless. That's not what I meant at all!"

"I'm sure," Libby reassured her. "We want to speak to Sandra because we're hoping she can shed some light on where Daisy Stone is."

"We just have a few questions we want to

ask Daisy about Manny," Bernie added.

Thelma cocked her head. "You want to speak to Daisy Stone?" she asked, surprised.

"Hopefully," Bernie replied, slightly disconcerted by Thelma's tone.

"About Manny?"

Bernie nodded. "Yes. Is that going to be a problem?"

Thelma sat back in the love seat and frowned. "My dear, talking to her about anything is going to be a problem."

"And why is that?" Libby asked.

Thelma reached for her cigarette holder. It was long, black, and shiny, with a series of red stars going down the side, and reminded Bernie of something out of a thirties movie.

"Because Daisy is," Thelma began, "not to mince words, completely off her rocker. Has been for some time. She's at the Pines. Such a nice name for such an ugly type of place, don't you think?" Thelma shuddered. "I keep on thinking of that old movie *The Snake Pit*, even though I know those places aren't like that anymore. It's such a pity. They keep her so doped up it's hard to get a 'hello' much less a 'how are you' out of her."

Libby took another sip of her iced tea for the sake of politeness. "So you've seen her?"

"That," Thelma said, giving Libby a confiding smile, "is why I said what I did."

Bernie raised an eyebrow. "How come you went?"

"That's simple. Sandra asked me to come with her when she visited." Thelma put her cigarette holder down on the coffee table, looked at it, and picked it back up. "God, I would love a cigarette," she said before putting the holder down where it had been. "Just thinking about that place makes me want to smoke." She took her glasses off and rubbed the bridge of her nose before putting them back on. "I smoked half a pack when we got out of there, which is one of the reasons I haven't been back. I'm ashamed to say it, but I don't do illnesses, either physical or mental, well. I'm not a caretaker."

Libby could sympathize. Neither was she. "Why did Sandra visit?"

Thelma shook her head. "Your guess is as good as mine. It's not something we discussed. Sandra has never been good with personal revelations."

"She had to have said something," Bernie insisted.

"She said"—Thelma paused to remember Sandra's exact words—" 'I need someone to come with me for moral support' and when we left she said, 'I don't want to talk about it.' So we didn't."

"What's wrong with Daisy?" Libby asked.

Thelma picked up her cigarette holder and waved it in the air. "Damned if I know. I'm sure there's a name for it. There always is, but really," she confided, "despite what all the experts say, I don't think naming something makes the least bit of difference. If you're crazy, you're crazy, and that's that."

"Can we see Daisy?" Bernie asked Thelma.

Thelma shrugged. "I guess. I don't see why not. I did. It's not like she's on a locked ward or anything like that." She looked at her watch. "Oh dear. I didn't realize how late it is. As fascinating as this conversation is, I'm afraid I'm going to have to ask you darling girls to leave. I'm Skyping with my friend in ten minutes and I need that time to powder my nose."

"Of course," Bernie said as she rose. "I don't suppose you know where Sandra is?"

Thelma shook her head. "Frankly, I have no idea. She comes and she goes as she pleases. However, now that you mention it, I did see her carting a big suitcase down to her car just before you arrived, so maybe she and her boyfriend are going on a trip. I can leave a message for her if you want."

"That would be great," Bernie said.

"Done," Thelma replied, punctuating the air with her cigarette holder for emphasis as she walked over to her front door and opened it. "And now, my dears, I must really bid you an adieu and get to my toilette. At my advanced age, everything takes quite a bit longer. Please drop by anytime."

"We will," Bernie promised.

Thelma wagged a finger at them. "I'm going to hold you to that," she told Libby and Bernie. Then she hugged them both and escorted them out the door.

"To Fannon's," Libby said once she and Bernie were sitting in the van.

"To Fannon's," Bernie repeated. She could taste the ice cream on her tongue already. Bernie decided that if ice cream were a religion she would join in a nanosecond.

Chapter 42

I t was a little after two in the afternoon of the next day when Libby and Bernie arrived at the Pines, the place Thelma had told Libby and Bernie Daisy Stone was staying at.

"I think the main house is the oldest structure in the five-town area," Bernie mentioned to Libby as they entered the grounds.

Libby gave a noncommittal grunt. She had other things on her mind at the moment—such as the ten pies they had to deliver to Greg Allen's house by five in the afternoon at the latest. Not that she was saying this to Bernie, but she really didn't care that the building encapsulated, to use Bernie's word, over one hundred years of history. She didn't care that it had originally been built as a workhouse back in the day, and when those fell out of fashion it had become a state-run charity hospital, after which it had metamorphosed into a psychiatric hospital.

She didn't care that twenty years ago, with the advent of community-based health care, New York State had closed Mercy and the patients had found other places to live, or that Mercy had remained empty for three years before a private company bought the building, gutted, remodeled it, and renamed it the Pines. The Pines, according to its ads, was a place where one could restore one's peace of mind, find balance, and free oneself from one's chemical dependencies, i.e. drugs.

"You have the basket, right?" Bernie asked Libby.

"You saw me take it," she replied as Bernie looked out the window.

It was a nice view. Libby drove by two deer browsing on the forsythia, a carefully manicured lawn with strategically placed tables and chairs scattered under the shade trees, and flower beds full of pansies, marigolds, soon-to-bloom impatiens, as well as beds full of tulips and irises. There was even a small pond with a tiny stream wending its way through the grass.

Bernie decided that if one disregarded the institutional tenor of the building, which the owners had tried to soften with window awnings and flower boxes, one would think that one was on the grounds of a Catskill resort. How Thelma could have compared this place to *The Snake Pit* was something that Bernie couldn't even begin to fathom.

"Maybe we should have called ahead," Libby said as the main building came into view. As she looked at the cluster of small white cottages scattered around the big building like ducklings around their mother, she wondered if Daisy lived in one of those or in the main house. As it turned out, Daisy lived in neither.

Bernie stopped watching the people strolling on the paths and sitting on lawn chairs and turned toward her sister. "Why?" she asked.

"Well, if they won't let us see her, then we could have saved ourselves the ride," Libby observed. Considering what Thelma had said about Daisy's mental state, she was having second thoughts about the feasibility, let alone the usefulness, of the endeavor she and Bernie were about to embark on.

Bernie smiled. "Because you have places to go and people to see?"

"Because I have pies to bake and salads to make," Libby retorted.

"Nothing ventured, nothing gained," responded Bernie.

"A penny earned is a penny saved," Libby came back with.

"The expression is 'a penny saved is a penny

earned,'" Bernie told her, "and what does that have to do with anything?"

"I'm just saying that we need to prioritize and this might not be the best use of our time. According to Thelma, Daisy is off somewhere in la-la land."

"Do you have any other suggestions?"

"We could talk to Ellen."

"We could, if we could get hold of her." Bernie's friend wasn't returning phone calls at the moment.

"True," Libby said. She'd run out of suggestions, and besides, they were almost at the building.

The receptionist sitting behind the desk smiled as Bernie explained why they were there. "Just don't bring up the topic of babies," she advised as she wrote out their visitor passes and explained how to get to cottage three.

"Why not?" Bernie asked, while she peeled off the backing and pressed the pass onto her wrap-around dress.

The woman shrugged the kind of shrug that conveyed she'd seen it all and none of it made any sense, and said, "Not a clue. It just sets her off, that's all I know." Then she turned to the man and woman standing in back of Bernie and asked if she could help them. The woman started to cry.

Libby and Bernie beat a hasty retreat back to their van. Cottage three took longer to find than it should have. Despite the receptionist's directions, Libby took two wrong turns before they ended up on the right road. It turned out that the compound was bigger than it looked and the cottages, all grouped in clusters of five, were scattered in a seemingly random fashion over the property. The fact that all the cottages looked exactly the same, that the numbers on the houses were small and hard to read, and that there was no one out to give directions made the task harder than it should have been.

Once they got to cottage number three, which turned out to be located near a tennis court, Libby realized that the place was actually less than a quarter of a mile away from the main building as the crow flies. She could have gone straight to it, but that was impossible given the way the roads were laid out.

Definitely very annoying, Bernie thought as she studied the tennis court. The lines were blindingly white, the packed clay immaculate. No tennis balls hid in the corners.

It looked as if it was never used, in contrast to the cottages, lined up like soldiers on parade, which looked as if they'd seen too much use. Paint was flaking off spots under the dormers, moss was growing on the roofs, and the lawn in front and around the cottages was overrun with speedwell and needed to be mowed. It was obvious to Bernie that the owners of the Pines had concentrated their efforts on the spots visitors would see and left the rest of the complex to its own devices.

"It's very quiet here," Libby noted as she parked in the designated parking lot. Mathilda was the only vehicle in it.

"Maybe the people in these cottages don't have visitors," Bernie said.

She didn't see chairs or tables set out, or people walking about. The only sign of life she observed were two squirrels chittering at each other in the pine tree behind the next cottage over and a turkey vulture circling in the sky. She decided that the compound reminded her of a stage. The road up to the main house and the main house and cottages were the front of the stage, whereas she and Libby were backstage, which was where the real business, whatever that was, was conducted.

"Maybe they don't," Libby said to Bernie. She grabbed the gift basket she'd made up for Daisy and got out. "Not a particularly promising sign if you ask me."

"Let's try to be a little less negative," Bernie automatically said over her shoulder as she started to walk toward the cottage, although in this case she had a feeling that Libby was correct.

"I'm not negative," Libby told her. "I'm just prepared for disappointment. Anyway," she said, changing the subject, "I hope she likes what we brought her."

"Of course she will," Bernie replied. "Everyone likes chocolate chip cookies and brownies."

At which point she and Libby were standing in front of the door. Bernie looked around for a doorbell to ring, but there wasn't one, so she knocked instead. A moment later, the door opened. The woman standing in the doorway didn't look at all the way Bernie or Libby had pictured Daisy. They had thought they'd be talking to someone with wild hair and mismatched clothes, but the woman who stood in front of them looked, if anything, prim and proper. *Or maybe,* Bernie thought, *bland is a better word.*

Bernie estimated she was about five foot four, on the slender side, with short blond hair cut in no particular style, and fine features. She was wearing a white camp shirt and a pair of pressed khakis. The thing that both Libby and Bernie found disconcerting though, was the lack of expression on her face.

"Yes," she said in a voice that echoed the lack of expression on her face. "What can I do for you?"

Bernie and Libby exchanged glances.

"Are you Daisy Stone?" Bernie asked.

After thinking about it for a few seconds, the woman nodded.

Bernie introduced herself and her sister, while Libby held out the basket of treats.

"Thank you," Daisy said, taking the basket but not looking at it.

"May we come in?" Bernie asked. "We'd like to talk to you for a moment."

Daisy nodded and Libby and Bernie followed her in. Daisy moved slowly, as if she had to concentrate on placing one foot in front of the other. When she got to the sofa she slowly turned around and told Bernie and Libby to sit. She followed suit, first carefully putting the basket Libby and Bernie had given her on the coffee table, then lowering herself down.

"Nice place you've got here," Bernie observed, even though it wasn't, unless you considered every-thing beige a style choice.

"It is nice," Daisy said. She'd folded her hands and placed them on her lap like a little girl would. She frowned as she spoke.

Watching her, Bernie had the feeling that Daisy had to concentrate hard on enunciating each word. As she was thinking about that she caught her sister's I-told-you-so look, but Bernie ignored her. So what if whatever Daisy was taking was slowing her down a little. That didn't mean she couldn't answer their questions. Anyway, even if she couldn't, at least they'd tried. Bernie was wondering what kind of meds Daisy was on when she realized that Daisy was speaking.

"What do you want to talk to me about?" she asked.

So Bernie told her. "We'd like to talk to you

about Manny, Manny Roget. We were wondering if you knew—"

Which was as far as Bernie got because Daisy let out a moan, put her head in her hands, and started rocking back and forth.

"Daisy," Bernie said.

The moaning grew in volume.

"This is not good," Libby said to no one in particular.

"No kidding," Bernie observed. Then she realized that Daisy was saying something, possibly a word. Maybe a phrase. But Bernie couldn't tell what it was.

"I'm calling the front desk and getting someone over here," Libby announced.

Bernie held up her hand. "Give me a minute." She knelt next to Daisy and put her arm around Daisy's waist. "What is it?" she asked. "Tell me. My sister and I can help."

Daisy rocked harder.

"Please," Bernie begged.

"No . . . no . . . no." Each *no* was louder than the last.

Libby had just taken out her cell and was looking up the Pines' number so she could call someone when the front door slammed against the wall and Jeremy Stone barreled in.

"What the hell are you doing here?" he demanded. "What are you doing to my sister?"

Chapter 43

Bernie could feel herself flush. "We aren't doing anything," she stammered.

"Well, it sure doesn't look like nothing to me," Jeremy snarled as he ran toward Daisy.

"We were just asking about Manny," she explained lamely.

"What is wrong with you?" Jeremy demanded of Bernie. "You can tell just by looking at my sister that she's in no condition to answer anything." He shook his finger at Bernie. "I want you and your sister out of here. I want you out of here now. Otherwise, I'm calling the police."

Daisy's moaning filled the room. Bernie felt terrible. She lifted her hands in a gesture of surrender. "I'm sorry. I didn't think—"

"That's exactly the problem," Jeremy replied, turning his back on her. "You don't think."

"If you had told me about Daisy in the first place, this wouldn't have happened," Bernie protested.

Jeremy didn't reply. By now he'd reached his sister and was cradling her in his arms like you would a small child, stroking her hair, and telling her it would be all right.

"Why did you lie about her?" Bernie asked him.

Jeremy looked up, shooting death ray stares at Bernie. "You want to know why? I'll tell you why. This is why. My sister has had enough bad things happen to her. She doesn't need you talking to her to make things worse." Jeremy pointed to the basket on the table. "And take that stuff with you. My sister is a diabetic. Do you want to kill her?"

"Sorry," Bernie said again as she retrieved the basket. Now she felt even worse—if that were possible.

"Well, that didn't go too well, did it?" Libby observed once she and her sister were outside. She noted that Daisy's moans seemed to be subsiding or maybe the cottage walls were absorbing them. Libby wasn't sure.

"She could have eaten the brownies," Bernie replied.

"That would have been worse," Libby agreed.

"So much worse that I don't even want to think about it."

"See," Libby said. "I told you we shouldn't come here."

"And you were right," Bernie told her. "Does that make you feel good?"

"Not particularly," Libby informed her as they got in the van. "Frankly, I wish I hadn't been."

Libby started up Mathilda and drove out of the parking lot. She couldn't get out of there fast enough as far as she was concerned. They were going past the main building when Bernie yelled at her to stop.

"What now?" Libby asked.

"I have an idea," her sister replied.

Libby snorted. "Haven't you had enough of those for one day?"

"I'm serious. I think I might have gone about this the wrong way."

"No kidding." But Libby turned into the lot and slammed on the brakes. "I'm waiting here though," she told Bernie. "I'm done."

"Fine with me." Bernie got out of Mathilda and went inside. The same receptionist was sitting behind the desk. Bernie read her name off her ID tag pinned to her chest while she summoned up her most charming smile. "Evie, I have an odd question for you," she said.

The receptionist cocked her head and smiled back. "Honey," she exclaimed, "that's all I get. Let's hear it."

Bernie folded her hands and leaned on the counter. "Daisy Stone in cottage three."

Evie nodded. "What about her?"

"Does her brother come to visit her often?"

"Once, sometimes twice a week. I gather you ran into him."

"We sure did," Bernie said.

"He was surprised to hear Daisy had visitors."

"Nobody usually comes to see her?"

Evie shook her head. "There was a big guy who

used to drop by once in a while. I was told Daisy really looked forward to his coming. And then he stopped coming, which was really too bad because Daisy didn't take it well. At all. As they say out in the world, 'she flipped.'"

"Was the guy's name Manny?" Bernie asked.

Evie thought for a moment. "I'm afraid I really don't remember. So many people come and go, I just remember the regulars."

"I don't suppose I could look at the sign-in sheets?" Bernie asked, even though she was pretty sure she knew what the answer would be. After all, nothing ventured, nothing gained. Evie stiffened and Bernie apologized. "That was out of line."

"It was," Evie replied. "There's no way I can do that."

"I know." Bernie looked contrite. Then she explained why she'd asked. As she talked, she could see Evie softening.

"Oh my," Evie said, her face creasing with concern when Bernie was done.

"Maybe you could tell me whether or not Daisy's visitor had a beard," Bernie suggested softly.

"A big full one," Evie replied. "And he was wearing an earring too. Does that help?"

"More than you know," Bernie assured her. "Thank you. Thank you so much."

"So?" Libby asked her sister when she got back in the van.

"So Manny definitely visited Daisy." Bernie

was in the middle of telling Libby what the receptionist had told her when Sandra called.

"Thelma told me you wanted to speak to me," she said.

Bernie switched her cell to her other ear. "That's right. We wanted to talk to you about Manny and Daisy."

There was a short pause, then Sandra said, "What makes you think I know anything?"

"Well, I know you went to visit Daisy with Thelma. I have to assume you went to see her because you cared about her welfare."

Another pause. Then Sandra said, "I'm getting ready to leave Longely."

"Please," Bernie begged. "Anything you can tell us, anything at all, will help me help my friend Ellen."

"Ellen's your friend?"

"Yes. For forever."

This time Sandra's pause was longer. Bernie could hear her talking to someone in the background. She was back on the line a minute later. "Okay," she said. "Can you meet me at the playground at Skylar at seven-thirty?"

"We'll be there with bells on," Bernie said.

"Bells?" Sandra repeated.

"It's an expression," Bernie said.

"I never heard it."

Sandra clicked off her cell and Bernie did likewise.

Libby clicked her tongue against her teeth. "I'm surprised she'll talk to us."

"Me too," Bernie allowed.

"I wonder why."

"I guess we're going to find out." Bernie turned to Libby as Libby put the key in the ignition.

"I certainly hope so," Libby replied absentmindedly. She wasn't thinking about Sandra or Ellen or Manny or Daisy. She was back to thinking about pies.

Chapter 44

Although Bernie and Libby had arrived at the park ten minutes early, Sandra was already there. Bernie spotted her immediately. She was leaning against the swings, sipping what appeared to be an iced coffee. When she saw Libby and Bernie, she waved and Bernie waved back. Then she and Libby threaded their way through the playing children, the strollers, and the joggers. The sun was setting, highlighting the sailboats moored on the Hudson River and haloing the clouds in the west.

"It's supposed to rain," Sandra said to Bernie and Libby when they got closer.

"But not for a while," Bernie replied. "Thanks for talking to us."

"You're welcome." Sandra inclined her head

and took another sip of her coffee. "I like watching the kiddies," she remarked. "They don't think. They just do."

"I suppose that's true," Libby replied.

She watched Sandra watch a five-year-old girl shrieking in delight as her eight-year-old brother chased her around a park bench. As she did, Libby reflected that Sandra looked twenty years younger than she had looked back at the Roost. The hardness in her face had dissolved. Maybe it was because she'd left her makeup off and pulled her hair back in a low ponytail, or maybe it was because she was wearing a mint green shirt-dress that belled out in the breeze, or maybe it was because she was smiling. She had, Libby decided, a nice smile.

"You look nice," Libby found herself saying.

Sandra grinned. "I'm off to my new life. Farming."

"Farming?" Libby repeated, nonplussed.

"Yeah. I know. Go figure. Weird, isn't it? But I met someone—Doug—through the *Agricultural Gazette*. He's looking for a wife, and well, I'm hoping it'll work out."

"You're going to live on a farm?" Bernie said. She couldn't quite believe what she was hearing.

"Yup." Sandra tugged at her ponytail. "The funny thing is that I always wanted to be on a farm when I was little. My aunt had a dairy farm around Saratoga and I just adored going there."

"You've met this guy in person though, right?" Bernie asked.

Sandra laughed. "Oh yes. I'm not that crazy. First we talked on the phone and then we Skyped, and last month he came up for a week. Now he's back and we're driving across country to Bozeman. He's got two sons—a six- and an eight-year-old who need a mother—and I'm hoping I'll be it." Sandra's eyes misted. She blinked the tears away and took another sip of her coffee.

Bernie thought back to what Thelma had said earlier. "Does Thelma know you're leaving?" she asked.

Sandra laughed. "Of course she does."

"Because I got the impression she didn't," Bernie said.

"You mean what she said about seeing me leave and giving me a message?" Sandra asked.

Bernie nodded.

"She was just covering for me in case I didn't want to talk to you. As a matter of fact, Thelma thinks I should go. I mean why not? At this point I've got nothing to lose. I can always come back if things don't work out."

"Like Manny did," Bernie said, and then instantly regretted it. "I'm sorry. That came out wrong."

"It's okay." Sandra went over and threw her coffee cup in the trash can. "But this is different.

Manny didn't come back because things weren't working out for him," Sandra explained. "Manny came back because Daisy asked him to." She studied a mourning dove pecking at a piece of hot dog roll someone had left on the path. "So sad," she murmured, and she lapsed into silence.

"Why did she do that—ask him back?" Bernie finally asked.

Sandra roused herself. "I don't think she ever got over him. She followed him out West when he left and that sure didn't work out. I think it was losing the baby that did it—she was never the same afterward." Sandra stopped for a moment to gather her thoughts. "Maybe her illness was there all along and it would have come out anyway—at least that's what Isaac and Mina say—but that just put her over the edge." Sandra took a deep breath and let it out. "You know technology can be a wonderful thing. It brought Doug and I together, but if Daisy hadn't looked up Manny online and started texting him, he never would have come back here and maybe he'd still be alive." She shrugged. "Jeremy was dead set against it from the start, but Isaac thought it might cheer Daisy up."

"And did it?" Libby asked.

"In the beginning. Even though it wasn't the same as before between those two. The romance thing had died. But Daisy liked having Manny around. She thought she could trust him."

"And could she?" Libby asked.

Sandra smoothed down her T-shirt. "I thought she could up until the day he didn't show up. She couldn't get him on the phone. Now I know why, of course, but I didn't know that then and neither did Daisy. She waited and waited, but Manny and the lawyer never showed. It was bad. Daisy freaked. She wanted to go out looking for him and the people at the Pines had to give her a shot to calm her down."

"Why did Daisy need a lawyer?" Bernie asked as she shook a pebble out of her ballet flat.

Sandra shrugged. "I don't know. You'd have to ask Isaac."

"How was he involved?" Libby asked.

"He was setting up something for Daisy. A trust, maybe."

Bernie raised an eyebrow. "Daisy wasn't related to him, was she?"

"No," she answered. "She wasn't, but he and Mina had taken her under their wing after her folks died. Even before that, because she and her family . . . well, let's just say they put the *D* in dysfunctional. But you'll have to talk to Isaac. I really don't know anything about what he was planning on doing. Isaac was pretty close-mouthed about stuff like that." Sandra brushed a mosquito away from her face. "I think he had a lot more money than he let on."

"I'd love to ask him," Bernie said, "but he and

Mina are off on a fishing trip somewhere in Alaska."

"Really?" Sandra looked surprised. "They never said anything about that to me. I guess that explains why I haven't been able to get hold of them to say good-bye," she said ruefully. "Weird."

"Why weird?" Libby asked.

"Because they said they'd be around. It's not like they're seventeen and taking off on a whim or anything like that. Well, I guess there's always the phone."

"Or Skype," Bernie added.

"They don't do Skype. Or cell phones. Are you sure you heard right?"

"Yeah, positive," Bernie said. "I guess you could call Cole up and ask."

"Who's Cole?"

"The guy running the place now."

"Cole?" Sandra frowned "Usually Isaac has the Dean brothers take care of the Riverview. I wonder what happened."

Bernie and Libby looked at each other. They could tell they were both thinking the same thing.

"Call the Dean brothers up and ask them," Bernie told her.

"Why?" Sandra asked. "You think something's wrong."

"Probably not," Bernie lied. "Just out of curiosity."

"Sure." Sandra reached for her phone and called the brothers. "They didn't know that Isaac and

Mina were gone," she said when she hung up. She shrugged. "I'm sure everything is fine. I'm probably making a big deal out of nothing."

"Probably," Libby agreed, but she couldn't shake the bad feeling she was getting. She sensed it was the same feeling Bernie had. "We're going by there anyway, so we'll take a look."

Sandra looked at her watch. "Gotta go. I told Doug I'd be back in half an hour to help finish loading." She impulsively hugged Bernie and Libby. "Wish me luck."

"Good luck," Bernie and Libby chorused.

Sandra grinned. "I'm going to need it."

There was a clap of thunder, the heavens opened up, and everyone ran for their vehicles.

"I give her a lot of credit," Bernie said as she blotted the water out of her hair with a paper towel. "I don't think I could do what she's doing."

"Me either," Libby agreed.

"So what do you think?" Bernie asked her sister.

Libby sneezed. "About Cole? Nothing good."

"Ditto," Bernie said. She sneezed too.

"I hope we're wrong," Libby said.

"Me too," Bernie said.

"Cole seemed so nice too," Libby observed.

"Too nice, Libby. Too nice. If they seem too good to be true, that's because they are too good to be true."

Libby turned to her. "What are those—words to live by?"

"Pretty much," Bernie told her. "At least in my experience."

Chapter 45

Libby and Bernie watched the rain pelting down on the windshield. It had been doing that ever since they'd left the park twenty minutes ago.

"It's got to quit," Libby said.

Bernie briefly stopped digging around in her bag for her brush. "It will sooner or later."

"Sooner would be better."

"Agreed," Bernie said after she'd found the brush and redone her ponytail.

She and Libby were sitting in front of the office of the Riverview Motel. The place was empty. Mathilda was the only vehicle in the lot. Looking out the window, Bernie could see the inside lights were on and the OPEN sign, blurred in the rain, was blinking red. She'd tried calling the motel but no one had picked up and the call had gone straight to voice mail.

"Maybe Cole went to do an errand," Libby said.

"Maybe," Bernie answered. She sat there watching the rain come down.

"We should call Clyde," Libby said.

Bernie turned to her. "And tell him what?"

"Good point." Libby worried her cuticle, realized what she was doing, and stopped. What Bernie said was true. Everything she and her sister were thinking was wildly speculative. "There's probably a simple explanation."

"Probably," Bernie said.

"But you don't think so?"

"Let's just say I hope there is," replied Bernie.

Libby sighed. "Me too."

"On the other hand," Bernie began, "I can think of another explanation."

And she began to talk. By the time she was done the rain had become a gentle patter on the van windshield. A few minutes later, the rain had stopped entirely and Libby and Bernie got out of Mathilda and headed toward the office. The door was open and they stepped inside.

Once again Bernie thought about how the office looked the way she remembered it looking. Nothing had changed. The old faux wood paneling was still on the walls, the pamphlets touting local attractions, half of which were no longer in existence, were still fanned out on the counter, and the little table with the coffee machine and the green ceramic bowl that was filled with chocolate chip cookies was still there. The radio that was always set to NPR was still on the counter. But it was silent now. Bernie supposed that Cole was using his iPhone instead.

"Cole," Bernie called.

No one answered. Bernie and Libby walked to the counter and peered over it. There were two empty paper coffee cups and a half-eaten taco on the desk.

"Well, he was here," Libby said. She sniffed. There was that odor again. "Maybe he's fixing something in one of the rooms."

"Maybe," Bernie said as she stepped around the counter and began rummaging through the desk. There was nothing much in there except a half-empty jar of aspirin, some paper clips, a small notepad, some pens, and a small lock. She took the lock out and weighed it in her hand. The bad feeling that she'd had talking to Sandra got worse. "Look at this," she said, holding the lock up.

Libby studied it for a moment. It was the old-fashioned kind and she'd seen it before. "It looks like the lock Isaac had on his freezer," she noted.

"Exactly," Bernie said. "Remember the key we saw in Clara Randall's kitchen?"

"The one with the note from Isaac telling her to take some salmon?"

"Yes, that one."

Libby thought about what Clyde had said about Manny's body being stored somewhere cold. "Manny would fit in Isaac's freezer, wouldn't he?"

"It would be tight, but I think he would."

"Oh boy," Libby said. "I don't feel so good."

"I could be reaching," Bernie said.

"I hope you are," Libby said as she walked into the back room.

The light was on, casting a yellowish sheen over everything. The cot looked as if someone had taken a nap on it recently and the trash can was half full of more takeout coffee cups and fast-food wrappers. The aroma she'd smelled out front was stronger in here. What was it? Not being able to name it was driving her crazy. She knew she knew what it was. She'd smelled it before; she just couldn't put a name to the blasted scent.

While she was trying to identify it, Bernie stepped into the room and pointed to a long covered object standing up in the corner of the room. "I bet that's Isaac's fishing pole," she said as she went over and unzipped the nylon cover. Isaac's name was clearly printed on the inside in block letters. "Yup. It is."

"Maybe he has more than one," Libby offered up.

"Maybe," Bernie said.

After all, it was possible. It was even probable. Bernie told herself she was becoming a Nervous Nelly like her sister. She took the rod out. The first thing she noticed was that the nylon line on the reel had unspooled. It hung down in a tangled mass. Feeling more and more disquieted, she found the end and looked at it. Then she showed the end to Libby.

"It's been cut," Libby noted.

"Exactly," Bernie said. "You said Manny was garroted. Using fishing line would have the same result."

Libby bit her lip. "Do you think Mina and Isaac are still alive?"

"I hope so, but I wouldn't count on it," Bernie replied, her tone grim. Something else occurred to her. "I think we need to go to Isaac's house and look at the freezer in the garage."

"I'll go with you," Libby told her, "but I'm not opening the locker up, because if there's . . . anything . . . in there I'll have nightmares for the next year."

"Get a grip. Manny is in the morgue. They're releasing his body for burial next week."

"I wasn't thinking of him," Libby informed her sister. "I was thinking of Isaac and Mina."

Bernie shuddered. She felt the hairs on the back of her neck go up. Somehow that hadn't occurred to her.

Chapter 46

Isaac and Mina's house was located five minutes away from the Riverview Motel in a cul-de-sac off Broad Street. The two-story light green colonial sat on the end of the street, rendered semi-invisible by evergreen plantings that had been allowed to grow up over the years. There was a car parked a little ways down from the house, but the driveway was empty and Libby pulled into it.

She and Bernie got out of the van and walked to the garage. The door to it was down, but Bernie grabbed the handle and pulled and the door slid up. She could see the freezer snugged up against the wall, underneath the small window that had been built to let in the light but was now covered over with ivy. Bernie swallowed and started walking toward it.

"I think I'll stay here," Libby said. She'd meant it when she said she didn't want to see what was inside the freezer.

"I'm probably wrong," Bernie responded, trying to convince herself to have a look. Now that she was here she was having second thoughts.

Libby was about to tell her she hoped she was when a shot rang out.

The sisters looked at each other, turned, and ran to the front of the house. The door was open and they raced inside. They heard moaning coming from the rear of the house and ran toward it, through the hall ending up in the kitchen. As they entered the room, the first thing they saw was a spray of blood on the wall behind the kitchen table.

Jeremy Stone looked up when he saw Bernie and Libby come in. "Call an ambulance," he cried. "Cole tried to kill himself."

Bernie walked over, while Libby dialed 911. Cole was lying in the middle of the floor with half of his head blown off.

"I think he succeeded," Bernie observed.

"He confessed just before he shot himself," Jeremy said, his voice cracking. "It was awful. He called me up and told me he had something to tell me. Then when I walked through the door, he told me how he killed Manny and Miss Randall. He said he did it for the money. Then he took out a gun. I was terrified. I thought he was going to shoot me, but he shot himself instead. It all happened so fast." Jeremy sucked his breath in. "It was the guilt. I guess Cole couldn't live with things any longer."

He bumped into Libby as he turned to go out the door and she stiffened in shock. Suddenly, she recalled what she'd been trying to remember.

"Excuse me," Jeremy told Libby, noting the look on her face. "I'm feeling a little shaky. I need some fresh air." And he started for the door.

Without thinking about it, Libby reached down, picked up the gun lying by Cole Webster, and pointed it at Jeremy. "I think you should stay."

"What are you doing?" Jeremy cried.

"I think the question is what are you doing, or more precisely, what have you done?" Libby replied.

"Libby?" Bernie said. "What's going on?"

"He shot Cole," Libby explained.

Jeremy smiled sadly at the accusation. "Libby, Libby," he said. "I realize this is a lot to take in. Maybe you and your sister should go home and let me deal with the police."

"Thanks for the offer, but I'm feeling fine," Libby replied. "Wearing Canoe aftershave was a big booboo on your part," she told him. "If you hadn't, you might have gotten away with the murders."

Bernie shook her head. "I don't understand."

"Dad's aftershave, Canoe," Libby explained. "The one Mom bought him for Father's Day that he wouldn't wear, so she started wearing it on Mother's Day and kept on wearing it. Don't you remember?"

Bernie smiled. "Yes. I do."

"Okay then. We smelled it in the motel room when Manny was killed, we smelled it in Miss Randall's house, we smelled it in the office of the Riverview just now, and I just smelled it on Jeremy. It's very distinctive."

"Yeah, we did, didn't we," Bernie replied. Libby's sense of smell never ceased to amaze her.

Jeremy made a dismissive noise. "Lots of men wear it."

"No. They don't," Bernie told him. "It's an old-fashioned scent. Anyway, aftershave has pretty much gone the way of the typewriter."

"You call that evidence?" Jeremy sneered.

"I call it a start," Libby said. "I think that putting

the blame on Cole for Manny's and Miss Randall's murder is a really good idea, but your choice of aftershave, not so much. The question is why did you kill Manny?"

Jeremy contrived to look bored. "I can't answer that because I didn't," he said.

But Bernie watched him fidget. She watched the slight trembling that had developed in his hands and the sweat breaking out on his brow and she decided that Libby was correct after all. A few seconds later, Bernie remembered the e-mails she'd read on Manny's laptop and what Brandon had said about Jeremy being involved in a big land deal, and everything came together.

"It was the land, wasn't it?" Bernie asked. "The land that the motel is sitting on. Someone wanted to develop it and you had the inside track. I bet you were counting on making lots of money. You probably expensed money you didn't have, because you were positive you'd be making double, even triple the amount. And things would have been fine if only Mina and Isaac would have done what you wanted.

"But they didn't. They wouldn't. They had other ideas, ideas that involved your sister. What did you think? That if you killed Manny your sister would go completely bonkers and Isaac and Mina would turn back to you?" Looking at Jeremy, she knew she had the right answer. "But why kill Miss Randall? What did she have to do with anything?"

"You're so smart—you tell me," Jeremy challenged.

Bernie tapped her fingers against her leg while she thought. "Let's see. Manny was living in her house. So maybe you killed him there and she saw? No. That wouldn't be it. The timing's wrong." She snapped her fingers as she remembered what her dad had said about Clara Randall being collateral damage. "I know. I bet you were looking for Manny's computer and Miss Randall caught you coming out. Maybe she grabbed you and you pushed her and she fell."

"That's a nice story," Jeremy told her.

"It works for me," Bernie replied.

"Good, because I'm going home. I need a drink."

"I don't think so, Jeremy," Libby said.

"I do," Jeremy replied.

"So how did you get Cole involved in your scheme?" Bernie asked him. She remembered the watch Libby had seen and Cole had claimed. "I bet he was the one who put Manny on the bed. How'd you get him to do that?"

Jeremy smirked. "Too bad you can't ask him. Now if you ladies will excuse me."

Libby raised the gun. "I think you're staying here until the police come."

Jeremy laughed. "Don't be ridiculous."

"I'm serious. We'll let them sort everything out."

"Are you going to shoot me if I try and leave?" Jeremy taunted.

"As a matter of fact, that's precisely what I'm going to do," Libby surprised herself by saying.

Jeremy chuckled. "That's a good one. Don't make me laugh."

"I will," Libby reiterated.

"You wouldn't dare," Jeremy said, and he turned and started walking away.

"Really?" Libby said, and she pointed the gun and fired.

Jeremy grabbed his ass. "Oh my God," he screamed. "You shot me. You shot me in the butt."

"I guess I did," Libby said, feeling secretly pleased with herself, never mind that she'd been aiming at the ceiling.

Bernie was trying not to laugh when Mina walked through the kitchen door.

"You're alive," Bernie cried. "Thank God."

"Of course, I'm alive," Mina snapped. "Why wouldn't I be? Now what is going on here?" she demanded as she surveyed the scene in front of her.

A moment later Bernie heard a door open and close and Isaac saying, "Mina, Mina, this time those dratted neighbors stole all our fish. They even took the lock. We are getting a new garage door and that's final."

Chapter 47

Two weeks later, when all the commotion had died down, Bruce, Ellen, their three sons, and Libby, Bernie, and Sean were having a picnic at Skylar Park. The weather was perfect. It was seventy-five and sunny with a slight breeze rippling through the trees. Sean, Bruce, and the boys were down at the dock going over Bruce's new sailboat while Ellen, Bernie, and Libby were gathered around the grill.

"I still don't believe it," Ellen said as Bernie took the corn out of the bucket of water she'd been soaking the ears in and placed them on the grill.

"About Jeremy?" Bernie asked absentmindedly. She was trying to calculate when to start cooking the pork she'd marinated in Pernod, thyme, olive oil, and garlic.

"The whole thing," Ellen said. "I can't believe the whole thing. It's like our own private *Dallas*. You know," she said to Libby, "I'm glad you shot Jeremy where you did. He deserves it."

"He deserves a lot more if you ask me," Libby said, giving the charcoal a vicious poke.

"And he's going to get it," Bernie declared. "He killed three people." She held up her hand and wiggled her fingers. "Three. Manny, Miss Randall, and Cole."

Ellen shook her head. "All of this because Mina and Isaac wanted to hang on to their motel and not turn it over to a developer."

"But then Jeremy would have lost all that money he invested," Bernie said.

"And it wasn't even his money," Ellen said. "It was Lisa's."

"I didn't know she was rich. I thought the money came from him," Bernie said.

"I think that's what Lisa wanted everyone to think," Ellen replied. "It's certainly what Jeremy thought." She sighed. "I feel so bad for her. She told me that as soon as she can she's leaving for her sister's place in Colorado and staying there."

"That's what I would do," Bernie said.

The women were quiet for a minute. They watched a group of sparrows twittering on a low-growing bridal wreath hedge. A moment later, a little girl came running by and the birds flew up in the air and landed on the next bush.

"Jeremy just hated Daisy," Libby said, remembering what Clyde had told her. "Hated her. He thought she always got all the attention. I guess thinking he might lose all the money because of her pushed him over the edge."

"Maybe being crazy runs in the family," Bernie said to Libby as she moved the corn to make room for the pork loin. She found that timing was always tricky when one was cooking outside.

"I don't think Jeremy meant to kill Manny,"

Libby said. "At least not in the sense of planning it out."

"That's what he told the police," Bernie said, "although there is the minor fact that he did cut the fishing line. Frankly, I'm not buying it."

"On second thought, that whole doing it in a blind frenzy of rage doesn't work so well for me either," Libby allowed. "But according to Jeremy, he'd just offered Manny twenty thousand dollars to go back to where he'd come from and Manny got furious and told him that not only wasn't he taking his money, he was telling Daisy and Isaac and Mina. Jeremy claims he doesn't even remember strangling him with the fishing line. He just remembers coming to and seeing Manny on the floor. He says he panicked and hid his body in Isaac's freezer until he could figure out what to do with it."

"I get that," Ellen said. "But why put the body on my bed like that? Why not just hide it in the woods? Or bury it?"

"That was Cole's decision," Bernie told her. "At least that's what Jeremy is saying. Who knows if it's true? The nice thing about having a dead partner is you can blame anything you want on him."

"That makes even less sense than having Jeremy do it," Ellen said.

"Well, again according to Jeremy, Cole had found Manny's body, figured out what was going on, and was holding Jeremy up for a percentage of the take. When the money was slow in coming, Cole decided to give Jeremy a little nudge—hence Manny on the bed."

"Kind of like the horse head in the bed in *The Godfather*," Ellen observed.

Bernie nodded. "Clyde said Cole thought it was funny."

"That boy never did have a lick of sense," Mina said, joining in the conversation. "Sorry we're late."

Isaac was right behind her. "It's lucky we're still alive."

"Pshaw. You're exaggerating," Mina said.

"Am not," Isaac snapped back. "That boy had a history. A criminal history."

"I didn't know that when he looked us up, did I?" Mina retorted. She touched her bun to make sure everything was still in place.

Isaac snorted. "It was obvious from the get-go," he said, appealing to Bernie, Libby, and Ellen. "We kept on coming up short on the count. On top of everything else, the boy couldn't even follow a simple direction. I told him to call up Thelma and tell her we were going away."

Mina patted Isaac's arm. "I think he did. She probably forgot."

"She forgets everything," Isaac said, playing to his audience. "Everything. I don't know how she remembers her lines."

"Which is why you should have written the message down like I asked you to," Mina told him.

"So," Ellen said, interrupting the conversation. "How long have you two been married?"

Isaac and Mina looked at each other.

"Forty years," Mina said.

"Thirty-nine," Isaac replied.

"No. It's forty."

"It's thirty-nine."

Bernie interrupted. "And you're still bickering?"

Mina and Isaac smiled.

"Oh yes," Mina said. "It keeps us young."

Ellen laughed. "I guess Bruce and I are going to be together for a long time then." She turned to Mina. "I know this is none of my business, but why were you giving the motel to Daisy?"

Mina looked at Isaac.

"Go on, tell her," he said.

Mina nodded. "Isaac and I never had any children," she began. "Over the years, we unofficially adopted Daisy. She used to come wandering over to the motel and we'd sit and chat and knit, especially after her parents died. I felt bad for her. She was like a lost soul. She was still coming over when she was a teenager. Then she met Manny and we didn't see her so much anymore. He was her first real boyfriend and she loved him."

Isaac squeezed Mina's hand and she squeezed it back.

"Maybe they would have broken up on their

own," Mina continued, "but Jeremy decided to do something about the relationship. In hindsight, I realize that even back then Daisy was showing signs of her illness."

"So he paid the two girls to accuse Manny of raping them," Bernie guessed.

Mina nodded. "It was effective. Manny got out of town, but unfortunately for Jeremy, Daisy went after him. I think she was pregnant at the time, though I'm not sure. Anyway, she lost the baby and things fell apart with Manny. She was never the same when she came back. We, Isaac and I, thought we should do something nice for her."

"She always loved the Riverview," Isaac said. "Which is why we're leaving it to her. I'm hopeful with the correct meds and competent help she'll be able to take the place over. She's coming to live with us next week, so hopefully we'll be able to sort everything out." He smiled. "Now," he asked Libby and Bernie, "exactly how did you figure out it was Jeremy? What is this I hear about aftershave?"

Libby laughed. "It's kind of strange," she said, at which point she proceeded to relate the saga of her dad, her mom, and the aftershave.

Ellen smiled. "So I guess you could say that your mom helped solve the case."

"I guess you could say she did," Libby agreed.

Half an hour later, the food was ready and everyone started to eat.

Recipes

Because this book is about Mother's Day, I had the brilliant idea of asking the men I know for recipes they would make for their wives on Mother's Day. I was quite pleased with myself. I was even more pleased that I put in my request three months early. All the guys I spoke to were very enthusiastic.

Three months later, I was still nagging. But the results I got are worth the wait. They are both simple to execute and tasty to eat. So these are all guy recipes except for the frittata. That comes from a good friend of mine—female—and I couldn't resist including it because it is both delicious and easy to make. It also has the plus of being good for breakfast, lunch, or a light dinner.

Bill Sheldon's Poor Man's Pulled Pork

This recipe was submitted on a paper napkin. It couldn't be simpler. Try it—it's really surprisingly good.

Put one pork shoulder, 3 pounds, in a Crock-Pot and fill with root beer. Set on low. Cook for 12 hours. Drain, shred it, throw out the fat, reheat with favorite BBQ sauce.

Frank Mt. Pleasant's
Tuna Fish Casserole

This recipe also came to me on a napkin. An oldie but goodie. Some would even call it a classic.

    1 box of flat noodles
    1 can tuna fish
    1 can celery soup
    1 can mushroom soup

Put soups together. Add correct amount of water (specified on the can). Cook noodles. Put noodles in a dish along with soup and tuna. Bake for 350 degrees for 45 minutes or until done.

Anton Ninno's Ziti
with Broccoli and Chickpeas

¾ pound (about 1½ cups) broccoli florets with
    no stems
6 quarts water
salt to taste
¾ pound ziti or mostaccioli
5 tablespoons extra-virgin olive oil
2 cloves garlic, sliced thin
1 15-ounce can chickpeas, drained and rinsed
freshly ground black pepper
⅛ teaspoon red pepper flakes (optional)

1. Place the broccoli in a steamer basket over boiling water. Cover and steam for 5 to 6 minutes, until it is cooked through yet still firm. Plunge broccoli into cold water to stop cooking and set color. Set aside.
2. Bring water to a boil, add salt, and cook pasta until it is al dente, about 8 to 10 minutes.
3. While pasta is cooking, make the sauce. In a saucepan or skillet large enough to hold all the cooked pasta, warm 2 tablespoons of olive oil over medium-high heat. Add the garlic and cook and stir until the garlic turns a toasty brown (do not burn). Press down on it with the

back of a wooden spoon about 2 to 3 minutes. Discard the garlic.

4. Reduce the heat to medium, add the chickpeas to the pan, and cook and stir for 1 minute. Add the cooked pasta, the broccoli, the black pepper, and red pepper flakes if desired. Cook and stir gently over medium heat for 2 minutes. Drizzle the remaining olive oil over the pasta. Serve at once.

Roger Markell's Venison Stew

For those of you who are fortunate enough to have a hunter in your family.

1 to 1½ pounds venison steak,
    cubed ½ to 1 inch
1½ cups diced potatoes
1½ cups green beans, cut into pieces
    (fresh or, if frozen, defrosted)
1 cup baby carrots
1 cup sliced mushrooms
1 medium onion, diced
2½ cups water
1 tablespoon lemon-pepper seasoning
¾ cup flour
bacon fat
salt and pepper

1. Mix the flour and lemon-pepper seasoning in a quart-sized plastic storage bag.
2. Fry several strips of bacon in a 3- to 4-quart covered skillet. Remove the bacon, keep bacon fat.
3. Roll the venison cubes in the bag of flour and seasoning to completely coat the venison.
4. Sauté the coated venison cubes until they start to brown in the bacon fat.

5. Remove venison; sauté carrots, potatoes, and onion until soft. Put venison back in pot, add water, cook over low-medium heat for 30 minutes.
6. Add green beans and mushrooms and simmer over low heat for an additional 15 minutes.
7. Salt and pepper to taste.

Barbara Beckos's Frittata
with Broccoli Rabe and Sausage

In Barbara's words: "Easy and protein rich. Can be made ahead by one hour. Cover and serve warm with a green salad. Eight wedges are a good serving size for a brunch, lunch, or light dinner."

12 eggs (large)
½ cup whole milk
½ cup grated cheddar plus ¼ cup grated
    cheddar at serving
1 tablespoon vegetable oil
1 tablespoon butter
½ medium sweet onion, chopped
½ pound sausage (remove casing), turkey
    sausage or sweet Italian sausage
1 bunch of broccoli rabe, chopped coarsely
salt and pepper

1. Preheat broiler
2. Whisk eggs and milk in medium-sized bowl and add ½ cup grated cheddar. Season lightly with salt and pepper. Set aside.
3. In cast iron skillet heat oil and butter, add chopped onions and sausage, and cook over medium heat until onions are softened and sausage is brown—about 6 to 7 minutes.

4. Add broccoli rabe to onion and sausage mixture and cook until broccoli is crisp-tender, about 8 minutes more.

5. Reduce heat to low and add egg mixture slowly over sausage and broccoli mixture. Cook for about 10 minutes more, occasionally shaking pan until edges start to set—8 to 9 minutes.

6. Add remaining ¼ cup cheddar to top of frittata and place under broiler for 3 to 4 minutes, until frittata is set and top is brown and cheese has melted.

Center Point Large Print
600 Brooks Road / PO Box 1
Thorndike, ME 04986-0001 USA

(207) 568-3717

US & Canada:
1 800 929-9108
www.centerpointlargeprint.com